The Kindred Killers

Graham Smith

Print ISBN 978-1-912175-46-8

I have decided to stick with love.
Hate is too great a burden to bear.
Martin Luther King

Dedication
To my son, Daniel. May he never grow up in a world where hate triumphs love and the acceptance of cultural differences

Praise for Graham Smith's Watching The Bodies , the first book in the Jake Boulder series.

"Graham Smith just knocked me off my feet and onto my ass with this super book that completely took me by surprise. What a brilliant talent he is."

Susan Hampson – Books From Dusk Til Dawn

"A belter of a start to a series. High-stakes cat and mouse games with a twisted killer and a really likeable protagonist. Definitely one to add to your TBR if you enjoy fast-paced action with plenty of twists and turns!"

Kate Moloney – Bibliophile Book Club

"I do love a good serial killer thriller and thankfully this is a brilliant example."

Joanne Robertson – My Chestnut Reading Tree

"The tough guy versus the matriarch makes for a thought-provoking dynamic and gave the reader something different to digest. An enjoyable book and a great start to a new series."

Sarah Ward – Crimepieces & Author of *In Bitter Chill*

"This is an extremely clever story. Well written with a killer that is one of the smartest and most twisted I've met."

Sarah Kenny – The Great British Book Off

"This book had just what I needed at the time, a book that had action but also had a lot of crime solving in it. I am looking forward to more of Jake Boulder and to what happens next."

Sean Talbot – Sean's Book Reviews

"Just what did I think of this book? Well I loved it! It's certainly a 5 star read for me."

Vicki Wilkson – I Love Reading

"With unwavering tension, fast-paced action, a creepy killer, murders galore and a great protagonist to boot, this book kept me hooked and interested from start to finish. Short chapters, many of which end in cliffhangers, kept me entertained and on my toes throughout. The breath-taking finale made me gasp...literally."

Joseph Calleja – Relax and Read Book Reviews

"I have always been a sucker for a serial killer story and in Watching the Bodies, I have found one of the best serial killer tales that I have read for a long, long time. I loved this."

Gordon Mcghie – Grab This Book

"It's one of the best serial killer thrillers I have read in a LONG time. I couldn't stop turning the pages and devoured this book in two short days. If this is what Graham Smith has in store for us with this new series, then consider me hooked. I can't wait to read more!"

Emma Welton – Damppebbles Book Blog

"I love, love, LOVED this book! I've always been a fan of serial killer novels and this one absolutely nailed it."

Ellen Devenport – Bibliophile Book Club

"The end of the book was so tense and fast-paced I couldn't get enough of it. I was dying to see how everything turned out and I was not disappointed."

Danielle Ryan – The Blonde Likes Books

"Watching the Bodies is packed with intrigue. The pace is there from the off with short chapters and the race against time to find 'The Watcher'."

Claire Knight – Crime Book Junkie

"This was a clever, well-written thriller that introduced a new lead character that I'm interested to see more of. If you enjoy thrillers that have a structured feel and feature serial killers, you'll want to pick up Watching the Bodies immediately."

Chelsea Humphreys – The Suspense is Thrilling Me

Chapter 1

I wake feeling like an NFL tackle dummy after a rigorous training session. Every muscle in my body aches and there appears to be an orchestra using the inside of my head as a rehearsal space. I don't know much about orchestras but I can tell the one in my head isn't the New York Philharmonic.

After a moment of rubbing at what feels like dried blood, I manage to force an eye open – only to wish I hadn't. I'm in a room I don't recognise. My first guess is that it's a motel room. I can't be bothered to make a second one.

There's a woman next to me and her face is covered with fresh bruises. A trickle of red has congealed on her top lip and there's no way she was born with a nose shaped like that.

Beyond her I see the detritus of passion. Clothes lie in a tangled heap on a chair. A bra hangs from the handle of a closet and, more telling, an open condom wrapper sits atop the bedside table.

The woman beside me is a stranger. While it's not unusual for me to pick someone up for the night, as a rule of thumb, I tend to remember their name the next day. Or at least their face.

I sure as hell remember their existence. All I know about this woman is she's not the one I'm supposed to be dating.

None of that matters. What's more worrying is the mess her face is in.

Who's been beating on her? Was it me? Was I so out of it that I raised my hand to her?

Another more worrying thought enters my head.

Is she still alive?

I put my fingers to her throat.

There's a pulse. Slow, regular and steady. Just the way it should be with a sleeping person. A wave of relief washes over me, but it's short-lived. I see raw and bruised knuckles when I draw back my hand. A check of the other hand finds the same.

If the marks on her face are my doing, I'll never be able to look at myself in a mirror again. It may be a cliché, but it doesn't stop me feeling like a low life. I've never liked men who beat women and the thought I may have become one is abhorrent.

I don't need to be Sherlock Holmes to work out that I had been fighting and gotten laid last night. What I need to do now is find out in which order and with whom.

A spear of agony runs through my body as I swing my feet to the floor. It's bad but not unbearable. Or unfamiliar. As a doorman, I'm used to getting into fights. It's a long time since I lost one, but when two men go toe-to-toe, more often than not, both will suffer.

I take a look around the room and confirm I'm in a motel. The bare threads in the carpet tell me it's not one of the most expensive motels I've ever stayed in.

The woman groans in her sleep, rubs an eye and flops her arm onto the top of the sheet. I see needle marks. Lots of them. I take a closer look at her face and the body below it. She might be draped in a sheet, but I can see that she's so thin she almost appears emaciated. The unbruised parts of her face are layered in thick makeup and there's a lankness about her hair.

Her appearance makes me wonder if she hires the room by the hour. My next thought is one of relief as I remember the condom wrapper. I may have been drunk enough to sleep with a drug-addled hooker, but at least one of us had the sense to use protection.

I totter into the bathroom and turn on the shower. Its pressure is feeble at best and never gets above lukewarm, but the water combined with slow movements does enough to restore a degree of suppleness to aching limbs.

When I return to the bedroom, the woman is sitting with her back resting against the headboard. Her head is held in shaking hands. I pull on my pants and look for my shirt.

'Thanks for last night.' Her voice is thin. I'm unsure whether she means it or not. She may be trying to keep me sweet; fearful of me and my intentions.

I look at the condom wrapper. It's not the same brand as the ones in my wallet, but that means nothing when I've been drinking. It could be one she's provided – in which case the sex was consensual after the fighting, and everything will be cool.

If it's one I've bought in a drunken stupor, there's a chance the marks on her face are my doing. A worse thought hits me, but it's not one I'm prepared to give brain space.

'What do you mean?' I keep my tone even and my posture unthreatening.

She looks at me with a bloodshot eye; the other is swollen to a slit. 'Don't you remember?'

I shake my head. It's a serious mistake. The movement knocks the orchestra further out of tune and makes my neck feel as if my head is being pulled off.

She gives a tight grin. 'You saved me from a beating.' A shrug. 'Well, a worse beating.'

'Did I?' I hear the relief in my voice. I didn't believe I'd been the one who hit her but, not being able to remember anything about last night, I haven't been able to rule it out.

I sit on the edge of the bed and look at her. 'I'm sorry, but I was wasted last night. I don't remember anything.'

'You sure were, honey.' There's a hint of southern drawl to her accent. 'Didn't stop you kickin' Benji's ass though.'

'Was that who did that?' I point at her face.

'Yeah.'

I rub my bruised face and body. Whoever this Benji was he either put up a good fight, or I was so drunk he managed to land a few blows of his own. It doesn't surprise me that I stepped in to protect a strange woman. I've never approved of men who hit women and the trace of MacDonald blood in my veins doesn't need much provocation.

That's the trouble with my drinking. I don't do it very often, but when I do I drink so much I lose all memory. I'm not even sure where I am.

'Where are we?' I remember driving into a town called Hayden, although I'm not sure it was yesterday.

Her face shows understanding and a little sorrow at the blankness of my memory.

'We're in Steamboat Springs. It's Wednesday, and after you'd kicked Benji's ass you carried on drinkin'. By the time you were on your second bourbon, he'd came back with his buddies.'

This information gives me some reassurance. I'd left home on Sunday night, so there are only two days unaccounted for. Steamboat Springs is about three hours east of Casperton, or two if I'm driving. My injuries are the result of fighting a gang rather than an individual. I can accept that. There's no shame in being beaten up by a gang.

Still, there's always pride. 'Did I take any of them down before they got me?'

'They didn't get you. You kicked all their asses.' She looks at me with a mixture of awe and respect. 'There was six of them. Ain't never seen anyone fight like you before. Every time they knocked you down you got back up. When you knocked them down they stayed where they was.'

I should ask why Benji had been hitting her, but I don't want to get myself embroiled in her life. Whatever happened between us last night was an isolated incident; I'll return to Casperton and she'll carry on with her life. If she has any sense, she'll keep away from Benji.

'You saved me last night. If it hadn't been for you, Benji woulda used his knife on me.' Her head dips. 'Nobody'd pay for a hooker with a ruined face.'

She doesn't need to continue; the holes in her arms explain why she's hooking. I can't help my eyes straying to the condom wrapper.

Her eyes follow mine. 'You passed out before I could say thank you.' She climbs out of the bed and stands naked before me. 'I still want to say it.'

I'm saved from having to decline her offer by a hammering at the door. As I don't even know where I am, it can only be bad news. I pull on my boots as the banging continues.

The noise abates and a familiar voice rings out. 'Jake! It's me. Get your shit together and get out here. Now!'

The voice belongs to my best friend and sometimes employer, Alfonse Devereaux.

I push away thoughts of how he found me and concentrate instead on the key points of his four sentences: he's sworn – something he only does when he's under great stress or is emotional; he's come to find me, and therefore needs me. As a rule, when I have one of my drinking binges, he leaves me to my own devices or comes to retrieve me when I call him.

The woman pulls the sheet back over herself. 'By the way, I'm Leigh.'

There's no point in pretending I've remembered her name. 'I'm Jake Boulder. If Benji bothers you again call me.' I pass her a card – unsure whether to kiss, hug or shake hands with her. In the end, I do none.

I open the door to be confronted with Alfonse's anxiety-creased face.

'C'mon. I need your help and I need it now.'

Chapter 2

Alfonse doesn't say another word until we're travelling west on the Forty. He hands me deodorant, breath mints and a scowl in one movement. When he does speak his voice is filled with urgency and worry.

My comprehension is a little slower than usual. I struggle to grasp what he's telling me.

'So your cousin and his wife have left home in a hurry. I don't see what the problem is.'

'Weren't you listening? They didn't leave home in a hurry. They were taken.'

I rub over my face with both hands until I reach the back of my neck. Alfonse isn't one to jump at shadows, but I can't believe a family of four have been abducted from their home. Kidnappers take one family member and they would target a wealthy family. I don't know Alfonse's cousin too well, but I know he's a regular guy who draws an honest wage for an honest day's work. All four of them being taken suggests something else.

I'm guessing someone else has hit the panic button, but it's not like Alfonse to get this worked up over a mistake.

'Say they were taken.' I raise a hand to forestall the indignant protest I know he's going to make. 'What reason is there for taking them? None of your family are rich enough to make kidnapping worthwhile. He's a lawyer and she works in a bank. There's no real motive.'

Alfonse shakes his head as he powers the SUV past a slow-moving suburban. 'That's what scares me. If they've been snatched for no obvious reason, there's something we don't know or someone intends to hurt them.'

'What makes you so sure they've been taken? Have there been any demands?'

'Not yet.' A shrug. 'Aunt Nina visited them and found the back door open. When she went in, it looked like there had been a fight.'

'Has anyone called the police?' It's a silly question I wave an immediate apology for. Alfonse makes a good living as Casperton's private detective. The new Chief of Police hasn't been in office long enough to sort out the nepotistically appointed detective squad.

He gives a grimace of distaste. 'It was the first thing Aunt Nina did. Farrage and one of his buddies trooped over, had a bit of a look around and then dismissed it as a domestic.'

'Sounds about right for him. I take it you want me to help find them?'

He doesn't say anything, but the look he fires my way screams 'well duh!'.

'I'm just playing devil's advocate here; what about the house convinced you and Nina they were taken against their will?'

'You don't know what Sherrelle's like. To say she has OCD would be an understatement. Everything in her house has its place and she freaks out if the slightest thing is in the wrong place.' He slows to avoid getting caught by a speed trap. 'She once lost the plot because I returned two DVDs in the wrong cases.'

I start to get why he's so worried. I had a great aunt in Scotland who was much the same. Visits to her house always filled me with dread as she had a sharp tongue for anyone who upset her carefully arranged home. As an act of revenge for one foul-mouthed rant, my sister and I waited until she was in hospital for a minor operation, and rearranged all her cupboards and drawers into a haphazard mess.

'When were they last seen or spoken to?'

'Monday night. Darryl spoke to Aunt Nina about a party he and Sherrelle were planning for Robyn's birthday. When she went round yesterday morning…' He tails off, knowing he'd be repeating himself.

At least we have a timeframe for when they went missing, or were taken. 'Why didn't you call me or come sooner?'

'I called you last night. We spoke for half an hour and you promised to get back by midnight.'

There is accusation in both his voice and his words. I've failed him as a friend. He called out to me in his hour of need and I made him a promise I didn't keep. Instead of getting my act together and going back to help him, I got into a fight and then went to bed with a drug-addicted hooker.

'I'm sorry, man.' There's not much else I can say; he knows what happens when I start drinking.

'You're here now. Let's concentrate on finding out what's happened to them.'

He doesn't say it, but the subtext is that at some point he's going to rail on me for letting him down. There's no answer to that; he has every right and we both know it.

Whatever happens, I have to make sure I redeem myself in his eyes. Right now the road to redemption is a one-way street leading to an investigation into a mysterious disappearance.

We cover a few miles in silence until we reach Hayden. It's a small town in the Yampa Valley. Once home to coal miners, it now supports small businesses and an airport bringing skiers to Steamboat Springs.

As we pass through the town he pulls into the car park of a bar. My Mustang sits askew in two parking spaces.

'Can I trust you to follow me back or are you gonna walk in there and have another beer?' His tone is mild, but his words cut deep.

'I'll be back at Casperton before you. Pick me up at my place.' I plan to race ahead so I can brush my teeth and change into clean clothes. My hangover is kicking in big time and I want to be presentable for his family.

I have another thought as I climb out of his car. 'How did you know where to find me, and where my car was?'

'You're the smartass, work it out for yourself.'

He's not the type to screech off in a cloud of tyre smoke, yet when he leaves it's as close as he'll ever get.

Five minutes later I pass his SUV on my way back to Casperton. With peace to think, it doesn't take me long to work out he must have been tracking me. The way he arrowed in on my precise location can only be explained by some kind of tracking device. I'm guessing both my phone and car are bugged.

Chapter 3

I'm waiting on the sidewalk when Alfonse draws up. I've shaved, changed, and swallowed a couple of Aspirin dry. I need a coffee but there's no time. Having let him down with my selfish behaviour, I need to repair the damage to our friendship. It's rare he asks for my help and I'm appalled at myself for letting him down.

'How long you been tracking me?'

'Since you got your new phone.' He skewers me with a glare. 'Knowing your talent for finding trouble, I thought it would be a good idea to be able to find you at any time. It was supposed to be a way to bail your sorry carcass out of trouble. Instead I had to use it to bring you back to reality.'

I don't answer him, and stay quiet as he drives towards his cousin's home.

While his words are barbed, I know he'll have added the trackers for a dual purpose. He's slated my drunken binges too often for me to not realise how much he worries about me when I have a drink. It's the one subject we're likely to fall out over.

We've been friends since the day we met in high school as a pair of imports: he from France and me from Scotland. Some of the redneck kids had railed on him because of the colour of his skin, but my fists soon ended the racial abuse and monkey noises for the bookish new boy.

The last thing my grandfather did for me, before I left Glasgow, was take me into the garden and teach me how to fight. Not any kind of martial art or restrained discipline like boxing.

He'd taught me how to use elbows, knees and my forehead. His lesson was filled with street-fighting techniques learned in

Glasgow's shipyards and back-alley boozers. He'd taught me well. The only time I've lost a fight since his tutoring, was when I got ambushed by a gang of football-playing jocks.

Alfonse parks behind the police sedan sitting across the drive. It's a good neighbourhood; there are children playing in the street and the gardens are all tidy. What cars I can see are new models and the general feel is one of refined domesticity.

While the street is twee, it's not one which reeks of opulence. I guess the occupants are professional folks like accountants, lawyers and doctors. Rich enough to enjoy a good lifestyle but not so wealthy they can give up work.

I'm sure there are secrets held behind the net curtains and clapperboards, but they'll be bland ones kept inside four walls for appearances sake. A short dalliance with a secretary or co-worker; a small gambling debt or a minor felony buried in their past.

There are two cops talking to Alfonse's Aunt Nina. Her voice has lost its usual sonorous quality and has risen to a shriek as she berates the pair.

The elder of the two tries placating her. 'I'm sorry ma'am, but there's not enough evidence for us to start the manhunt you are asking for. I'll pass on your concerns to Lieutenant Farrage but that's all we can do at this stage.'

'Don't be bothering that fool. I want the chief to look into this. Farrage is a waste of space and you know it.'

I feel for the cops. Nina might be speaking the truth, but there's no way they can be seen to agree to her assessment – despite its accuracy. Her demands for the chief's personal involvement are also unrealistic. He has a whole county and town to run, that's why he has deputies and a squad of detectives. As soon as the public start calling the shots there will be an inevitable breakdown in law and order, as competing factions waste the chief's time fighting for his attention.

Alfonse takes Nina's arm and calms her down with promises I'm not sure he can keep. I hear my name mentioned but I avoid eye contact with Nina; lest she see the bloodshot pits I saw in the mirror. If I'd had my head screwed on I would have grabbed a pair of shades before leaving the house.

Alfonse takes a small step back from his aunt. 'Why were there cops here?'

'I called them. They weren't doin' nuthin' to find Darryl so I called them.' She beams at her own cleverness. 'Called 911 so they'd have to respond.'

Alfonse clasps her hands in his. 'Aunt Nina, you've got to trust me and Jake. Don't bother the police again until we have some evidence they were taken against their will. As soon as we've got that, the police will have to act.'

'Is this true, Jake, are you going to help Alfonse find my boy and my grandchildren?'

'Of course I am, Nina.' I shift my gaze to Alfonse. 'Whatever he wants me to do, I'll do it.'

Give Alfonse his due, he makes sure Nina doesn't hear his snort or see the glare he throws my way.

She gives a decisive nod and takes a step to one side. 'Then quit gabbin' with an old woman and go find your evidence.'

Alfonse leads me to the back of the house and into the kitchen via a utility room. What he said about Sherrelle's OCD strikes a chord before I'm two steps into the house. Everything is aligned in neat perpendicular rows. The footwear on a rack in the utility room is even arranged from small to large.

The kitchen is cleaner than a lot of the showroom display models and more orderly than a hospital ward.

The smear of blood on the wall by the door stands out like a nun in strip club. It has four tails where someone's fingers have been scrabbling for something to grab onto.

Alfonse leads me into the lounge where another example of showroom perfection is marred by an upturned coffee table. A ceramic coaster and a women's magazine lie on the carpet beside the table.

I get why Alfonse and Nina are so worried. Someone with Sherrelle's fanaticism for neatness and order could never have left the house in this mess. It would have driven her to distraction. Something tells me if I look in Sherrelle's closets, I'll find clothes arranged by size, purpose and colour.

While I like to keep my own apartment clean and tidy, I prefer a lived-in look to the sterile atmosphere of this house. The Xbox games and the DVDs lined up on the shelf beside the TV are sorted by age then A to Z.

Even now, with it looking as if they've been abducted, I feel like a voyeur peering into her home uninvited.

To make matters worse I've had a thought which doesn't improve my mood, but any investigator has to look at situations with an open mind. Alfonse may have come to the same conclusion himself, but there's a strong possibility his emotional connection with the potential victims has affected his judgement.

Unpalatable as the suggestion may be, I still have to raise it.

'What are your thoughts, Alfonse?'

'I told you what I thought when I picked you up from Steamboat. I want to know what you think.' He doesn't snap at me, but I can tell he's not far off it. If anyone else had spoken to me like that they'd be unconscious by now.

'The blood trails on the kitchen wall look quite narrow as if they were made by a woman's hand. I'm guessing Sherrelle, or possibly Robyn.' He nods in agreement. 'Therefore, Darryl was incapacitated and unable to help, or he was the aggressor.'

Alfonse scowls at me. 'The thought did cross my mind. Then I thought about how they were together. I've never known a more loving couple. Whenever I teased Sherrelle about her OCD, it was always Darryl who sprang to her defence. They did everything together and were so well matched they would each have died to save the other.'

'Sorry.' I spread my hands wide. 'I had to consider it.'

'I know. It just sounds crappy when someone else says it.'

'Is there blood anywhere else?'

He looks shamefaced. 'What with looking after Aunt Nina, and coming to get you, I haven't had time to conduct a thorough search.'

Again, I'm left feeling like a douche for letting him down. The time used retrieving me would have been far better spent working the case. Yet he'd wanted me alongside him badly enough to waste half a day getting me. I make a silent promise to myself that he'll get unconditional help and support from me until we find Darryl and his family.

I look him in the eye. 'You speak to your family, find out everything you can, and I'll search the house. When you're done speaking to them, start on their tablets, phones and finances. I know the idea sucks, but keep an open mind. Nobody ever knows what goes on behind closed doors.'

His face is grim as he turns away. The tasks I've set him are what he does best, but there's no easy way to pry into your own family's secrets without upsetting those you love.

With Alfonse gone, I turn back to my examination of the lounge. The creams and beiges of Sherrelle's choosing are a godsend when looking for blood specks. Not finding any, I move to the stairs.

Halfway up is a large globule of dried blood. Judging by its size and the way it has splashed on the carpet, I'd guess it's been spat from a bleeding mouth.

Skirting the blood spatter, while taking care not to upset any of the perfectly aligned pictures on the wall, I reach the landing and try the first door on my right. It opens to reveal a closet filled with towels and bedding.

The next door I open belongs to a bathroom. Again, the earthy tones fail to show any sign of blood.

The third door reveals the room of a pre-teen boy. The posters are of WWE stars, supercars and a model whose swimsuit covers just enough flesh to get the poster past any maternal censorship. While it may be the least tidy room I've seen in the house, it would take a determined person less than a minute to bring it into line with the rest of the home.

I double back and try the next door. It must be Robyn's room. Here the posters depict what I figure are R&B and rap artists, coupled with teen heartthrobs. The mess of the room must be like nails on a blackboard to her mother, or it's the girl's way of rebelling. The colours are darker in here but I still don't find any traces of blood. Perhaps a proper forensic examiner might find something with a can of Luminol and a UV light, but there's nothing which stands out to my naked eye.

The next door leads to a room which is made up ready for use, but has empty closets and a lack of family comforts. Figuring it's a guest room, I try the final door on the landing and enter the master bedroom. It's as neat as I expected it to be. Everything is in the required place and is lined up ready for use. Deodorant and perfume bottles on the nightstand are arranged in order of size; their labels all front-facing.

They don't hold my attention for long though. The splatter of blood against the pale peach wall is much more demanding of my interest. I've thrown enough punches to recognise what happens when a fist ruins a mouth. There's always a string of bloody saliva accompanied by a spray of droplets. From what I can gauge, the owner of the blood was standing a couple of feet from the wall as the tails of the splatter indicate the drops were on a downward trajectory when they hit the wall. A glance beside the unmade bed shows a chick-lit novel at the side where the blood-spattered wall is.

The blood would be Sherrelle's. The handprint in the kitchen from where she'd nursed her mouth.

With the beds in the kids' rooms also being unmade everything pointed to them being abducted in the middle of the night.

This wouldn't favour any neighbours observing them being hustled out of the house. Still, there's always the chance a parent was nursing a young or poorly child. Perhaps an elderly neighbour had risen to visit the bathroom and seen something.

Hope dies within me as soon as it flares. In a street such as this, the neighbours would have been falling over themselves to report anything suspicious. These residents aren't gang-bangers struck dumb by questions from an investigator; they're law-abiders and carers.

Not for the first time I wonder if Lieutenant Farrage, and the others who make up Casperton's detective squad, had to fail an intelligence test to qualify for the job. With the correct response from them, a team of forensic investigators would have swooped through the house and gathered enough samples to help identify a suspect or secure a conviction. Now it may be too late, or the scene may be too contaminated by me, Nina, Alfonse and any other of their family members who've been for a look.

I have no idea how much it would cost to hire the forensic team, but I'm sure it's more than Alfonse and I have. Especially now the scene is so contaminated.

It's something he and I can discuss when I've finished my search.

Now I'm finished looking for blood, I turn my attention to the next big tell in any household.

The medicine cabinet in the en-suite contains prescription drugs, feminine hygiene paraphernalia and a box with a blister strip of contraceptive pills.

With the medicine cabinet a bust, I reach into the drawers of the fitted units and, working by touch, I try to find a diary. Looking would be quicker, but there's something degrading about a man looking through a woman's underwear drawer. The voyeuristic feelings I had earlier have come back in spades.

I find a hard-backed diary.

The diary has a picture of a meadow printed onto the front and back covers. When I open it and scan a few pages I find the one thing in Sherrelle's life which isn't tidy. Her handwriting.

It takes me a few false starts, but I begin to understand the scrawls. I pick out pages at random, but the general feel of the ones I read are that of a journal, rather than a diary of feelings and otherwise untold emotions.

She's chronicled the achievements of the family and their day-to-day events – the only hint of personal details are expressions of love and pride.

I skim the pages looking for anything which speaks of arguments with colleagues, neighbours or people represented by Darryl. There's nothing apart from banal dealings recorded on those fronts. A snippet of gossip here, a pleasant comment or two about a co-worker there.

Were the contents of the diary not so potentially important in finding who'd snatched the Fourniers, I'd launch it across the room in disgust at its saccharine wholesomeness. Sherrelle loved her husband and kids, championed them and crowed about their achievements.

If there had been any animosity in their relationship it hadn't come from her. There were no suspicions written down nor complaints about Darryl working late. Her comments on the subject were supportive of his dedication to providing for his family.

I put the diary back and return to Robyn's bedroom. Her diary is harder to find, but when I remove the bottom drawer of her dresser it is lying on the floor behind the kickboard.

Robyn has a neater script than her mother, yet her diary is no better as a source of information. She talks of what I assume are school friends. The main topics are unrequited love for a classmate, and her girlfriends' relationships – both actual and desired. Her parents barely get a mention, and when they do it's for tension between her and them rather than arguments between Sherrelle and Darryl.

I'm about to head back downstairs when my cell rings. It's Chief Watson.

Chapter 4

The chief is waiting for me when I arrive at the police station. His face is grim and there's a set to his jaw which speaks of determination. When I meet his eyes, I see pain and despair for the depths of depravity he encounters.

'You sure you want to come with me?'

'No, but if I don't come Alfonse will.'

He gives a terse nod to show he understands the sacrifice I'm making for Alfonse. His craggy face softens. 'If it's any consolation, I don't want to go either.'

Alfonse had argued to come with me when I'd broken the chief's news to him. It was only the disintegration of Nina which had seen him back down. She needed him more than he needed to see what may be the bodies of Darryl and his nearest and dearest.

I sit in silence as the chief drives us north on the 191. The radio in the pickup crackles with chatter, but there's nothing interesting enough to wrest my thoughts away from what lies ahead.

Halfway to the Flaming Gorge National Recreation Area, he slows to a halt behind a police cruiser. An officer standing beside the cruiser points us towards a rough track leading into Ashley National Forest. I notice how he doesn't look at either of us. His thoughts elsewhere.

The chief engages a low gear and sets off up the track. Before he's travelled fifty feet I realise it's a mistake.

'Stop. Stop right here.'

'Why?' There's a mix of ornery and curiosity in his voice.

'How would you get four bodies to where we're going?'

'I'd use a pickup truck or an SUV.' He looks at me without understanding. 'Goddamn it, Boulder, what's your point?'

'How many trails are there to the dump site?'

He shrugs, getting exasperated. 'I don't know. One, two maybe?'

'I don't think it's a good idea for us to use them.' I pick my words with care. While I may have assisted with stopping a twisted serial killer a few weeks back, I am only here on the chief's sufferance. 'You never know what evidence or clues you may hide or contaminate by driving over them.'

An expletive escapes his lips as his hand reaches for the SUV's radio. 'I want four good men with hiking equipment to search the trail. They're looking for tyre prints, discarded litter and possibly footprints. If any of the men you send are in the detective squad, I'll consider their presence as your letter of resignation.' His eyes flick towards me. There's a touch more colour than usual in his cheeks. 'I can't believe I didn't think of that.'

I try a spot of reassurance. The chief is a good man and a better ally. 'If I had to think of everything you have to, I'd probably not have thought of it either.'

We climb out of the SUV and look at where the track disappears into the forest. 'You know we're two miles or so from the dump site?'

'That's good. It means there's more chance of getting a tyre print.' I point to the right of the track. 'If we walk a few feet out from the track we can still follow it and see any big pieces of evidence.'

'Don't push it, Boulder. You might have gotten the jump on me once, but I give the orders round here.'

I step back and let him lead. He chooses to follow my suggestion. It's tempting to point this out, but I remember I'm only here at his request.

The going is easy at first with gentle slopes and a clear passage through the trees. As we travel further into the forest the hill becomes steeper and the trees closer together. Fallen branches and treetops, snapped off by high winds, litter the ground causing minor obstructions.

My boots are good enough to keep my feet dry, but their soles are worn smooth from walking on paved areas. As we make our way up a steeper bank I can feel them slip and slide on the loose pine needles. If I'd known I'd be hiking in the woods I'd have worn something more appropriate. The jacket I'm wearing is fine for town but, up here with the sun hidden from view, it's too thin, and the exertion of the climb is all that's keeping me warm.

The chief is wearing a windbreaker pulled from his jeep. For a man of his age he's showing remarkable resilience to the strains of the exercise. The pace he's setting is a fast one.

With no landmarks to guide us, there's no way of knowing how far we've travelled. Considering the terrain I reckon we're making about two miles an hour which means it'll take around an hour to get to our destination. A glance at my watch shows we've still got at least another half hour of hiking ahead of us.

We encounter a small glade, and use a few exposed rocks to cross a stream without getting our feet wet. The bright sun in the glade raises my temperature enough to give me the sweats.

Five steps after re-entering the forest I'm drenched with perspiration. The beer and liquor I've consumed over the last few days is now leaking from every pore. My thin jacket now feels like a heavy winter coat as the alcohol escapes my body. While there's a certain level of discomfort and embarrassment to my situation, I welcome the sweats. Combined with the exercise and fresh air, they are chasing away the hangover which has dogged me since I first opened my eyes in that crummy motel room.

The roiling in my gut is easing and the orchestra in my head has better learned its tune and settled down to play a gentle number which has a familiar but unidentifiable sound. With every passing step I can feel strength returning to my body.

'You okay?' The chief looks at me with scant concern.

I toss him a grin. 'Fine. It's just a while since I've been hiking.'

'From what I've heard it's a while since you done much but drink yourself stupid.'

His words sting. I respect him, but from his tone I can tell I'm losing his respect. I could make hollow promises about never drinking again, but neither of us would believe them.

He stops walking and looks at my face. 'This hike is helping you. Your eyes are a damn sight clearer than they were when I first saw you.'

'You should try looking at them from my side.' I set off again, making sure I set a brisk pace. He may be the chief of police and a man I respect, but I'm too old to accept lectures from anyone.

We're both quiet as we walk. My thoughts are on what lies ahead – as I'm sure are his. So far, we're working on descriptions of the scene only. I catch a whiff of cooked meat and have to fight a gag reflex. I hear the chief give a big sigh and know he's caught it too.

He pulls a tub of vaporub from his pocket and dabs some on his top lip before offering it to me. It's a trick used by law enforcement officers and coroners the world over.

I take it and thank him. The strong fumes of the vaporub clear my sinuses with a minty aroma, but they can't eradicate the scent I've already caught.

We press on. A natural reluctance to face what lies ahead slows our pace a little, but not enough to stop us.

Voices carry to us. They're engaged in conversation, but we can't make out what they're saying or see the people they belong to.

'Teasle, Mavers, is that you I can hear?'

'Yes, Chief.' Two cops appear from behind the trees. The way they're dusting the seat of their pants tells us how seriously they've taken their guard duty.

As the chief berates the two men for their dereliction of duty, my eyes are drawn to a huge oak tree. Four charred crosses hang from one of its lower branches. On each cross is a blackened, twisted body.

Chapter 5

The chief instructs his men to put crime scene tape from tree to tree in a fifty feet radius of the giant oak.

I stand in silence beside the chief. Neither of us comment on the horror before us. From where we are there's no way to conduct a close inspection, but I'm not sure either of us wants to get any nearer. There's always the danger we'll contaminate vital evidence which will either thwart the investigation or allow a slippery lawyer to have his clients acquitted.

There's a strange eeriness to the area. There's none of the birdsong I heard on the way up; the only sound is a gentle breeze rustling the upper branches of the trees. The smell of burnt pork, hanging in the air, threatens to evict what little alcohol the hike hasn't removed from my system. The lack of animal presence in the area makes me wonder if they can sense the evil which ended four lives. Even the flies and insects, which have been ever present in the forest, are missing.

I examine the ground first; the action nothing more than a distraction to delay the moment when I have to look at the crosses and their grisly burden. Everything I'm looking for is missing. I see no obvious footprints and no empty cans used to transport gasoline or other accelerants.

When I scan the ground below the crosses, I see burnt needles where burning clothing has dropped from the crosses.

The fact there is more than one person involved in this is obvious. The crosses dangle two feet above the ground, hanging from wire ropes thrown over a sturdy branch. The other ends of the wire ropes are shackled to chains which are wrapped around the base of other trees. No one man could haul a body on to a cross and then fit the shackle. Therefore there must be more than one person involved. My guess is at least four.

I don't want to but, unable to think of another reason to delay the moment, I turn my attention to the body on the nearest cross. There are large nails protruding from each wrist and both ankles. The body is nothing more than a twisted, blackened husk. It doesn't take much to imagine their pain and terror as they were nailed to the cross and incinerated. The agonised contortions remain in death, and their mouth is open in a wide scream.

Beside me, I notice the chief shaking his head in disbelief. 'Well?'

His one word carries every emotion I'm feeling, including the determination to find whoever did this and punish them.

I shrug, unable to tell him the one thing he wants to know. 'It could be them. If my memory serves me right the bodies look to be about the right size for the Fourniers, but I'm loathe to make any definitive identification in case I get it wrong.'

'I don't expect any more than that.' He wipes his face with one hand and kneads his temple with the other. 'What other thoughts do you have?'

'That whoever did this was organised enough to bring the wire ropes, crosses, nails, chains and some kind of accelerant with them. There were also enough of them to haul the crosses up and secure them in place. They also policed the area when finished. There's not a footprint or tyre mark to be seen anywhere. The cleanliness of the scene makes me wonder if the killers used branches to sweep the forest floor.'

'That's a given. What else did you get?'

I pick my words with care. 'The burning of the bodies on crosses speaks to me of racial hatred. I hate to say it, but if that is the Fourniers on those crosses then you're looking at a possible revival of the Ku Klux Klan.'

'The last time I heard of them being proactive was the early eighties.'

'Maybe so.' I look into his eyes. 'But if a black family has been crucified and then incinerated it's got to either be Klan, or someone trying to make us think it's Klan activity.'

'Us? There's no us in this, Boulder. You're here in the hope you can make a provisional ID on the bodies. I don't want to drag a member of your buddy's family down to the morgue to make a formal identification only to find out I've distressed the wrong family. If you can't do that you're not involved.'

'If it is the Fourniers, do you think Alfonse and I are going to sit back and let Lieutenant Farrage lead the investigation? He's already dismissed the possibility a black family were abducted, and now you're up here with four victims whose deaths bear all the hallmarks of a racial crime. We'll be investigating the disappearance of the Fourniers, and, if that's them,' I jab a finger towards the oak while staring into his eyes, 'we'll be investigating their deaths too.'

He sighs, long and low. 'I cannot allow you anywhere near this investigation. The last time you got involved, you killed the main suspect.'

'Bull. I defended myself when a serial killer tried to add me to his list of victims.' I lower my tone to a more reasonable one. 'I'm sorry to say it, but I believe they will turn out to be the Fourniers on those crosses. You know as well as I do, Lieutenant Farrage isn't up to leading an investigation of this scale. If it is the Fourniers we'll give you every possible assistance. If it isn't, we'll keep out of your way and let Farrage screw things up.'

'You don't get to set the terms around here, Boulder.'

'Neither do you. You still haven't been able to hire a decent detective, have you?' It's a low blow. Mayor Farrage will always protect his son, and everything the chief tries to replace him will always be thwarted. 'Look, Chief. You've been dealt a poor hand you can't fold on. Save the bluffing for others and accept a better card if it comes your way.'

'Damn you, Boulder. Even when you're recovering from four days spent in a drunken fug you make sense.' He fronts me up, but there's no threat in his body language. 'If it's them, we'll exchange information. If it's not, and your buddy's family turn up, you may well find yourself deputised.'

I nod. More from a feeling I need to make a gesture than any great sense of agreement to his proposed deputation. 'Can we go closer, see if we can find anything to help with an ID?'

His lips purse as he considers the trade-off between getting information sooner and the possibility we damage the crime scene.

'Step only where I step.' He takes measured strides towards the cross bearing the largest body.

I understand his logic but I have more knowledge of the potential victims. 'Chief. If you're going towards the biggest body thinking it's Darryl, you're mistaken. Sherrelle is the taller of the two.'

He changes direction without comment.

I follow him, taking care to step where he does. My eyes flicking between the ground and the stomach-churning scene before me.

Rage is building within me. That anyone could have committed such a despicable act as this is beyond my comprehension. Whether or not it's Alfonse's relatives on those crosses, I believe the victims will have been selected because of their skin colour.

What makes it worse is that two of the bodies are notably smaller than the others. It's bad enough for adults to be murdered, but the killing of children elevates an already terrible crime to one which has a horrific intensity.

The chief stops and examines the body on the cross. Using a gloved hand, he spins the cross so he can see every angle. The body is wider than the lumber used to make the cross.

There's less burn damage on the back and the remains of a pair of pants show. The chief tries to pull something from the pocket but the material comes away in his hand. He snorts in disgust until he turns the material over. Half visible through the soot-blackened grime is a hand-sewn label.

I'm not close enough to read it, but the chief is. When he speaks there's sorrow filling his voice. 'I'm sorry, Boulder. The name on this label is Darryl Fournier.'

My eyes close as the confirmation of identity sinks in. Not only has my best friend lost family members in the most horrible fashion. There's the added insult of the fact they may have been targeted because of their skin colour.

'I take it you'll need to do a formal ID on them all?'

'We will. The label is enough to point us in the right direction, but we'll have to get the coroner to match DNA from each body with samples taken from their home.'

I know what that will entail. They'll collect some personal items to get test samples of the Fournier's DNA. Tooth and hairbrushes will be their best options.

Officer Teasle comes across. 'Chief. I've just heard the coroner has arrived and the CSI team are on their way.'

'Thanks. You and Mavers are to stay here and guard the scene from wild animals and other hunters. I'll send someone to relieve you later.'

As the chief and I start the hike back down the hill, he pulls a radio from his windbreaker and starts issuing a string of orders to various people.

While he's doing that, I busy my own mind with people to question and the answers I need to find. The reports from the coroner and the CSI team will be worth double, or treble, what Farrage and his cronies produce. Whereas Alfonse and I will learn far more from people and technology than he could hope to.

Chapter 6

The chief and I make good time as we head back to the road. Both of us are too wrapped up in our private thoughts to speak much. There's the odd comment or question, but all we're doing is affirming ideas and seeking support from each other.

Around half-way down we meet the CSI team working their way along the track.

The chief beats me to the obvious question. 'You guys find anything worth finding?'

A man in a protective suit lifts his gaze from the trail and shakes his head. 'Sorry, Chief. There're too many pine needles on the ground for there to be any tyre marks. We've picked up a couple of cigarette butts and a food wrapper, but they look as if they've been lying there a good while.'

I know what he means about the pine needles. The track has had too little traffic to create ruts and muddy patches where tyres would have left a discernible tread. It could be years since it last saw regular use.

Having seen the organisation and preparation behind the executions – I can't think of them as murders – I'm not expecting the CSI team to find anything left by the killers.

As we reach the treeline we see a half dozen cars parked at the side of the road. I hear the chief utter a curse under his breath, and follow his gaze.

A certain Ms Rosenberg is busy haranguing a sergeant. The Casperton Gazette's lead reporter is a short New Yorker of Jewish extraction. Legend has it, it's so long since anyone used her Christian name even she's forgotten what it is. A fearsome nature combined with an evangelical desire to unearth the truth makes her one of the main reasons there's so little corruption in Casperton's political figures.

Her flitting eyes spy us as soon as we emerge from the treeline. She turns away from the sergeant and marches over to us trailing a cloud of cigarette smoke and noxious perfume.

'Chief Watson, can you confirm the rumour that a family of four has been crucified and then incinerated?'

I see from his face he's loath to tell her anything at this stage of the investigation. Yet it seems she knows too much for him to give a flat denial.

With a long sigh he faces her. 'At this moment in time, we do not have a confirmed identity for the victims of what has been a heinous crime. As soon as we have identified the bodies and informed the families, we will release a statement to the press.'

Her eyes shine as she digests his words. As expected she reads between the lines on her first pass. 'You're not denying four people have died that way.' It may be a statement she makes but there's no doubt she means it as a question.

'I'm neither denying nor confirming anything at this time, Ms Rosenberg.' He gives her a tight smile borne out of politeness rather than pleasure. 'If you'll excuse me, I have a busy schedule.'

'One last thing, Chief. Why is Jake Boulder here with you?'

It's a good question. Ms Rosenberg has championed my investigative ability in the past. Once again, she's found me accompanying the chief at the scene of a serious crime.

'He's here at my request because he hikes up here all the time. His local knowledge has just saved me an hour's hiking. As you so rightly pointed out in your column, he has the makings of a good detective.'

I try not to show any surprise about my new-found love of hiking. Her eyes narrow as she assesses our faces. She'll have been shovelled enough bull in her time to have good instincts for when people are telling the truth and when they're lying. She must take the chief at his word, as she turns on her heel and heads towards her car.

I look at the chief. 'You may regret that last part.'

'I doubt it. She's right.' He kneads his temples. 'I'm guessing you've come to the same conclusion as me regarding a rough time of death.'

I haven't, but a moment's thought gives me enough time to make an educated guess. 'They were taken in the middle of Monday night, stroke Tuesday morning. I reckon they were taken straight there and executed.' I wipe a hand over my face. 'What I don't understand is how the fire didn't burn them, and the crosses, more thoroughly.'

The chief gives me a strange look. It un-nerves me and I wonder what he knows that I don't.

'Do you remember anything about yesterday?'

I feel my cheeks burn. I want to lie to protect myself, but there's no point; he'll see right through me. 'No. I can't remember any of it.'

'Well if you could, you'd remember waking up to a huge rainstorm.'

He doesn't need to continue. While most people would assume gasoline drenched bodies and timber crosses would burn away to nothing in a matter of minutes, the truth is they'd take a lot longer without other fuel to create a heart to the fire. It might be an effective way of ending lives, but without the wood usually found in a funeral pyre the bodies would never have been disposed of.

Left to burn, the fires would have smouldered for hours. The heavy rain would have cooled them; robbing their heat and extinguishing them far earlier than the executioners had planned.

Chapter 7

I catch up with Alfonse at his place. He looks dejected and frightened in a way I haven't seen since our high-school days. As his friend I need to salve his wounds and rid him of the despondency he's feeling.

We've always given each other straight talk when required, yet I know he doesn't need me to tell him to stop moping, and start thinking of ways to catch his cousin's killers. He needs reassurance they will be caught, confirmation I'll help no matter what it takes, and guidance in the best way to find these excuses for human beings so they can be brought to justice.

What he needs most of all, is to know that the remaining members of his family are safe. That has to be the first priority in our investigation. Once we can determine whether the Fourniers were selected at random, or specifically targeted, we will be able to assess the risk to his mother, Aunt Nina and both his brothers and their families.

'What did you learn from your family?' I lead as he is still too shocked to think properly.

His head shakes. So do his hands which isn't normal for him. 'Nothing. There's nothing to tell. No affairs, no known money trouble. They were excited about planning Robyn's birthday party.'

His voice is on the point of breaking and taking his composure with it. I pour him a mug of coffee and help myself to one. While he has my pity for what he has gone, and is going through, I need him operating at a higher level if we're to have any success with our investigation. My mind can't comprehend the trauma of having loved ones go missing, only for them to be reported as the victims of what appears to be a hate crime.

'Have you had a proper look at their finances yet, or a look through their online presences?' I don't mean a scan of their bank accounts and a glance at their social media profiles. I mean an in depth forensic look at expenditure, cross-referenced against social media posts and family events. To be specific, I'm looking for the stuff other members of the family may not know about. Things like debts, illicit trysts and a hundred and one other clues which may give our investigation a focus.

'Not yet.' His voice is flat. Devoid of his usual excitement for life.

I pass him a sheet of paper. 'Write down where they worked. I'll go and see the people there. Ask a few questions.'

I would question their neighbours but the police will be doing that. Instead, I plan to look at their professional lives in case their killers are someone they've crossed.

He takes the paper and scrawls down the information I've asked for. I consider asking if he knows of anyone I should speak to at their workplaces but change my mind. It's better I go in cold and work through the hierarchy myself to find out who to speak to.

I fold the paper as I stand. He doesn't lift his head to follow my movement.

It's time for some tough love and hard logic. Not something I want to do, but he needs to lose the melancholy and find some fire in his belly. 'I'm going to go speak to whoever I can find at these places. I need you to get off your backside and start working. It's only a matter of hours before Lieutenant Farrage and his buddies take all the computers, tablets and phones from your cousin's house, along with all their financial records.'

'They'll never think of that. Wouldn't know what to do with them if they did.' There's self-pity in his voice as he mocks the detective squad.

'You're right. But Chief Watson will, so you better do it first while you still have access. I know how much it sucks. How work is the last thing you want to be doing right now, but,' I rest a gentle hand on his shoulder as I let the word hang, 'you can do your grieving when this is all over. Right now, we're the best and only chance there is of justice being delivered.'

'I don't want justice. The assholes who did this don't deserve justice. They deserve to die screaming in agony. Just like Darryl and his family did. If they were here right now, I'd kill them with my bare hands if I could.'

I've mistaken him. I thought he was beside himself with grief. In reality he's overcome with rage and thoughts of vengeance.

He should be careful what he wishes for. Normal people like him and I aren't equipped to take lives. There is a toll. A cost which I was neither expecting nor forewarned of.

A murderous revenge may seem like a good idea to Alfonse at this particular moment in time. I know from experience that as soon as the deed is done, he'll regret it. That's what I now have to live with. I'm the tougher of the two of us, both mentally and physically.

The man I killed deserved to die. He'd killed others and was trying to kill me. None of these facts matter when you wake up tangled in sheets and soaked in perspiration. Nor do they count when you look in the mirror and see the face of a killer. They matter least of all when you are considering your own worth to society and realise you've committed a worse crime than many of those incarcerated in prisons across the land.

You can try to justify it any way you like. It all boils down to one thing. You killed someone. Took a life. The worth of the life is irrelevant.

I've got to live with the knowledge of what I've done. He shouldn't have to do the same.

He's not equipped to handle the guilt. The constant self-recrimination.

Every day since I took another man's life, I've examined my actions with a forensic scrutiny in a vain attempt to justify every choice I did and didn't make.

The results of this examination oscillate between crippling guilt and a powerful certainty I did the right thing.

Even so. I killed in a life or death situation. Alfonse is talking about something different. He's talking about pre-meditated murder.

I know him too well to believe he means what he says. It's just surreal to hear him saying it.

Chapter 8

Gazala puts the three shirts returned by the obese man back on the correct rails. She returns to her post by the cash register straightening various displays as she passes.

Her preference would have been to work in a fashion house, or at least in a store which sold women's fashions, but in a town like Casperton you have to take what jobs there are.

C-Dude is all about men's clothing for those who want to look good. It sells shoes, hats and everything worn in-between. The quality of the clothing is reflected in the pricing. C-Dude isn't a discount store and everything on sale has a definite brand.

The one upside of the job is the number of good-looking and financially-sound men who walk through the door. Sometimes, if she's lucky, she'll get to help out with a spot of personal shopping. This allows her to play dress-up, with the man in question assuming the role of her personal model.

Her sales technique is a mixture of honesty and knowledge garnered from a fashion course at Salt Lake University. With a flirtatious nature and pretty face she makes sure none of her customers leave empty-handed. Her skills at upselling ensure her monthly commissions are the best in store by a considerable margin. By never being greedy or pushy with her colleagues she retains good relationships with all but one of them.

The exception is the matriarch of the group. Neither liking nor liked by any of her colleagues: Marjorie does things her own way. Often discussed rumours of an affair with the owner are the only explanation for her continued employment.

Gazala knows when the day comes that she opens her own store there will never be a place for anyone with as poor people-skills as the ageing woman.

The dream is still a couple of years from being realised, but the groundwork is being laid every day. Still living with her parents, she's managing to save almost every penny she makes. Her father has agreed to put money into the business providing she can raise fifty thousand dollars of her own. Bank loans are not an option. She has to raise the money herself with no ties.

Gazala's days off are spent researching female fashion trends and travelling to Salt Lake City to observe the higher-class stores she plans to emulate. Her own group of friends have long bemoaned the lack of a decent women's clothing store in Casperton and it's a gap in the market she intends to fill. Nights are spent mining her father's vast experience in starting businesses and making them a long-term success.

A man walks in and starts to look around. It's Jenny's turn so she approaches him asking if he needs help with anything. A smile is flashed and the two of them head towards the section of the store where the shoes are kept.

'You there.'

Lost in her thoughts Gazala jumps and lets out a squeak. The speaker's voice is gruff and domineering. She suspects that whomever it belongs to will be a demanding customer who'll take up a lot of her time and buy little.

'Yes, sir. How may I help you?' Her smile is bright as she tries to turn this customer into a decent prospect.

She feels the man's eyes bore into her face as he points towards her. 'I want a new suit and I want a good one.'

'Very well, sir. We have a range of suits for all occasions. Can you tell me what you need the suit for?'

It's a standard sales technique. Find out the occasion and the intended venue so you can best advise the customer. Once they're taking your advice it's easier to upsell to them. A nice shirt and

tie combo to complement the suit, or a pair of shoes which are a better match for the colour.

'None of your business, girl. Just show me the suit.'

Gazala doesn't answer him. Doesn't see the point in explaining herself to someone who won't listen. The best way to deal with rude, obnoxious cretins like this guy, is to serve them what they want and get them out of the store as quick as possible.

As she shows him the suits, Gazala can feel his eyes examining her body. The blouse she's wearing is open enough to flash a tiny bit of cleavage. Her pencil skirt is above the knee, but only just. The way it accentuates her thighs and butt often helps with the light flirting she uses to make sales. She knows her light brown skin looks good against the white blouse and grey skirt. Depending upon the time of year, Jenny spends hours sunbathing, or a fortune on tanning lotions, so she can darken her skin to a similar hue.

Today, with this customer, she feels like she's exposing herself to a predator. He looks at her as if she's a piece of meat. When he's not looking at the suits he's towering over her; his eyes travelling past her face into her blouse. There's no lust in his face. Just a cold expression of bored indifference. He's ogling her, but doesn't seem to be interested in dating her.

It's not the first time she's been ogled and she knows it won't be the last. Yet the lack of manners, and the dominant manner of this man, turn an everyday occurrence into something more sinister. Gazala can feel her skin prickle as the man makes no attempt to disguise where his eyes are landing. Backed up with friendly conversation, and a little flirting, his wandering eyes wouldn't bother her. But his eyes are cold and give nothing away at all.

To fasten another button would be obvious, so she keeps moving around to minimise the number of times his gaze finds its target. Every time she turns her back on him she can feel a visual handprint on her butt and legs.

'Do you know your sizes, sir?' God forbid she has to measure him.

From across the room a peal of laughter comes from Jenny as she jokes with her customer. To Gazala it sounds almost mocking. Matters are made worse by the rude man looking at Jenny and smiling.

'Of course I do, girl.'

Gazala listens as he give her his measurements. Her teeth biting the inside of her lip to prevent her giving voice to her dislike for the man and his derogatory use of 'girl' to address her.

She picks out a couple of suits and shows them to him. He snatches one and stalks off towards a cubicle.

Gazala takes the opportunity to fasten all the open buttons on her blouse. It's a small show of defiance but there comes a point when the customer is no longer right.

When the man exits, he's wearing the suit and it's a good fit on him. He admires himself in the full-length mirror before returning to the cubicle.

A minute later he throws the suit at her. 'Bag it.'

As she's removing the anti-theft devices the man switches his gaze from her to Jenny. He's all smiles for her. There's a flirtatious nature to him now. That is until Gazala gives him his receipt. The simple act of looking at her wipes the smile from his face and the warmth from his eyes.

It's at this moment she realises the man's issue. He doesn't like her because of the colour of her skin. To him she'll just be another 'damn A-rab'. In his secular world, all brown-skinned people will be either terrorists or illegal Mexican immigrants. If he wasn't such a douche about it she'd pity him.

Chapter 9

I pull into a parking space and switch off the engine. While Darryl's co-workers may have heard of his death, my turning up asking questions will bring it home to them. I'm sure he'll have been popular. He was a stand-up guy with empathy for others and had a generous nature.

People are often granted a saintly status upon their death. In a lot of cases, bad tempers, drink problems and all kinds of other anti-social behaviour are airbrushed from their lives. Nobody wants to speak ill of the dead; to be critical of them.

These are the very details which can drive, or at least direct, an investigation. Amid the grief and shock I'm going to have to dig for dirt that may or may not be there.

I've been home and changed into clean clothes after my hike with Chief Watson. A quick shower has washed the smell of death from my body, but there's nothing I can do to rid the scent from my memory.

By rights, Lieutenant Farrage, or one of his cronies, should be here by now. It's their duty and job to seek the same answers I am. Their absence says more about their ineptitude than anything I could say ever will. They'll get here in time. But the smart money would be on it being at the chief's insistence rather than their own inspiration.

I enter the law office and approach the desk. A receptionist with a false smile greets me and asks me if I have an appointment.

'I don't. I'm here from AD Investigations and I need to see the managing partner at once.'

Something flits across her eyes but there's no guessing what it is. 'I'm afraid Mr Ligotti is in a meeting. I have strict instructions not to disturb him.' Her eyes flit down the corridor.

A part of me wants to storm down the corridor knocking on doors until I find this Mr Ligotti. The more sensible part is aware that this is a time for guile rather than aggression.

'It is imperative I speak with Mr Ligotti at once. It's a sensitive matter regarding Darryl Fournier, and he will be pleased you let me speak to him.'

My tone is level and I keep a bland but serious expression on my face.

There's hesitation as she reaches for the telephone on the desk so I give her a smile of encouragement.

She relays my request and answers a couple of questions. There's a slight whine that's crept into her tone – as if she's being chewed out by the person on the other end of the phone.

'You've got two minutes. They're in the end room on the left.'

Her arm points along a corridor; after me earning her a telling off, she's not going to get up and show me the way.

This act of rebellion doesn't bother me; I'll get there quicker without her. If there's any justice in the world, whoever gave her a hard time will apologise after hearing what I have to say. I'm not holding out much hope though. Lawyers can be an arrogant bunch.

I knock on the door and wait for it to be answered.

'Come.' The voice is loud and commanding. It's the voice of someone who is used to being in control and dominating conversations. Such a manner seems out of place in a law firm with two partners and four lawyers. Perhaps in a large city-based practice that kind of demeanour will be necessary. In Casperton it reeks of egotism.

When I enter the office I see a table with a dozen chairs and two men around it. Other than perhaps a full staff meeting I don't see the need for such a large table. There's a desk at one end of the room; it looks way too neat to be used on a day to day basis, but it supports a metal nameplate with Ligotti's name on it. On another occasion I might spend a moment or two wondering if the oversized table is some kind of penile substitute, but I've got more important things to consider today.

'What do you want?' Ligotti's tone has traces of impatience and hostility. A horseshoe of hair, too dark for his age, rings a bald head.

The temptation to deliver the bad news in a style and tone as blunt as his almost gets the better of me. Something holds my tongue though. Perhaps it's a realisation that his bluster and manner will ensure he lives a lonely life with no true friends. Or perhaps it's because to do so would be irreverent to the deceased.

'I'm afraid I have to inform you that Darryl Fournier has been the victim of a brutal homicide.'

The colour drains from their faces as they digest the news. It's the other man who speaks first. He looks every inch the corporate lawyer and his tone is authoritative in a way Ligotti's will never be. 'That's terrible news. How is Sherrelle? If there's anything we can do to help her, please tell her all she has to do is ask.'

'That's very kind of you Mr—?' I let the sentence hang so he'll identify himself. I don't want to tell him everything without at least knowing his name.

'Hall. Eddy Hall.'

The law firm is called LH Associates so it doesn't take much guesswork to figure out Mr Hall is where the H came from.

There's no easy way to break this piece of news, so I go for direct. 'Unfortunately Darryl was found with three other bodies. At this moment in time, we're working on the assumption they are his wife and children.'

From the corner of my eye, I see Ligotti reach for the phone on his desk. 'Bring a pot of strong coffee in here at once.'

Hall's face has a ghostly hue and he looks as if he's had a gut punch from a heavyweight. His mouth keeps opening and closing as he goes to speak and then loses conviction in the words he's about to use. In other circumstances I'd enjoy leaving two lawyers speechless. Today I feel dirty.

I know the questions going through their minds; most of them have already gone through mine. I'm pretty sure that while Hall is considering the horror to befall the Fourniers, Ligotti is already wondering about the implications for LH Associates.

'I don't mean to be insensitive, Mr Boulder, but why are you here instead of a police detective?' Ligotti has gotten control of his tone, and his question is a good one.

'I'm sure they'll be here soon. My partner, Alfonse Devereaux, is Darryl's cousin.' There's no point saying anything else; lawyers should be smart enough to figure the rest out.

'So you're here ahead of the police.'

I shrug at Ligotti's comment, ignoring the snide element which has crept into his tone. He will know better than I, the competence of Farrage and the other detectives.

'What do you need to know?' Hall points to a seat at the conference table as a knock on the door is followed by the receptionist entering with a tray of coffee and a timid expression.

I wait until she leaves, and Hall finishes passing out the cups. 'I know Darryl was a lawyer for your firm, but I don't know what kind of cases he dealt with. Which field did he practice in?'

'He was corporate through and through, he specialised in mergers and takeovers but did a lot of work advising local companies of their, and their customers', rights. Most of the small businesses he worked for got him to draw up their terms of service.'

My brain is firing off all kinds of ideas as I listen to Ligotti speak. Mergers and takeovers can be hostile affairs and, if someone has been screwed over by a store or company who hid behind their terms of services, Darryl may well have been targeted on purpose.

A counterpoint to this line of thinking is the fact we're talking about Casperton not New York. Mergers and takeovers here were likely to be a small business changing hands or expanding when a rival decides to retire. It would also be a massive leap to kill the lawyer who wrote the rules under which a small store operates. To also target his family with that kind of brutal execution even more improbable. It will all still need to be checked out though.

'Do you recall any instances where things got nasty or acrimonious?' I'm fishing here. With luck, a particular client Darryl has advised will have had a beef with him. I don't expect it, but you never know. 'A client who felt screwed over, or perhaps someone who felt aggrieved at how good a deal he got one of his clients?'

'Did you know Darryl yourself?' I nod at Hall's question, unsure where he's going. 'Then you'll probably have found him to be a stand-up guy. Someone who cared about people, was fair with them, and generally tried to help whenever he could.'

'I did yes. I guess you're about to say he was the same in his work life?'

'He was. He always played fair with his clients and often acted as a mediator to ensure both parties were happy with the final deal. The other lawyers in town all liked dealing with him.' He shrugs. 'Casperton is too small a town to screw people over.'

'Fair enough.' I'm not sure Ligotti agrees with his sentiments, but that's their issue not mine. 'What about clients of his who wanted to screw people over – how did they react when he sought to find an acceptable middle ground?'

'He either brought them round to his way of thinking or he refused to work with them. There was one guy who pushed it though.' He strokes his chin in thought and turns to Ligotti. 'Made a complaint to you, didn't he?'

'He did yeah.' Ligotti scowls at a memory. 'Guy was an asshole looking to force a buyout. He thought his lawyer should do as he was told, no questions asked.'

'What was the outcome?'

'I backed Darryl so he went and hired some out of town shyster. The guy did what he wanted and would have screwed over a family business if they hadn't hired Darryl themselves.'

I feel my pulse quicken. 'What happened?'

'Darryl gave his client good advice on a fair deal and, when the asshole didn't get his way, he went back to wherever he was from.'

'Do you remember his name, when this happened and where the guy was from?'

Ligotti looks at the ceiling. 'Sorry. I don't recall any details. It took place a few years back.'

'I'm sure we can retrieve the details from our files though.' Hall moves towards the phone. 'Elizabeth, can you come to Mr Ligotti's office please?'

My pulse slows back to its normal pace. If this all happened a number of years ago, it's unlikely it has anything to do with the case. It will have to be checked out though. For all we know, it could have been the catalyst to a downward spiral.

A moment later the door opens and a woman comes in. She carries a notepad and an air of professionalism.

'What can I do for you, Mr Hall?' A pen hovers over the notepad awaiting instruction.

Her accent is local. I guess she's Casperton born and bred. Something about her body language tells me she's never married. A glance at her ring finger finds it bare.

'I'm afraid it's bad news, Elizabeth. Darryl Fournier has been killed.'

A hand flies to her mouth. 'Oh his poor wife. Those poor children.'

From my seat I can see the tears glistening her eyes. Her sense of pride will not let them be shed before her bosses.

'Sadly he was the victim of a homicide. We need to go through his files in case it's connected to any of his cases. Are you able to bring me a short synopsis of each of his cases for the last few years?'

'Of course.' A desire to seem efficient battles with her grief. 'It'll take me a couple of hours to get them printed, but I'll start work straight away.'

'Thank you. Please start with the cases he handled six years ago.'

I like how Hall didn't mention the possible deaths of Sherrelle and the two children. Or that there is a particular case we believe may be relevant. His request she starts with cases from six years ago brings a frown to her brow.

'Is there anything else we can help you with?' It's Ligotti who's speaking, his tone less polite than his words.

'I'd like to know how he got along with his colleagues, with you two as his bosses, if he ever confided anything personal with anyone, who his friends at the office were.'

Hall gave a long deep sigh. 'He got on well with everyone, from partners to interns. He treated us all with respect and wasn't the type to share confidences in the workplace. Anything he did share was the mundane stuff about everyday life or work. As far as I know he didn't socialise with anyone from the office on a one to one basis. Any time I saw him socially, most of the others were there too.' His eyes flick to Ligotti. 'What about you, do you know anything different?'

'Not at thing.' Ligotti looks at me. 'Sorry, but what Eddy says is true. Darryl was a valued member of the team and he got along with everybody just fine. Such is his standing, we were going to make him partner next year.'

I sense Ligotti is starting to hide behind corporate speak, and needs some time to discuss things with Hall, so I rise from my chair. 'I have other people to see, so I'll leave you gentlemen to sift through the reports from Elizabeth and will call back later. If I was you, I'd expect the police to visit. The sooner you get the required information for me and the police, the sooner we can get a vicious killer behind bars.'

Chapter 10

The bank is just how small town banks are. A row of customers waiting to be seen by a row of tellers. Some are bringing money in, and some taking money out. With the invention of digital banking it's nowhere near as busy as it was when I first walked in, all those years ago, with an acne-covered face and a wad of dollar bills earned by cutting lawns.

It's ten years since I was last in here. With my mortgage secured, I have my salary paid into my account and go to the machine when I need a few bucks. Everything else is managed online.

As ever, there has been a human cost to the digital mechanisation of yet another industry. Now, the majority of those who enter the bank on a regular basis are store owners depositing cash, and the elderly who don't understand computers or are just longing for some interaction with other human beings.

I join the short queue and take a look at the four tellers to see if I know any of them. Two are strangers but the others are semi-regulars at the Tree. I've tossed drunks from the Tree long enough to know most faces in the town, but I can't put a name to either of these two.

In an ideal world I'd get one of the known faces, or at least the pretty blonde I could melt by thickening my Scottish burr. Instead, I get the dude who seems to be more interested in clock-watching than working.

'Good morning, welcome to the Utah Community Bank. How may I help?' His obvious boredom sucks the joy from the corporate greeting.

I can't blame him; if I had his job I'd end up growling the mantra. Still, good manners cost nothing. 'Good morning. My name is Jake Boulder and I'm here representing AD Investigations. Could I speak with the manager please?'

'I'm sorry, but if you don't have an appointment then you won't be able to see her.' He looks at the screen on his desk. 'I can arrange one for Monday at three o'clock if that helps?'

'It won't. I need to see her today. Ideally within the next two minutes.' He hesitates; unsure of how to deal with my forceful tone. A glance is tossed over his shoulder towards a closed door. The frown that flashes across his face tells me plenty about his relationship with whoever is behind the door. 'Trust me. You'll be in more trouble from her if you don't let me in.'

I can see his indecision, so I lean against the counter in a relaxed manner. The suggestion that I'm prepared to wait him out works. He rises from his seat and knocks on the manager's door.

Five minutes later he's ushering me into her office.

'Mr Boulder. I'm Miss Oliver.' She doesn't rise to greet me and just waves at one of the chairs on the other side of her desk. 'Take a seat.'

She's prickly to the point of frosty. She looks to be in her mid-thirties but her clothes and styling are those of a woman twenty years her senior. Everything about her screams career-driven and I guess she runs the bank as if it's a personal fiefdom.

There are no rings on her fingers or pictures on the desk. She'd be pretty if she removed the stern expression from her face. I'd bet a hundred bucks that the only thing that gives her pleasure is a balanced balance sheet.

When I tell her why I'm here the hard mask she wears crumbles, but doesn't break. Her already pale skin drops a couple of shades.

I let her have a minute or two to digest the news then start asking questions.

Most of them are answered without hesitation but there are a couple she jots on a pad for later investigation.

Just like her husband, Sherrelle was popular with colleagues and customers alike. There were no known issues.

'What about friends in the workplace? Was she close to anyone in particular?'

Miss Oliver almost smiles at a memory.

'Sherrelle would always hang with Charlie when she got chance.'

Excellent. I've now got the name of a friend of hers who may be able to shed some light into areas of her life where the killer may be found.

'Is Charlie in today? Can I speak with her?'

'Charlie is a he.' She taps a few keys on her computer and scribbles a note. 'Here's his address and cell number. I'll speak with the others and get you the answers to your questions.'

The fact Charlie is male gives me a shred of hope. Perhaps he tried his luck with Sherrelle and was spurned. The executions his way of taking revenge. His thinking that if he can't have her nobody can.

It's a stretch though. There's no way one person could have captured all four of them and got them on the crosses, let alone hauled them up and secured them. Charlie may have attacked them after being rejected, but it doesn't explain the motivation of whomever he enlisted to help him.

I'd hoped for nothing more, so I rise and say my goodbyes. As I leave the bank my cell beeps; I have a new message.

I read it as I walk to my car. There are two parts to it, and neither is good.

Chapter 11

Gazala slings her bag over one shoulder and sets off along Main. Her thoughts are fixed on the new lines that were delivered this afternoon. With so many of Casperton's executives being male, female fashion in the town is always at least two steps behind.

While others may be jealous of the bias, she revels in it as it will give her the opportunity she craves.

Crossing at a junction she toys with the idea of getting a bottle of wine from the 7-Eleven, but decides against it. Her mother never gives voice to her disapproval of midweek drinking, but she does allow her face to display her opinion.

Gazala is so wrapped up in her thoughts she doesn't notice the van following her.

There's nothing remarkable about it. No decals advertising its owner's business; no pimped-up wheels or tinted windows. The tyres may be off-road ones and the suspension may have a slight jacking to increase ground clearance, but many vans have those modifications. It's a typical white panel van similar to a million others in the country. Except this one is driven by someone who is proud of his racism.

She's unaware of the two masked men sitting in the back. Unknowing of the bag they hold ready to pull over her head.

Perhaps if she was more alert to her surroundings she'd recognise the threat presented by the slow-moving van and its occupants.

After buying some of the latest fashion magazines at the 7-Eleven, Gazala bumps into a neighbour.

They talk as they walk the half mile back to their street. A hundred yards behind them is one of the men from the van.

Shorn of the coveralls and mask he'd worn ready for the pickup, he looks like any other guy as he strolls along the street.

His detail an obvious one.

He has to follow her home. Once they know where she lives, as well as where she works, they can pick her up at any time. It's a blow not to get her tonight, but there'll be plenty of other chances.

With her address memorised, he walks until he's three blocks away before calling for the van to come and collect him.

Gazala doesn't know it, but meeting her neighbour has saved her life.

Chapter 12

Alfonse meets me at the door of the Joshua Tree, or 'the Tree' as everyone calls it. The Tree is a rock bar where even the music has to be twenty-one to get in. A diner-cum-restaurant through the day, it stops serving meals at eight and the music is turned up at half past. Friday and Saturday I mind the door, and eject six-beer-heroes who start fights they mostly can't finish. The work pays well and satisfies my natural blood-lust.

The two-part message from Kenneth, the owner, has both irritated me and piqued my interest.

'What you got?' Alfonse asks the question before I've even climbed out of the Mustang.

I shrug. 'Got a few possible leads but nothing I believe will pan out. You?'

'I got nothing.'

The dejection in his voice tells me of the strain he's feeling. Of the way this most personal of cases is getting to him despite only being a day old. I want to reassure him that we'll catch whoever is behind the murders. At the same time I don't want to make promises I can't keep.

However much I want to make up for letting him down, I'm not prepared to offer him false hope.

'You're gonna have to work tonight, aren't you?'

'Not if I can help it.' I don't want to and plan to do everything I can to get out of it as I figure Alfonse's need is greater than Kenneth's.

The only reasons I haven't pulled a sickie are that Kenneth would find out, and I want to know more about the man that the second part of his message said was looking for me.

It seems too short a space of time for Benji to have tracked me down for a spot of revenge so it must be someone else who's asking around.

When you've kicked as many asses as I have, there's always some fool with a grudge or a point to prove. Whoever it is, they'll have to stand in line. I don't have time for petty vendettas.

Alfonse follows me as I lead the way to Kenneth's office.

I don't bother knocking as Kenneth is too down to earth to exercise authority with such formalities.

Kenneth lifts his hands in apology. 'I'm sorry, Jake, but I need you tonight. Mabel has taken a table of twenty. It's booked in the name Augiers.'

The name tells me everything I need to know. The Augiers family are a bunch of deadbeats. If they lived further south they'd be best described as rednecks. Every one of them is slow of mind and quick of temper.

'He'll be here, Kenneth.' Alfonse's words cut across the tension in the room. He looks me in the eye. 'I'm not pointing any fingers, but if I was I'd point some at them.'

I get what he's saying. The Augiers are backward in their thinking and casual racism is never far from their lips. The last time they were in the Tree, Kenneth had three staff refuse to serve them. By the time I threw them out, six chairs, two tables and a couple of dozen glasses had been smashed.

'Why did Mabel take the booking?' I fix Kenneth with a determined stare. 'Can't you cancel on them – blame a double-booking or something?'

Whether I'm here tonight or not, there's going to be trouble. The family are troublemakers, and once alcohol is consumed at least one or two of them will kick off.

Kenneth's eyes blaze back at me. When he speaks his voice is laden with impotent frustration. 'I tried. When I called them to tell them of a double-booking they told me to cancel the other one. Maisie-Rae also told me they'd wreck the place if they turned up and there wasn't a table for them.'

He's between a rock and a hard place. I can't let him down, not after everything he's done for me.

'I'll be here.' I rest my knuckles on the desk and lean close to Kenneth. 'If they as much as belch too loudly, I'm throwing them out and barring them. You okay with that?'

It's not his permission I'm asking for and all three of us know it. He should have barred them last time around but he bottled out of it.

'Damn straight I am. I've had to rearrange the roster for tonight as it is.'

'Time's their booking for?'

'Seven.'

I jerk my head at Alfonse and make for the door. 'I'll be here at six. I want to greet them personally.'

When I reach the door, I turn back with a change of subject. 'Who was the guy asking for me?'

'Just someone who asked if you were around and left when I told him no.'

I feel like pushing for a description but there's little point. Kenneth's eyesight isn't the greatest and I don't remember fighting with Benji, let alone what he looks like. Whoever is trying to find me knows where I work so it's inevitable our paths will cross.

Chapter 13

Noelle Holten rubs a loving hand over her stomach and thinks of the new life growing inside her. The home pregnancy tests' results had been confirmed by Dr Potter earlier in the day.

She lays two places at the table and checks the oven. Dinner smells wonderful and will be ready for Oscar when he returns from work. Tonight is when he'll learn of her pregnancy and she wants everything to be perfect.

Her first instinct was that they should dine out, but it was soon dismissed. She knows by cooking his favourite meal and cleaning the house from top to bottom she's already starting to nest, but doesn't care.

Even Buster, her black Labrador, has been scrubbed in preparation for the moment she tells her boyfriend he's about to become a father.

All she has left to prepare is herself.

The clothes are laid out on the bed ready. There's just enough time left for her to grab a quick shower, do her hair and makeup, and dress before Oscar returns.

The one thing she's been unsure of all day is what to wear. Oscar's Latino blood runs hot when he's happy – which made her think of a dress she knows he likes combined with her best lingerie.

Another part of her is questioning whether it's appropriate for an expectant mother to prepare for seduction. She doesn't want to go too far the other way though, and appear frumpy before the little man, or lady, swells her belly.

In the end, she chooses a less seductive dress but keeps the lingerie to go underneath it.

Twenty minutes after stepping into the shower she's pulling a pair of heels onto her feet. Whatever else happens tonight, she wants to be ready to welcome Oscar with a kiss and a beer when he arrives back from the oilfields.

Today more than any other, since meeting him eighteen months ago, she realises just how much she loves him.

The numerous failed relationships she has behind her, had made her worry she was destined for spinsterhood. Yet Oscar is everything those other men weren't. Dependable, loving, funny, passionate, gentle and honest are just some of the qualities he possesses.

The hardest part of tonight will be not blurting out the news before dinner, or showing her goofy happiness and causing him to guess.

A proposal from him is the only thing in the world that could make her feel any happier.

Chapter 14

I knock on Charlie's door and survey the neighbourhood while I wait. It isn't quite in white picket fence territory, but we're no more than a street or two away. It's a solid working class area where collars will be white.

The door is answered by a slim man wearing designer jeans and a branded shirt. He has one of those complicated beard arrangements which must take forever to keep trimmed. I'm already starting to dislike him and I don't even know his name.

He nods when I ask if he's Charlie.

'I'm here to ask you a few questions about Sherrelle Fournier.'

'Is she hurt? In trouble? Why do you want to ask me questions about her?'

I gesture at the open door. 'Can we talk inside?' Charlie can't have heard about the murders and I think he may break down when he does. If that's going to happen it will be best for him to be in a private environment.

He's not stupid. He reads between our lines with ease. A hand rises to his mouth. 'She's dead, isn't she?'

'I'm afraid so.'

He bumbles his way into the house so I follow him. He makes for the kitchen and throws his arms around the guy standing beside the stove. 'Sherrelle's dead.'

The house is a home. Not a woman's home with splashes of colour and soft furnishings; a guy's home with pale colours and clean lines.

The man doing the cooking makes comforting noises as he returns Charlie's embrace. No great insight or deduction is required to connect them as a couple.

I don't judge. There's enough condemnation in the world without my adding to it. As far as I'm concerned, people can do whatever they like – providing it doesn't break any laws and they don't force their opinions or beliefs on me.

When they break from each other it's the cook who speaks first.

'Sorry to be impolite, but who are you?'

I identify myself and learn that his name is Pete.

Charlie slumps into a chair by the table and looks at me with glistening eyes. 'The fact you've come here to talk to me means she wasn't killed in an accident. That you're looking into her death … or should I say her life, means she was murdered. I'm right aren't I?'

'I'm afraid you are.'

There's no easy way to tell him how she died so I skirt round the how, and focus on the fact that Darryl and their children were also killed.

He's astute enough to recognise I'm sparing him the gorier details and doesn't push me for them.

The existence of Pete has changed my thinking. Where my initial thoughts had centred on Charlie and Sherrelle engaging in an affair or Charlie lashing out against unrequited love, I now realise those scenarios aren't likely. The relationship on display in front of me is filled with intimacy and tenderness.

Charlie may be bisexual, which re-opens those lines of investigation, but I just can't see it. Pete's hand rests on Charlie's shoulder in a gesture of support and companionship.

Even as I ask a few questions, I'm striking a mental line through his name as a suspect.

If he's not a suspect he can still be a source. I change both tack and tone as I redirect the conversation.

'Forgive me if I sound rude, but did you and Sherrelle ever discuss discrimination?'

Again his intelligence shows as he digests my words.

'You're asking me about discrimination for a reason. You're thinking they were killed because of the colour of their skin.' His tone takes on an aggressive note for the first time. 'You think a gay man and a black woman are only friends because they're both discriminated against?'

I shake my head while raising my hands in a placatory gesture. 'I'm asking because I'm not gay, black or female. Some folks have tried to call me on being Scottish, but that's not the same thing.' I choose not to mention how much it pisses me off to be called English. This isn't the time to explain about Highland clearances and a thousand other slights.

Pete gives Charlie's shoulder a slight push. There's enough force to show admonishment but not enough to fan the flames of anger.

'I can see why you're asking.' The admission comes after a moment's thought. 'I guess it's a valid question but I'm not sure it's relevant in the twenty-first century.'

'How do you mean?'

'Maybe once or twice a year I get called faggot, or some such insult because a customer doesn't get the answer they want.' He gives a shrug. 'Anytime it happens, I get the feeling I've been insulted with whatever obvious trait I display. You know – like fat, or black, or bald.' Another shrug. 'It's just dumb people giving vent to their frustration and lashing out without imagination.'

I know what he means. I've been called lots of names by drunks I've thrown out of the Tree. None of them serious – although the ones who call me English will always earn a somewhat more forceful ejection than necessary.

'Did you ever feel intimidated, or worried that the person would attack you with more than words?'

'Never.' He wipes a hand over his face. 'And if Sherrelle ever felt discriminated against, intimidated or threatened, she didn't share it with me.'

I can't help but notice how soon he's adapted his speech to talk about Sherrelle in the past tense. When my time comes, I hope my friends take longer to adjust than he has. 'You said earlier that people called you a faggot at the bank because they didn't get the answer they wanted from you. Did you ever see, or hear, anyone abusing Sherrelle the same way?'

'Not that I noticed, but she worked mostly on small business accounts while I deal with personal ones.'

I try a different angle and enquire about her relationships with colleagues at the bank. Friends and colleagues know stuff that bosses don't, but again Charlie's answer is negative. 'Nobody had a bad word to say about her. She got on with everyone and was good at her job. No one had to pick up her slack and she always helped others whenever she had a spare moment.'

I thank him for his time and leave. I have ten minutes to get to the Tree. My plan to see what Elizabeth has turned up in Darryl's past cases will have to wait until morning.

Chapter 15

I watch as the Augiers family clamber out of a collection of decrepit pickups. As is typical of their uncaring arrogance, they've abandoned their vehicles in a way that shows no consideration for others.

The entire family is here and their brooding malevolence travels across the road like an advance party.

Maisie-Rae comes first like a general leading troops into battle. Flanking her are eldest sons, Jim-Bob and Butch. Jim-Bob's face is still raw from the last silver medal he collected. By contrast, Butch's face is unmarked and his nose has its original shape.

He's the real threat; people with battle scars have been hit, guys without, are either too quick or too clever to let their opponent make contact.

I shift a half pace so I'm blocking the door; my feet planted shoulder width apart and muscles tensed.

Jim-Bob scowls at me in a way that's meant to be intimidating but isn't.

Butch gives a measured stare.

Maisie-Rae opens her mouth wide enough to show all three of her teeth. 'What's your problem? We got us a booking.'

'I know.' I lift my head and look straight at Butch. 'The last time you were here three staff walked out after your family abused them and a bunch of stuff got broken. That's not going to happen tonight. If there's one hint of trouble, I'll throw the cause out and then I'll come looking for you.'

'You don't want to do that, buddy. You'll get your English ass kicked all the way home.'

Graham Smith

In one swift movement I have Jim-Bob pinned against the wall. What little patience I have is removed when I'm called English by a moron. Doubly so considering the fact I've spent the day recovering from the mother of all hangovers while battling guilt at letting Alfonse down. Besides, people listen a lot more closely when you have your hand around their throat.

'I'm Scottish, not English. You'll behave yourselves tonight or leave with your asses kicked.'

There's enough menace in my growl to put uncertainty into his eyes as I release him.

'Ignore Jim-Bob, he still hasn't learned how to behave.' There's enough contempt in Maisie-Rae's voice to convey a lifetime of disappointments. 'We're here for a meal and a few drinks. Nothing more, nothing less.'

'That's fine. Just make sure nobody abuses the staff, or other customers, and you'll have a great night. Cross the line just once and your night will end immediately.'

I don't bother to say they'll be barred, they'll expect nothing less.

The family file past me into the Tree. Some throw malevolent looks while others make an elaborate show of ignoring me.

Kenneth has used his common sense and made sure their table is as secluded as possible, so other diners aren't disturbed. The waiting staff are male with one exception, but I don't have to worry about Kenneth's wife. She's more than capable of holding her own with the Augiers. He's also taken the precaution of making sure the waiting staff are white to prevent any racial slurs.

The Augiers family are well known for their lack of tolerance towards other races, and as such I have their names in mind for the killings. To that end, I want them to behave themselves long enough to get drunk. With luck, one of the two dictaphones I've taped to the underside of their tables will pick up something incriminating. It's a longshot, but at this moment in time I'm willing to try anything to get a solid lead.

****

60

The evening passes with me never being too far from the Augiers table. I don't get close enough to be antagonistic or overhear their conversations. At the same time, I'm near enough for them to know I'm watching, and waiting for them to screw up.

Until ten o'clock their behaviour is restrained enough. There are a few bursts of sudden laughter and one curse-laden story, but nothing that gives me good reason to toss them out. When all is said and done, the Tree is a bar and people laughing and swearing is par for the course. Butch quells any potential trouble with a quiet word, or a scowl as appropriate.

I see one of the younger family members coming back from the bathroom. He's unsteady on his feet and tries to engage a girl in conversation. She gives him a polite smile and turns to go back to her seat.

The smile was a mistake. It encourages him.

I know the girl. She's a regular and she's here with her boyfriend.

The Augiers lad follows ten paces behind her as she heads back to her seat. I'm five behind him.

He reaches her table. I hang back but make sure the boyfriend can see me. If he gets up and takes a swing at the kid, all hell will break loose.

The drunk Augiers kid slurs something to the girl. She responds by gesturing to her boyfriend.

The kid points at the boyfriend and jerks a thumb over his shoulder. The boyfriend doesn't move so the kid pushes at his shoulder.

I've seen enough. I stick my own thumbs out and bury them into the kid's armpits. Applying just enough pressure to lift him onto his toes, I direct him back to his family. If he had any brains he'd raise his arms to neutralise the pain of my thumbs digging into his soft skin. He though, is a drunk kid with more arrogance than intelligence. His attempt to salve the pain consists of clenching his arms by his sides. A move which intensifies, rather than alleviates his pain.

When I release him, he whirls round to face me with raised fists. The drink he's taken makes him rotate a few degrees too far. By the time he's corrected himself, a meaty hand has landed on his shoulder.

'Sit. Down.'

The kid obeys Butch without hesitation, leaving me facing the real head of the family. There's a challenge in his eyes. I dare say he sees one in mine.

'You gonna put us out over that?'

'No. But if there's anything like it again you're out.'

He gives a small nod. 'Fair enough.'

While I'm happy enough to fight him if needs be, I would like to keep him onside if possible. If he and his family aren't behind the killings, they may know who is. He travels in different social circles to me and his is a community I don't know. My only access into that element of society will have to come through him.

The rest of the night passes without incident until it's time for them to leave. Most, if not all, of them are fully in their cups. As they walk away from their table Jim-Bob fronts up to me.

I back away from him as he tosses abuse towards me. It centres on the fact that I manhandled his kid. He thinks I'm retreating when all I'm doing is leading him outside so I don't have to worry about damaging anything belonging to the Tree.

As I back-step down the three steps at the entrance, he uses them to launch himself forwards onto me.

Thanks to the steps he's got a height advantage to add to his weight. My advantages are sobriety and intelligence. His advantages aren't going to be enough.

He swings his right fist as he flies through the air. I take a swift step to one side and reach for his other arm. I grasp his wrist and lever him round to further emphasise the spinning momentum caused by the wild punch.

Because he's airborne he can't counteract the move by shifting his weight. When he lands, he's on the half turn and staggers with his arms out as he tries to stay upright. Before he can react, I step forward and deliver a sharp uppercut to his jaw.

I turn without waiting for him to drop. There's too many of them to stand around admiring my handiwork.

The kid is two paces away. His fists are raised, but he's so drunk and inexperienced he's lifted them so high they're blocking his view. A solid dig in the gut leaves him doubled over, regurgitating everything he's consumed.

The females in the group are shouting abuse at me as Butch elbows his way forward. There's a sadistic gleam in his eyes as he gazes over his fists.

He's leading with his right but I know it's a trick because I've made a point of identifying his dominant hand.

I don't have time to reflect on the wisdom of researching possible opponents as he feints twice with the right and steps forward to throw a couple of left jabs.

I lean back to dodge the blows and duck under the right cross he follows them with so I can deliver a couple of hard lefts to his ribs.

He grunts but doesn't stop swinging. I manage to dodge the first couple of punches until he lands a roundhouse that restarts the amateur orchestra in my head.

The realisation he wants to keep this as a fistfight makes me change my tactics. When he sends out his next punch, I grab his arm and wheel inside twisting and bending as I go.

I'm sure the move wouldn't work against anyone with martial arts training, but he spins over my shoulder and lands on his back as intended.

My knee drops into his gut and then I'm on him. My blows rain down on him as my self-loathing for letting Alfonse down finds an outlet.

It takes all my willpower for me not to pound him into mincemeat, but when I feel his struggles wane I stand up and wait to see which, if any, of the family are willing to continue the fight.

None are, so I push through them and make my way back into the Tree.

Chapter 16

Gazala closes the door behind her and retrieves the slice of toast from her mouth. The sun is alone in the clear blue sky but it's too early in the day for its warmth to be felt yet.

She sets herself a brisk pace to counteract her late start. She hadn't meant to oversleep, but she'd worked into the small hours composing the first draft of her business plan. Every point on her father's list had been addressed. She'd known that she ought to have stopped hours sooner, but she'd hit a stride where solutions to the myriad of problems were coming to her.

As her feet pound the sidewalk she is working on refinements to last night's work. The tiredness she feels is insignificant when compared to the elation of having gotten through so much work.

The business plan was a chore she'd been putting off until her savings were sufficient to make the dream become a reality. Its daunting presence has loomed over her since her father first suggested writing it six months ago.

Now the task has been started, she understands her father's insistence that she writes the business plan as soon as possible. Like the wise owl he is, he'd known how it would focus her mind on the financial aspects of the business, and help her to identify the flaws in her current thinking.

A copy of it rests in her handbag, ready to revise at lunchtime. Already in her head she's redrafted the paragraphs on cash flow and unforeseen expenditures.

So wrapped up is she in her thoughts, she doesn't notice the panel van fifty yards behind her.

Gazala takes a left turn and sets off through the park. At this time of day, it's deserted – bar one lady walking a golden retriever. She passes the woman and exchanges a nod with her.

As she nears her intended exit, a panel van comes to a stop beside the sidewalk. It has no markings on it but she doesn't give it any thought.

As Gazala leaves the park, the racist from yesterday leans out of the window. 'Excuse me, girl. Can you tell me where I can get some gas?'

Against her better judgement, Gazala steps forward with her left arm pointing. 'Go three streets down and take a left…'

The side door of the panel van slides open and strong hands grab her. She's hauled into the van before she can offer any resistance or even finish her sentence.

Gazala is thrown onto her stomach and has a rag stuffed into her mouth and secured in place. Her arms are held behind her back while packing tape is wound around her wrists. She tries to kick out but she feels powerful fingers grasping her ankles.

The only thing she's sure of, is that she's about to be raped.

Chapter 17

I enter LH Associates and make my way along the corridor to Elizabeth's office. I'm hoping she's got the information I requested. There's precious little in the way of leads so far and I've lost a few hours with having to work last night.

Alfonse had spent the evening talking to Darryl and Sherrelle's friends, looking for enemies, but had turned up nothing. None of the people he'd spoken to had said a bad word about them. That was to be expected as nobody wants to speak ill of the dead.

What's strange, is that none of their friends knew of anyone who didn't like them. At times like this people fall over themselves to help, and in their efforts to offer information they can often conjure up scenarios which never existed.

With no obvious enemies to focus the investigation on, their deaths are taking the shape of a hate crime. The list of suspects for such an act is an unknown quantity – made worse by the resurgence of open Klan activity. Marches have taken place throughout a number of states. Utah has a history of being a Klan stronghold and Casperton is a remote enough town for members to believe they can act as if it were still the twenties.

Another thing chewing at my mind is the conversation I had with Kenneth after I'd dealt with the Augiers. He told me a little more about the man who'd been looking for me. A man with an accent like mine.

I need more time and less of a workload to try and figure out who the man may be. The fact he sounds like me means he's Scottish, which suggests a relative across on vacation. Yet it can't be as simple as that. If a relative was across visiting, I'd have known about it.

My mother would have organised a big dinner and a party for them; if for no other reason than to be the centre of attention. The relatives would have been regaled with tales of my sister's successful business, and my refusal to settle down and provide my mother with grandchildren to spoil.

The fact this hasn't happened suggests the person looking for me is an unknown quantity. From Kenneth's sketchy description of the man it's hard to determine if he's someone sent over by a lawyer, or if he's a former acquaintance who's travelling across the States and has decided to look me up.

It's a stretch though, as it's twenty odd years since I left Glasgow and I've not heard from any of my old friends. I made promises I didn't keep and as soon as I realised what my Scottish brogue did to the local girls, all thoughts of Glaswegian mates were forsaken. If I'd been a few years older, there's a better chance I'd have somehow kept in touch, but I wasn't the only one to blame. None of them had written to me either.

If social media, or even emails, had existed, keeping in touch would have been a lot easier. Teenage boys are not renowned for their letter-writing skills.

The one ghost from my past that I expect to never turn up is my father. He walked out of the family home when I was six and hasn't been seen or heard of since. It was Mother remarrying which brought us to Casperton.

Elizabeth greets me with a tight smile tinged with sadness. My presence here is a reminder of the horror which has invaded her world.

She's brisk and business-like as she hands over an envelope.

I take a seat and break the seal. Inside is a single sheet of paper.

Below the letterhead is a name and address. Below that, a date and a brief outline of the case Darryl had fought against a Mr Jefferson.

'I'm guessing this is all you can give me without breaking attorney-client confidentiality?'

'I'm afraid it is. However, I can tell you from personal experience that when Mr Jefferson lost the case he flew into a rage, and shouted a lot of dumb threats.'

I like what she's saying, but all of this happened long ago. It's a stretch to think this Jefferson guy has killed a lawyer who defeated him five years ago.

Still, it's not beyond the bounds of possibility. Perhaps Jefferson has pinpointed losing that case as the beginning of a slide his life has taken; I need Alfonse to dig into the guy's life.

A chime from my phone as I leave LH Associates makes me reconsider my plans for the day.

Chapter 18

Dr Edwards looks at me over steepled fingers, as is his way, his face as inscrutable as ever. I would have blown off the appointment but I know Dr Edwards may be able to help me understand the killer's motive.

'I need your help.'

'Do you realise the implications of what you've just said?' His face still hasn't changed. I must remember to never play poker with him.

'You don't understand, Doctor. I need your help with a case I'm investigating.'

His lips purse beneath his beard and fine lines appear at the edges of his eyes. 'Would I be right to assume you're looking into the murders of the family found up at Ashley Forest?'

I nod. 'I need your opinion on what mind-set the killers may have – to commit a crime like that.'

'I'm not a criminal psychologist, Jake. I'm just a plain old regular psychologist who's trying to help a man who has some issues he needs to work through.'

'And I'm a layman. Your knowledge and insights can help me.' It's not the first time we've done this dance. 'They have before.'

He rests back into his chair. 'Same arrangement?' I know I've got him on board although it's going to cost me more than I want to pay. It would be easy if it was money he was after. Instead he wants the truth about my feelings. Why I have stayed single and how it's connected to my father's abandonment of us. It works like a quid pro quo deal; I get his insights on the case but in return I have to give honest answers to his probing questions.

I tell him how the bodies were arranged at the dump site. His eyes widen as I speak. It's good to see him have a human reaction to a horrific situation. I would think less of him if he didn't.

'So, you're investigating their deaths and, by extension, their lives.' His words are a statement rather than a question. 'I presume you're looking at possible enemies and, because of the way they were killed, you'll also be considering hate groups.'

'You're right with your presumptions. So far, we've uncovered no known enemies, and everything we've learned points to them being well liked. This, in turn, suggests it's a hate crime rather than a targeted one.'

He leans forward, placing his elbows on the desk and resting his chin on steepled fingers. I let him think in peace. What I'm asking him is outside his area of expertise and I want him to give me a properly thought out answer.

I look around the office while he thinks; its muted tones are supposed to be calming. A couple of framed certificates hang on a wall. A watercolour of Kangle's Bluff is the only splash of colour.

'I can only judge hate groups from what I've seen in the media as I have no personal experience of them. Taking the Ku Klux Klan as an example, it would seem they are organised and have some kind of code of conduct. Their activity seems limited to marches. Their days of burning crosses and hangings, thankfully, seem to be in their past. I also think that if it was them, there would be other incidents across the country.'

He makes sense and I tell him as much. 'What about other groups?'

'Neo Nazis wouldn't stage it to make it look like a Klan killing. They'd do it their own way and leave something there to claim the credit.'

'Are you suggesting it's an unknown group?'

'I'm not suggesting anything. I'm just giving you my interpretation of the facts.' He looks me in the eye. 'My turn. What's the longest relationship you've had?'

'About three months. What about the mentality of these killers?'

'I can't answer that because I've never met, or treated, anyone who'd do such a thing. The best I can imagine is that they are aggrieved at the Fourniers for no other reason than their skin colour. It may be the twenty-first century but there's still a lot of nineteenth century thinking. Racism isn't something that can be quickly eradicated from a person's beliefs. Especially not if they are surrounded by like-minded people.' He scratches his ear and picks up a pen. 'Why do you think three months is the longest relationship you've had?'

'Because I've never wanted to settle down with anyone.'

My answer is trite even to my own ears and I just know he's going to follow it up.

'Why is that, Jake? Have you not found the right woman, or is it a fallout from your father's abandonment?'

'I've never pictured myself with a wife and kids. Don't get me wrong, I like kids, I just don't think I'm cut out to look after one.'

He gives a little chuckle. 'That's what everyone thinks. Most of us pick it up as we go along.'

I'm making excuses and we both know it. The real truth is that I remember the pain when Dad left and I know how badly my mother blamed herself. I don't want to be the one to cause such hurt. On the flip side, I never want another person I love to abandon me.

'These killers, what about their mind set? I mean, c'mon, they've nailed a family of four to crosses and then set them on fire. They must be psychotic, right?'

'I can't answer that without asking them how they feel about it. If they're now feeling remorse, then strictly speaking they are not psychotic. I suspect they will be though. The level of preparation needed for what they've done speaks of premeditation rather than impulse. My fear is this may only be the start. To kill in this way shows signs of egotism – megalomania even.'

'How?' The Glasgow use of the word slips out unbidden. It's a long time since I lived there, but it's where my roots are.

'To take a life is a big step. To do so deliberately is a bigger one. To pre-plan to kill, and persuade others to help, shows a huge ego. The driving force behind this attack is an extremely dangerous person. I suspect they enjoyed what they did. Not in any sexual way, just as a means to an end. They'll be fanatical in their beliefs like religious zealots. I believe they'll see the murders as just.'

As I'm digesting what he's said, he catches me with a broadside.

'I trust you're not serious about Taylor?'

I don't answer him. I can't without confirming I'm dating his receptionist and putting her job in jeopardy.

'Don't worry, I'm not trying to trick you. I overheard her talking to a friend about you.' He gives a rueful smile. 'If I'm honest I didn't expect it to last this long.'

He's been honest with me, so I give him the truth. 'I don't plan how long I'll be with someone. It's just when women start looking for commitment from me, or for the relationship to progress, I find myself drawing back. Things peter out and we part company.'

'Then all I can say is let her down gently.'

As I make for the door he offers a final word of caution. 'These people you're hunting are dangerous, amoral killers. Like it or not, your accent marks you out as a foreigner. Stay safe.'

Chapter 19

The van takes a sharp turn causing Gazala to slide into the boots of one of her captors. He straightens his leg, pushing her back into the centre of the floor.

Try as she might, Gazala can't keep the fear from her eyes. Now the initial shock of being abducted has worn off, and her efforts to fight back or escape have proved futile, she has realised she is going wherever the men are taking her.

The gag in her mouth prevents her from begging for her life. The only part of her body she can use is her eyes.

She can see the three men guarding her. Two are older and the third is around her age. One of the older ones looks as if he's been beaten up, the other has a bald head.

Figuring that the younger man offers her the best chance of some sympathy, Gazala tries to give him a beseeching look.

The bald man beside him is the one who reacts first. 'Look, boy, she's giving you the eye. Reckon she wants you.'

'She can want. I ain't puttin' my dick in no chink slut.' The youth's disgust at the suggestion fills the back of the van with enough contempt to start a fight with the stench of sweat.

'You dumbass. She ain't no chink. She's brown not yellow.'

'Yeah? What is she then?'

'Damned if I know. Korean maybe, or somewhere like that. She'll be one of them Muslim bitches though.' The bald man scratches at his ear, a lecherous grin splitting his face. 'So you wouldn't, huh?'

'No way. Dunno what I'd catch from screwing a Muslim.'

Gazala bites down on her gag. Even though she's Hindu, not Muslim, she knows these men are prejudiced against her. Telling them her true religion will achieve nothing apart from increasing the number of potential rapists.

The man with the battered face speaks for the first time. 'You might think different if you could see what I can see. It might be the wrong colour but I'm sure it'll work mighty fine.'

Gazala turns her head and sees the man has knelt on the van's floor and is looking up her skirt.

She forces her knees over and manages to roll onto her side.

'Don't matter what you can see, I ain't interested.'

'You don't know what you're missin', boy. That warm pussy will squirm like a snake. Do you see her eyes? She's a fighter. Fighters make some good lovin'.'

'You do her then. I ain't puttin' my dick in no Muslim bitch.'

'You sure? We'll hold her down for you.'

'No way.'

Their callous words bounce off Gazala as she realises a new truth. She expects to be raped. Without being conceited, she knows she's pretty and has a decent figure. That they plan to rape her is a terrible thing for her to know.

It is the youth's disgust which makes the synapses in her brain make the necessary connections. He doesn't want to rape her. He's disgusted by the idea. Not the rape itself, but the contact with her.

While they're talking about raping her, they're not actually touching her yet. When they hauled her into the van, held her down and bound her, there was no sexual molestation.

Her biggest concern is that their faces aren't covered and their tattooed forearms are on display. Even the most dim-witted abductor would know to hide their face, and recognisable features like tattoos, from their victims.

This can mean only one thing. They don't care about her being able to identify them because they plan to kill her.

A thought crash-lands in her head; a vague memory of a news item half-heard over family chatter.

Something about a family being murdered. Something about crosses and fire.

The bad news synapse fires again.

The murdered family were black.

Their bodies were found on charred crosses.

Only racists would do such a thing.

She's been snatched by a group who despise her for what they perceive to be her religion.

The man driving the van had looked at her as if she was the lowest of the low. He'd been checking her out as a victim not a conquest.

Religious and racial hatred often walk hand in hand.

Her brain shuts down as complete terror envelops her. She'd renew her struggles to break free of her bonds if her body wasn't suffering such extreme shakes. Her teeth are sawing at the gag as her head thrashes about.

Her final indignity is her bladder emptying itself.

The drawl of the bald man rises above the thuds of her body on the van's aluminium floor. 'Looky here, boys. Our girl is getting all wet thinking about us.'

'Dirty Muslim bitch. She's filth and deserves to die.' The youth's heavy work boot swings out and catches Gazala's chin knocking her out.

Chapter 20

I switch off my phone and think about my conversation with Alfonse. He has computing skills far beyond the average person and can track, trace and find out information which is inaccessible to ninety-nine percent of the population. There are very few databases he can't hack his way into when the notion takes him. Ideally he should be in Washington or New York working for a three letter agency, but he's never been drawn to that kind of life.

I've asked him to find Jefferson for me. I have the address from Elizabeth, but it's several years old and a three hour drive away. Once he's confirmed an address, I can go and speak to him. Another thing I've asked him to do is to look into the Fournier's finances and through their computers. It's a long shot, but we have to consider every possible avenue of investigation.

The main thing I want him to look at though, is the Deep Web. That area of the internet where sites don't try to be found. Rather they stay undercover. This is the area where the worst of the internet lies. The sites featuring Islamic activists beheading their captives; suicide forums; the worst kinds of extreme porn and a hundred and one other illegal services. If you need anything from fake ID to a contract killer, the Deep Web is the place you can buy it.

The brief I gave Alfonse is very specific for someone looking in a hidden place, for something that doesn't want to be found, but if anyone can find it, he can.

I'm about to turn onto Main when my phone informs me of a message from Mother. As usual she's typed in block capitals. Whenever Sharon and I explain that block capitals are akin to shouting, she just nods and tells us we always did respond better to shouts.

MEET ME AT SHERRI'S. 30 MINS

I send one back saying I'm too busy. Her reply comes back within seconds.

IF YOU DON'T COME I WILL REDECORATE THE TREE WITH YOUR BABY PHOTOS.

Knowing her, it's not an idle threat. What I thought was a lunch invitation is really her summoning me. There are only two reasons for the summons. One is a set-up with the daughter or niece of one of her friends. The other is that she's heard about the investigation I'm working on and wants to berate me for risking my life chasing killers. I hope it's the first one.

As I'm walking into Sherri's another possibility strikes me. Perhaps she knows who the mysterious stranger asking about me is, and is going to tell me about him.

Sherri's is a fifties diner which has preserved its original décor, rather than a modern place fitted out to look like one. It's ruled by the iron fist and soft heart of Sherri's daughter and is the kind of place where you get reprimanded for not cleaning your plate. I eat here on a regular basis.

Mother is sitting in one of the leather seated booths at the back of the diner. She's alone and wears an expression that would frighten a gargoyle.

I slide in beside her and offer a peck to her cheek.

She turns her head away. Not good.

Her eyes flash with anger and worry as she looks at me. 'You're investigating those murders, aren't you?'

'Of course I am. I can't let Alfonse down. He needs me.'

'The police are paid to chase killers. You're not.'

I can't prevent the scorn in my voice. 'Oh c'mon. You know how useless they are. You're not seriously saying I should leave Alfonse to investigate it himself, are you?'

'I'm saying you shouldn't go risking your life again. You were lucky once, you might not be so lucky a second time.' There's a fierce intensity to her expression and tone. 'Promise me you won't risk your life again. It's bad enough not being a granny without having to bury my one chance of grandkids.'

There it is again. Even when she's worried about my safety she manages to bring children into the conversation. The desire for grandchildren fuels everything she says to me. With my sister unable to conceive, I am Mother's only chance and she's forever on my back about settling down and starting a family.

'Nobody's getting buried. I'm helping Alfonse identify the people who killed the Fourniers and that's all. As soon as we have a suspect we'll hand the information over to Chief Watson and step back.'

Her snort draws the attention of other diners. 'Forgive me if I don't believe you. Remember the last time you said that to me? You damn near got yoursel' killed.'

She has me there. I have no defence, so I don't offer one. Instead, I wave away her concerns.

'This is different. He ended up hunting me.'

'You carrying that gun I gave you?'

During the search for a serial killer, she gave me a gun to protect myself when I ignored her entreaties to drop the case. It's now under the spare in the trunk of my car. Guns scare me. I don't know how to use them and, as such, I'll be a greater threat to myself, and those I'm trying to protect, than my intended targets. Besides, pulling a weapon of any kind escalates the situation.

'I'm involved in the investigation, not the hunt. Taking down a bunch of racist killers is a job for law enforcement officers with a SWAT team at their disposal. I'm a doorman at a bar – not a vigilante or an avenging angel.'

'You've got MacDonald blood in your veins.' She takes a sip of her coffee. 'Plus a nose for trouble and a stubborn streak that's got you into more than your fair share of fights.'

'I'm telling you, don't worry. One fight to the death is more than enough for me. It's not an experience I plan on repeating.'

I stand and leave before she can reply. That last outburst was perhaps a little harsh considering how I've dodged her questions on the issue, but at the same time it may well give her the reassurance she craves.

What I haven't told her, or anyone else, is how I can't sleep due to reliving the moment.

Were there a Catholic church in Casperton, I dare say I'd end up in a confessional booth. A Glasgow upbringing isn't something you can escape.

Considering Mother's concerns, I'm glad I didn't quiz her on who might be asking around town for me. She's worried enough as it is without me adding to her burden.

When I have a spare moment I'll call my sister. She's the one who keeps in regular contact with the family back in Glasgow. If it's anything to do with the family, she'll know.

Chapter 21

Chief Watson is at his desk when I stride into his office. The desk is neat with only a large sketchpad, telephone and framed photo on it. As ever, the sketchpad is littered with scribbles and notes in his scrawl. I know from experience they are placed in no kind of order. He just writes wherever his pen lands. It wouldn't work for me, but everyone has their own methods and he's the only law enforcer within fifty miles who I trust to run a proper investigation.

'You got anything, Boulder?'

His tone is full of stress and it's only a matter of time before he starts kneading his temples.

I fill him in on what Alfonse and I have learned and give him a moment to digest it.

'You reckon it's this Jefferson?' He scratches his chin. 'It doesn't seem likely to me.'

'Nor me. I'm still gonna check him out though.'

'I like the idea about the Augiers. They seem much better candidates for this kind of thing.'

'Are you thinking it's Klan related?'

The chief fixes me with a scorn-laden stare. 'Of course I am. What else can it be? Those rednecks sound like they're the type to get mixed up in that kinda thing.'

'Perhaps they are; perhaps they're not.' I shrug. 'I know they're not the finest part of society, but I'm not sure they're that bad.'

'If not them, then who?'

'That's the big question. As horrible as it seems, it'd be better if the Fourniers were targeted because of a grudge rather than the colour of their skin. I've got Alfonse going through their computers and their finances.'

'I wish I could share your enthusiasm for it being anything other than a hate crime. The nature of their deaths screams Klan activity to me. Nobody else would do such a thing. Can you imagine how they suffered?' He doesn't pause long enough for me to answer. 'Those poor, poor people. Tell me something, Boulder. If that's not a hate crime, then what is it?'

'I think you're right that it's a hate crime. I just don't want to jump to any conclusions before there's evidence to back up the theory. If I wanted to shift the blame for a murder I'd committed, this seems like a pretty good way.'

'You're saying the method was chosen as a distraction to the investigation?' His knuckles begin to knead his temples. 'If it's not hard enough looking for unknown Klan members, now we also have to identify a group who're impersonating them.'

I don't bother to answer his question. It's three parts rhetorical and we've already been over this ground. Instead I tell him about the things I've asked Alfonse to look into.

He nods in agreement as he listens.

'Can he really search in those places?'

Being mindful of who I'm speaking to, I hesitate before answering. The chief waves a hand and tells me not to worry about him going after Alfonse.

'Alfonse can get into all kinds of places. If anyone can pinpoint things on the Deep Web, it's him. Haven't you got your tech guys looking at their stuff?'

He follows my change of subject. 'Yeah, but they're not what you call quick. Or efficient. Tell you the truth, Boulder, I only ever understand one word in three when they send me a report.'

I keep the smile off my face but it isn't easy. Chief Watson is of a generation where computer usage is a necessary evil. He'll have limited skills with those programs he needs to use. Internet browsing and email will be familiar to him as will whatever software the police uses.

The science behind computers will seem like witchcraft to him. How things actually work, and the technical terms used, may as well be Sanskrit for all his understanding of it.

'What about the pathologist? Have you got any results from the autopsies yet?'

'I have. They were alive when they were nailed to the crosses and alive when they were set alight.' He pauses to let me ponder his words. It's not a pleasant experience.

'What about the toxicology reports?'

I'm stretching here. Hoping they were sedated before their murders. The chief shakes his head, his eyes full of sorrow. 'Still awaiting results.'

I leave it a couple of minutes before speaking. The silence in the office is almost ethereal in its quality. Sure, the noises and chatter of the police station rattle on in the background, but I feel as if I've been transported elsewhere. From the look on his face, the chief is in a similar place.

'Have you any ideas on the dump site?'

Do you mean why it was chosen?'

'I do. It seems odd to me.'

'Not to me. It's in the middle of nowhere. Those poor folks could scream their heads off and there wouldn't be a single person to hear them.'

I fix him with a stare. 'That's my point. Klan activity is usually more overt. Burning crosses used as warnings. Gangs of people at hangings. You saw the track up to the dump site. Didn't look like a whole lot of people hiked up there.'

'What are you saying, Boulder?'

His use of my name is a warning so I pick my words with care. 'If those hunters or hikers hadn't found the Fourniers they could have been there for weeks – or months. It was a horrific act carried out in secrecy. The Klan are no longer about being secretive; they have marches, websites and even spokespeople. The Klan want people to know about their activity. To be scared by it. Their goal is to have only white Christian men in positions of power. They consider themselves to be knights. They use terms like Imperial Wizard to describe their big kahunas. Their websites preach non-violence and show dates and times of future meets.'

His hands slam on the desk as he stands up. 'What, you're telling me they're all just horribly misunderstood? You'll be telling me that piranhas make great bath toys next.' There's enough scorn in his voice to flay a walrus.

If anyone else spoke to me like that, I'd have made them horizontal by now. Laying out the chief of police however, is a bad idea. Doubly so when you need his help.

'You're not a stupid man, Chief. I suggest you stop acting like one.' If I can't slug him, I'm sure as hell going to bring him down a peg or two.

We stare each other out for a moment until we're interrupted by the desk sergeant. He passes the chief a message.

The paper is tossed onto the desk as the chief slumps into his chair. 'An Indian girl has gone missing.'

'Don't you mean native American?'

'I mean Indian, as in, from the country India.' He's calmer but not by much. 'She left for work this morning and didn't get there. Her purse and cell were found lying on a sidewalk halfway between work and home.

The implications of the girl's heritage isn't lost on either of us. Her purse and cell being found on a sidewalk indicate she's been abducted and her belongings discarded. These days even the densest of criminals knows to dispose of their victims' cell phones.

It's too early for a normal missing person's report to be filed and acted upon. Twenty-four hours is the starting point for that. Neither of us say that though.

My immediate thought is that, if she's been snatched by a person or persons unknown, she'll be terrified she'll be raped, or if she's seen the news, of being crucified and burned alive.

If she's been grabbed by the gang who killed the Fourniers, her chances of survival are so low as to be negligible. Provided she hasn't already been murdered.

The chief is on his feet – the hat in his hands a sign our meeting is over. I promise to call him later, and leave.

My next stop is Green River. It's a hundred and eighty miles or so to the south. I plan to be there within two hours.

Chapter 22

Gazala comes to, only to find she's still in the back of the panel van. The floor pitching and yawing causes her to slide around, bumping into the boots of her captors.

Their conversation has moved from rape to sports. They're discussing the pitcher for Salt Lake Bees and his recent game stats.

Her jaw hurts and she's desperate for a cold drink. Neither of these things worry her too much. In the greater scheme of things such minor discomforts as thirst and a sore chin are the least of her problems.

It doesn't take her long to work out they must be travelling along a rough track. The movement of the floor tells her as much.

This can mean only one thing: she's being taken somewhere remote. Somewhere her captors can rape or kill her without being disturbed.

Every time the van lurches into a hole, or over a rut, she picks up another bruise. It doesn't matter; she wants the journey to last forever. Whatever happens when she is taken out of the van will be far worse than anything she's endured so far.

The van draws to a halt and her captors clamber out. The bald man slides the door shut behind him.

Now she's alone she begins to fight against her bonds. Her efforts cause her body to wriggle across the floor. Something pointed digs into her back and snags at her blouse.

She can feel where it's drawn blood and the realisation is a welcome one. If it's sharp enough to cut her skin through the blouse, it'll be sharp enough to cut through the tape binding her wrists.

It takes a lot of wriggling for Gazala to manoeuvre her body so she can saw at the tape binding her wrists. Once in position, she saws her arms back and forth until she feels the tape begin to part.

After what seems like an age, the last strand of tape parts and her hands are free. As she picks at the end of the tape around her ankles with her right hand, she rubs her left hand against her side in an effort to restore some blood flow.

After a minute she changes hands and uses weak fingers to grasp the end of the tape which her nails have worked loose. Thirty seconds later her ankles are free.

She grits her teeth and pulls at the tape holding her gag in place. However much it hurts, she mustn't cry out. If they hear her cry out they'll know she's broken free of her bonds.

One quick yank and the tape is on the floor of the van, along with the other pieces. The skin around her mouth burns but no sound escapes her lips.

Now she has a decision to make. Does she try and escape now or does she wait until the men come for her, and burst out of the door as soon as they open it?

Both options are fraught with danger. If the men are outside the van, they'll react as soon as she opens the door. Waiting for them to open the door is also full of risk. Instead of getting away unseen she'll be entering a race right from the start. As her captors have the van, the only way she'll be able to escape is to go across the countryside.

Not the best of ideas when the men are sure to know this area much better than her. It's still a better idea than letting them do whatever they're planning to do though.

To help her decide she puts her ear to the back door and listens.

She hears voices. Not loud, not quiet, just the voices of a group of men chatting. She guesses they are about eight or ten feet from the back of the van.

Too close for comfort. By the time she's opened the door and taken a step they'll be on her.

This means she'll have to burst past her captors and hope she can outrun them.

Now she knows what she has to do, she starts looking at ways she can give herself every possible advantage.

Her shoes are ballet style flats. Great for comfort and work but not good for running. If she loses a shoe and has to run barefoot she may as well stop and let the men recapture her.

She remembers the man who bound her dropping the roll of tape into a tool locker at the front of the van. The youth and the bald man had used the locker as a seat.

When she heaves the lid open she finds the roll of tape sitting on a bag of tools. She removes the tape, a screwdriver and a utility knife.

The knife blade is an inch in length. Long enough to do some damage with a slash but no use as a stabbing weapon. That's where the screwdriver comes in. It's the kind of long, thin, narrow type used on wall sockets or other fine work.

A hammer, or something else that could be used as a club, would have been a good find, but there wasn't one. It could be a good thing; the extra weight may slow her down or at least upset her rhythm.

She moves on, conscious the men may come back for her at any moment.

Using the weapons is a last resort to prevent recapture. There are at least four men outside the van and she knows there's no way she can fight them all off. The weapons are there for defence should one of them manage to grab her.

She puts the weapons on the floor and winds the tape around each foot in turn. With her feet secured into her shoes, Gazala turns her attention to her skirt. It's tight enough to hinder her legs at full stride.

That can't be allowed to happen. She can either remove the skirt or hitch it up over her hips.

Gazala is about to hitch up the skirt when her eyes land on the knife. Rather than risk the skirt lowering itself as she runs, she slips it off and cuts a slit in both sides before pulling it back on. Now her dignity will be more or less maintained and her skirt will provide no hindrance to her planned sprint.

With her preparations complete, she goes through a series of stretching routines to make sure her muscles are ready for the sudden burst of exercise she's going to give them.

Five minutes into her exercises she hears a hand grab the handle of the van's back door.

She tenses herself, ready to dash; to stab and slash if need be.

It's the youth who opens the door. Gazala's hand turns at the last moment so she delivers a backhanded punch to his face rather than a slash.

Unprepared, and off balance, he staggers backwards before tripping into the bald man.

Gazala sees none of this. She's travelling past him as soon as the blow lands. Ahead of her is open land. A track runs from left to right and there's a ranger, or forester station a few yards to the right.

She runs straight ahead. Towards the open land where the van can't follow her.

With the possible exception of the youth, she reckons she'll be fitter and faster than any of them.

Shouts follow her. Gunshots don't.

She hears heavy footsteps, and heavier breathing, for twenty paces but it starts to fade as she outruns her pursuers.

If she can just keep going for a few more minutes she'll be far enough ahead to slow to a pace more suited to the rough terrain. That she might turn an ankle is a constant fear.

Chapter 23

I pull into the car park of a motel. Jefferson's listed address is next door and I want to have a scout of the area.

Green River is one of those cities that populate all the main interstates. Spaced every hundred miles or so, their main trade comes from gas stations, diners and motels servicing the passing travellers. Garages and mom and pop stores also do a decent turn and the rest of the economy supports itself with local services. Casperton would be the same if it hadn't got lucky by establishing itself beside some oilfields.

A rumble of my stomach tells me it's time I ate. I want to ignore it, but I know I need sustenance of some kind. Discussions with strangers always go better if your body doesn't embarrass you. A bathroom would also be good. I made the drive from Casperton in a little over two hours, but only because I'd shattered the speed limit and managed not to get pulled over.

I take a look along the wide street and spy a diner halfway along the next block. The walk is a short one taken with long strides as I welcome the chance to stretch my legs.

The diner is like Sherri's without the authenticity; or the high standards of hygiene; or the friendly staff.

Most tables are occupied, although none of the patrons seem too enamoured with the place. Off to one side a mid-forties couple are engaging in a hissed argument while another couple are struggling to contain their young children from burning off steam now they've escaped the confines of a car.

A trucker shovels food into his mouth as if it's the first meal he's had for weeks, while a man who must have waved goodbye to his eighties several years ago, stares into his cup with rheumy eyes.

The server greets me with a bored expression. She looks as if she's spent her life making bad decisions, and waiting tables is her punishment.

'C'n I getcha?'

Even her voice sounds defeated. There's no effort to add warmth or basic civility. I stop short of pointing out that friendly waiting staff can double, or treble, their wages with tips, and order a well-done burger and some fries. It's hard to get food poisoning from well-cooked meat, and the heat of the oil in the fryer will see off any germs on the fries.

While I'm waiting, I focus my mind on the same things I've been looking at all the way down here: the questions I want to ask Jefferson, the missing girl, whether Alfonse has learned anything, and whether the search team found any clues on the trail up to the dump site.

The questions are all no brainers – depending upon Jefferson's answers I may have to think on my feet. I've tried to foresee as many comebacks as possible, but don't expect I've thought of them all.

The Indian girl who appears to have been snatched is a worry. I should have asked Chief Watson for more details. The obvious ones like her name, age and where she was travelling from and to.

It was stupid of me not to do so. My job at the Tree means I know a lot of the people in Casperton and there's a chance I know her. I can think of three girls whose race could put them in the frame, but know only one of them well enough to do anything more than pass inane greetings. I hope it's not the one I know as she has two young kids.

The chief won't be able to start an official investigation into her disappearance until the obligatory twenty-four hours have passed. In normal circumstances he'd be able to start looking for her pretty much right away. He'll be annoyed and frustrated there's no way he can redirect any of his resources away from the investigation into the multiple murders, regardless of how much he may suspect the Indian girl's life is at stake.

My last thought jars with me. I'm thinking of this missing girl as the Indian girl. That's wrong. She's a girl with Indian parents. I think of myself as a guy, rather than a Scottish guy. Why should she be any different?

This is the kind of natural and casual racism that creeps into society and goes unnoticed. It's nowhere near as bad as it used to be, but it's still there in all of us. My grandfather's tongue was laden with terms like darkie, chink or wog. While those terms are now outdated and offensive, racial stereotyping and grouping still goes on in our subconscious.

Alfonse is my best friend and I've never thought of him as anything other than a guy, a mate, a buddy. Not once in all the years I've known him have I used his skin colour as an identifier or as the butt of a joke. Yet when someone adds a country of origin to a person's sex, my subconscious pounces on it and gift wraps the whole package into one racist parcel.

My burger and fries arrive as Darla answers my call. The chief's assistant gives me the information I need and manages to call me sweetheart twice, and honey four times, in a three minute conversation.

The missing girl's name is Gazala Kulkarni. She's twenty-two and was born and bred in Casperton. I wasn't, and as such will never be classed as a true local. Gazala lives with her parents and works at C-Dude. According to the report filed by her father she left home at eight-thirty and never arrived at work. Her boss had called at ten after nine demanding to know why she wasn't at work.

I'll refocus on her disappearance as I drive back to Casperton. For the meantime, the Indian girl shall no longer exist. Her name is Gazala and that's the way she deserves to be thought of.

The burger and fries are better than expected and the plate is in good condition with no bacteria-laden chips or cracks. The chef must care more about hygiene than the waiting staff.

I call Darla again and get answers to the questions I forgot to ask the chief.

The search of the trail uncovered three faded candy wrappers, six cigarette butts, one cigar butt and, best of all, a few flakes of white paint. The paint was from where a vehicle appeared to have slid from the trail and scraped against a tree.

What is most encouraging is that the searchers' report stated the tree showed a recent gouge which had led them to finding the paint flakes.

I'm no expert on the subject, but I've read enough crime novels to know automobile paint can be traced to a particular vehicle. It's just a matter of time before the lab results come in and give us a make and model.

Saliva from the cigar and cigarette butts would be better than an ID on the paint. A quick run through a DNA database or two and the chief could be on the phone to the nearest SWAT team.

The torrential rain on the night of the murders is likely to have ruined any chance of a DNA trace. I'm sure Chief Watson will have sent them for tests anyway. The odds are it'll be a waste of time and money, but he'll have procedures to follow and he might just get lucky.

I'm tempted to call Alfonse, but I know he'll call me as soon as he has some news. I also know disturbing him when he's deep in a project is a bad idea. Once he gets himself on the digital highways he's lost to the world. Interruptions are met with biting sarcasm. The fact I've directed him off the highways, onto the back roads, will at least double his displeasure at my calling for an update.

I decide against calling him and count out the exact change to pay the check. As an insult to the least-welcoming waitress in Utah, I leave a solitary dime three inches to the side of the check. It's tight of me, but no more than she deserves.

Once I'm outside, I walk round to the back of the diner and find the trade entrance. My knock is answered by a homely woman with a natural smile.

'Yes, sugar?'

I hand over a five dollar bill. 'Your waitress will come back here in a minute. She'll be bitching about a customer who left her a dime tip. Tell her it's a statement of customer satisfaction, and share the real tip among those who've done their jobs the way they're paid to.'

The waitress's voice comes storming out the door carrying its own weight in expletives.

I get a knowing smile and a wink as the homely woman pulls the door closed.

Chapter 24

The house is a nice one, even if it is next to a motel. The Mercedes on the drive is a recent model. The guy who lives here won't be rooting down the back of his couch for loose change. If Mike Jefferson is the man who answers the door I've wasted my time coming to Green River.

He stands five-three in his sandals and has the build a supermodel would consider too thin. Not only that, his skin is two shades of ebony darker than Alfonse's.

Still, I've made the journey, so I might as well ask my questions, stupid as they now seem.

I've learned that telling the truth about why I'm asking questions, can distort, or even prevent, the answers. I proffer my hand and get ready to shovel some bull. I've done this enough times to know I need to speak fast and with conviction.

'Hi. Are you Mike Jefferson? I'm Jake Boulder, you don't know me, but my lawyer has told me about you. Said you were the right man to offer me a lifeline.'

He's intrigued. Who wouldn't be, upon learning that a lawyer has said they could save a stranger.

He smiles. 'You got two minutes, Mister, and then I'm going to close this door.'

For a little man he's got plenty of arrogance. I may have to give him a focussing dig in the ribs if he gets too cocksure.

'You tried to buy the Railroad Inn in Casperton a few years back. I bought it last year and can't make a go of it. My lawyer told me you might be the man to take it off me and turn it around.'

His eyes narrow as I speak. He'll be remembering his conduct at the time.

"Fraid you've had a wasted journey. Best thing that happened to me not gettin' that place. I'm guessing your lawyer is the guy who kicked my ass in court. Didn't know it at the time but that dude did me a big favour. When you see him, tell him I apologise for all the stuff I said back then.'

He goes to close the door. My boot gets in the way.

'I'm curious, why is it the best thing that happened to you?'

He glares at me until I change my expression. All of a sudden his cockiness goes. Perhaps he's realised I might just be pissed enough to lash out. He'd be right.

Problem is, it'd be like smacking a child. There's no glory or satisfaction to be had from winning an unfair fight.

'When I didn't get that place, I bought a motel instead. Got four now and it's easy money. Once you own all the places along a section of highway, you can charge whatcha like.'

I try another angle. Honesty. 'I'm not really looking to sell the Railroad to you. I'm investigating the murder of the lawyer you threatened.'

'I knew you was spinning me some line.' He taps his nose. 'Got me a damn fine bullshit detector. When was he killed?'

There's no worry in his face. Curiosity, yes. Concern for his own implication, no.

'Two nights back.'

'Figured it might have been. You're wastin' your time again. Just had me a few days in Vegas. Only got back a couple of hours ago.' He pulls out his phone. Shows me his Facebook feed. It's filled with selfies in front of Sin City's various landmarks.

It's a dead end. It was always a long shot, but Jefferson's alibi makes it feel like a wasted effort.

I point the nose of my Mustang towards the 191 and lean on the gas pedal.

It doesn't take me long to start second-guessing myself.

Jefferson could have taken those pictures at any time and just uploaded them over the last few days. He could have been lying about owning four motels.

I make a mental note to get Alfonse to check out his story, for no other reason than to stop me doubting myself. Whichever way I look at it, I can't see a black man setting up a murder scene in a way that suggests Klan activity.

What if it's a deliberate set-up by members of the ethnic community who are trying to trigger a race war with the Klan?

The thought is so extreme it makes me question my own sanity.

I prod at this theory for a mile or two and then discard it as stupid. My brain has more important things to think about than ridiculous ideas. Today's multicultural America is too advanced for a full hate war. Sure, there are pockets of idealists all over the country, but they lack the support of the general public and, as such, are only a threat in isolated areas. Most of these will be on the radar of at least one government agency and will receive close scrutiny.

Chapter 25

Gazala's arms pump as she hurtles her way through the brush. The rough branches of scrub tear her skin as her legs thrust her forwards, but she doesn't feel anything except terror.

She can hear the panting of her captors and the heavy thuds of their boots as they chase after her. Their shouted curses fly past her ears, each one creating an extra prickle of urgency. And terror.

The ground is rough underfoot with a myriad of loose stones and small pebbles to slip on, yet the tape binding her shoes in place does its job and she's able to run at three quarters of the pace she could manage on a racetrack.

Her eyes are fixed ten feet in front of her. They're looking for the easiest path, the worst obstacles and hidden dangers like snakes and animal burrows.

A hundred yards from the van she finds a narrow animal track. It may be less than a foot wide and nothing like straight, but, compared to the terrain she's already crossed, it's a godsend.

She stretches her legs, further increasing her speed.

The shouts behind her are getting fainter.

She risks a look over her shoulder. Sees the youth fifty yards behind her. The bald man some twenty paces behind him.

Looking back is a mistake. When she returns her eyes forward she sees a twist in the trail later than is wise at the speed she's running.

Her ankle bends as she makes a sudden change of direction to avoid the foot-high cactus. She misses the spiky plant but sprawls in a tangled heap; her grip on the makeshift weapons loosening as instinct opens her hands ready to break her fall.

She tries to rise. To resume her dash for safety.

Her ankle gives way as soon as she puts weight on it.

The scream which escapes her mouth is divided equally between pain, frustration and sheer unadulterated terror.

The younger of her captors catches up with her. Sees her clutching her ankle and starts to laugh around his gasps for air.

His panting adds greater insult than the laughter. It shows he is nowhere near as fit as she is. If she hadn't injured herself, there is no way he would have caught her.

He leaves her half lying, half sitting, until his breathing settles. When his chest stops heaving, his fingers grasp her arms as he stands her upright.

She expects him to hit her. Or kick her ankle.

He does neither. His back bends and she feels his bony shoulder dig into her gut as he straightens with her over his shoulder.

'You hit me just once, I'll stand you up and drag you back by your hair.'

The pain receptors in Gazala's ankle make the decision for her.

She knows there's no way she can manage to walk back to the van. If the youth is true to his threat, she'd end up being hauled over the rough ground like a sack of garbage. Her skin would be flayed by a thousand sharp rocks and thorny bushes.

The youth hasn't gone three paces before the other two men from the back of the van join him.

Every step the youth takes sends a jolt through Gazala as his shoulder echoes his footfall. She doesn't know whether the nausea she feels is due to the bounced impacts of his shoulder on her stomach, or fear for what awaits her.

The youth drops her in a heap on the dusty track. Another scream forces its way out when her injured ankle bangs off a stone.

The van is on one side of her and to the other is the hut she glimpsed earlier. Her feet point to a forest but she doesn't know which one. Doesn't care. Whatever happens now, knowing the name of the forest isn't going to make it any better.

Gazala can feel the adrenaline leave her body. In its wake are shaking hands, tiredness and the tears she's held back since being abducted. The spasms of her stomach cause her to retch.

The pain in her ankle settles from white hot to a deep dull ache. It was better when it hurt more. She'd been able to fantasise about passing out and escaping this nightmare.

She watches as the bald man pulls a knife from his pocket and unfolds the blade. His familiarity with the weapon is almost as frightening as the blade itself.

'Please. Please don't kill me. Whatever you want, I'll do.'

'I know you will.'

It's the driver who speaks to her. His tone is measured, calm, confident.

'Tell me. Tell me what you want me to do and I'll do it.' A thought comes to Gazala. She's disgusted she didn't think of it sooner. It's obvious why she's been snatched. 'My father is a wealthy man. He'll pay your ransom. Don't worry about that.'

'We don't want your filthy money. Do we?'

Three heads shake in answer to the driver's question.

Gazala swallows. If they don't want money, the only other thing they can want is her body. 'Is it me you want?'

'You'll serve a purpose. Nothing more, nothing less.'

His words are non-committal, neither confirming nor denying a desire for her.

The bald man tosses the knife, end over end, and catches it by the blade. If the gesture is meant to scare her it works.

She knows she's powerless. That she can't escape these men and save herself. Therefore she has to make a decision. When they start to rape her she can either fight back or lie still in acceptance of the inevitable.

It's a terrible choice and not one she knows how to make. Fighting won't change the end result and is certain to add to the number of injuries she has. Yet, it would be good to bury her good foot into one of their crotches. To gouge at eyes and scratch any exposed skin, or even grab that knife and bury it hilt deep into one of them.

The chances of it working are slim and there are enough of them to hold her down while turns get taken. The thought of letting them mount her unchallenged goes against every instinct she possesses.

Logic says otherwise. It's telling her to go along with their wishes and give them what they want. To give them so much pleasure they'll keep her alive. Logic tells her she's seen their faces and that they plan to kill her. It whispers to her that she must give them a reason to keep her alive.

Gazala can't decide which will be worse. Giving herself to them, or death.

She wants to fight, but knows she can't.

When the bald man reaches down and uses his knife to cut away the rest of her skirt, Gazala's survival instinct makes the decision for her.

She doesn't offer resistance.

When the knife is pointed towards her blouse, her fingers get to the buttons first. They fumble but achieve their task. She pulls her blouse off and uses it to wipe her tear-stained face.

'Well looky here boys. This here Muslim whore is gettin' herself all pretty for us.'

The bald man's words are full of glee, but they bounce off Gazala. Now a course of action has been decided upon, she has a focus. In the greater scheme of things, a little name calling is the least of her problems.

The driver is less impressed. 'Just you watch her. She's already tricked you once.'

Gazala focusses on the bald man and his knife. He points it at her chest and cocks his head. She understands his meaning and reaches behind her back, unclasps her bra and lowers it onto her blouse. Her mouth is kept closed, lest they see how hard she's gritting her teeth.

She's looking at her feet rather than him but she can feel his gaze locking onto her exposed breasts. It's like the prickle of a thousand insects' feet walking across her chest. Every last pore is being examined and lingered over. It takes all her self-control not to shudder in disgust and shield her breasts behind folded arms.

'You ain't finished yet.'

When she looks up the knife points at her crotch and then bounces twice.

She can't prevent the frustrated sigh from escaping her lips, as she slips her thumbs into the sides of her panties.

Her attempts to remove them without aggravating the injury to her ankle fail, and a pained yelp passes her lips.

'Now!'

The single word from the driver is a barked command.

Three pairs of hands grab at her. Pinion her.

The youth has her shoulders. The bald man and the guy with the battered face hold her feet.

She bucks and twists in their hands. It's not what she planned to do; the suddenness of their attack has thrown her planned acquiescence.

A twist of her foot from the bald man stops her resisting him as he parts her legs.

The driver comes into view.

He's holding something in his hand. It's a long bar with a pointed end. Not sharp like a spear, but kind of tapered to a blunt point. He lays it between her legs. She feels the point against her thigh. It's cool, even in the morning sun.

When Gazala sees the driver lift a large hammer with his free hand, she realises the bar being cold is the least of her worries.

Chapter 26

None of life's daily irritants matter to Noelle today. The computer crashing five times in a row, her boss acting like a fool in front of a new client, the customer who spent twenty-five minutes bitching about something which turned out to be his own mistake; every one of them are irrelevant.

Oscar had been delighted when she'd told him her news. He'd beamed with joy, kissed her stomach and dropped to one knee.

She'd said yes before he was even finished asking the question.

Dinner had to be thrown in the bin. By the time they came back downstairs it was ruined. Neither had cared. They'd ordered a pizza and set about calling their families.

Whenever she can grab five minutes without her boss hanging around she is researching wedding venues on Google.

Oscar was insistent that they must be married before the baby arrives. The time frame is a double-edged sword; she wants to be married to Oscar as soon as possible, and agrees with his sentiments that their baby shouldn't be born out of wedlock, but there is no way she wants to waddle down the aisle eight months pregnant.

Together they've decided to marry in two or three months' time. Their wedding is to be a small affair. Close family and one or two friends will make the guest list. Neither want a grand affair with hundreds of guests; they just want a simple ceremony, observed by those closest to them.

She knows that the biggest problem she's facing, is finding a decent venue which has a free date. Horrible as it is, Noelle is aware that her best chance of finding somewhere may lie with the cancellation of someone else's dream.

So far she's managed to find three venues she likes, and she plans to call them in her lunch break to check availability.

Her sister and best friend have agreed to join her on a trip to Salt Lake City to look for a wedding dress on Saturday.

Noelle leaves the office and heads towards a sandwich bar. Ten minutes later she's on a bench in the park wiping traces of mayo from the side of her mouth.

She's too involved with mentally planning her wedding to notice the man watching her. He's just another piece of background in a world which has a new focus; a minor detail of little consequence.

If she was paying attention she'd notice his dead eyes, the way he's pretending not to observe her every move, and the way everyone else is keeping out of his way.

The man thinks of her as a canuck and Oscar as a beaner. She can be tolerated. Her fiancée can't.

Chapter 27

I let myself into Alfonse's apartment; there's coffee brewing so I help myself after using the bathroom. Alfonse is in his office. I can hear his fingers rattling across a keyboard.

He'll be using his PC rather than the laptop. Whenever he does a big hacking job he always uses the PC as he ends up pounding the keys in such a frantic manner he breaks them.

Two keyboards tossed into a corner tell their own story.

Various sheets of paper are pinned to the wall. He flicks glances at them as he types.

A look at his computer doesn't educate me as to his progress. He's got several different windows open and he's jumping between them, firing in commands or printing results.

I make him a coffee and drink mine as I watch him work. As usual, he has total focus on what he's doing. The serious expression on his face is a mixture of concentration and revulsion at the things he's looking into. It can't be easy for him to read the propaganda and hate on the various Klan websites he's investigating. From time to time his face wrinkles with disgust.

His first acknowledgement of my presence is a sheet of paper thrust my way. I whip it from his hand before he drops it at my feet. His racing mind accelerates everything he does and he expects others to match his pace.

I read with hope, rather than expectation. He's given me the intimate details on the Fourniers.

Their bank accounts are healthy enough to suggest a comfortable, if not affluent, life. Bills are paid direct from their bank and their credit card spend is nothing to write home about.

A look at their respective browsing histories shows nothing untoward. The sites they visited were entertainment, retail or informational. Tyrone had managed to get round the parental lock on his iPad, and looked at a few websites with wet T-shirt videos. If I didn't know his morals so well, I'd suspect Alfonse's hand in the hacking.

Alfonse's report also covers the family's social media feeds, email and cell communications. Or rather it doesn't. A single line states, no hate mail, no bullying, no issues.

The line is typical of Alfonse's dryness. He's detached himself from the personal element and is treating the case like any other. Or at least that's what he's trying to appear to do. I've been his friend too long to be fooled by words on a page.

The printer kicks into action with a whir and a snap as the paper is grabbed by the mechanism.

'Yours.'

Alfonse doesn't even look at me as I take the pages.

I leave him to his task and look at the spreadsheets he's generated. There's only a handful of people in the country who can get into the places he can. Without his skills, we'd be chasing our tails – three steps behind the idiots who comprise Casperton's detective squad.

The spreadsheets are filled with the details of Klan, Neo Nazi and various other hate groups. He's got their websites, basic propaganda, contact details and many other points listed. One of the key things he's done is dig into the people who created, maintain, or are the listed contact for the websites. In most cases it's the same person.

The printer's next whir is accompanied by a command from Alfonse. 'Read that and tell me what you think.'

I lift the paper from the tray and scan the page. It's a draft copy of a letter. Not just any letter. An email which purports to be from the FBI.

You and your organisation are on our watch list. To date we have not had any strong concerns regarding your activity which is why we're requesting your help. We're looking for potential or ex members of your organisation whose behaviour, actual or intended, was so extreme you took the sensible step of disassociating yourselves from them.

We urge you to contact us by return at once. Time is of the essence, so if we do not hear from you within twelve hours, we will impound all your electronic communication devices.

Special Agent Devereaux

This is a big step he's planning to take. One from which there can be no going back. Not only could he be in serious trouble with the FBI, if any of the groups who receive this manage to trace it back to him, his life will be in danger.

I read the letter again, aware he's stopped typing and has risen from his seat.

He leaves the room as I work through my reactions to this letter. When he returns, he's got two fresh cups of coffee.

'I presume you've fully thought this through?' I put concern in my voice rather than a challenge. 'Once you send that email there's no recalling it.'

He gives a thin smile. 'Actually, I can recall emails.'

'So what do you expect to happen when this gets read? I take it you realise the first thing the recipients will do is delete their files?'

'Of course they will. That's what I'm planning on. I'll be attaching a hidden program to the email. Anything deleted or removed from the devices that open the email will be sent to me. It'll also send me anything from linked devices. The few who reply will be quicker to deal with than the ones whose deleted files I get.'

'And what happens if someone traces the email back to you?'

'They'll find the IP address belongs to the FBI press office.' He shrugs. 'Or the Office of Public Affairs, if you want to give them their proper title.'

I don't bother grilling him further. He's on top of the obvious stuff I can think of. If this were a chess game, he'd be working out how to corner my king while I am still moving my first pawn.

'Have you had any luck on the Deep Web?'

'Some. It's tougher to find stuff on there. I had to write a program to search for sites that show recent usage, along with key phrases and words. Once that's done, I'll have to examine them to see if they're relevant to our search. After that it'll be a case of getting their details and emailing them.'

'That sounds like a mammoth task. How are you going to deal with all that yourself?'

'Henry is coming over. It's better that he's here. Gives him something to do.'

I know what he means. Henry is Darryl's brother and the most volatile of Alfonse's family. There have been one or two occasions in the past when I've thought I may have to subdue him.

By enlisting his help, Alfonse will be able to keep an eye on him while also giving him a focus. Henry isn't a bad guy, he just possesses more energy than he knows how to manage.

I tell Alfonse what little I've got, and leave. He needs peace and I need to keep moving.

Chapter 28

The Augiers' place is only forty miles from Casperton, but the journey takes me the best part of an hour. The road is narrow, and littered with sharp corners which prevent me from building up a decent head of steam.

I'm quite happy to drive fast on a good road, but only a fool drives round blind corners at speed. The last three miles being nothing more than a gravel track doesn't help.

Sometimes you can judge people by the kind of home they keep. This is one of those times.

The Augiers live in the kind of place Jed Clampett left when moving to Beverley Hills. It looks as if a violent sneeze could demolish it. Some of the repairs to the timber walls look as if care has been taken, while others look like the hasty efforts of an uncaring oaf.

There's a shack in a similar state of disrepair off to one side. Around it are a number of trucks, four tractors, and a couple of what I guess are farm implements. None of them look at all modern.

There's not a lot of farming land around here once you get too far from the river valleys. What little there is will be fraught with hard labour and poor returns.

A door opens and Maisie-Rae steps out with a hand raised to shield her eyes from the late afternoon sun. The scowl on her face when she recognises me shows I'm going to get the welcome I expect.

I'm not surprised by her reaction, it shows a mother's instincts.

I lift my hands in a surrender gesture. 'I'm not here to cause trouble. I come with an olive branch.'

She looks puzzled. Her eyes dart to my hands, looking for the branch I'm talking about. Not finding it they flick across the yard towards the shack.

'Butch. Jim-Bob. Freddie. Get your asses over here.'

I lean against a sun-bleached post and wait for them with my legs crossed at the ankle. Before they get all uppity, I need to show them I'm relaxed – that I'm not here for confrontation.

The door of the shack opens and three denim-clad bodies file out. As they walk across, I realise I'll have to examine every word before I speak. Butch looks angry, but also curious as to why I'd show up. He has a hand on Jim-Bob's arm, lest he get yet another silver medal.

It's not them I'm worried about though. It's Freddie, the drunk wannabe Lothario from last night, who has my full attention. Or rather the shotgun he carries does.

Even from twenty feet away I can see the redness of his eyes and the shake of his hands. The barrel of the shotgun points at the ground, which is something, but it's the ground near my feet not his.

I can't see if his finger is on the trigger and I have no way of knowing if the shotgun is loaded. The only safe option is to presume the answer to both of these questions is yes.

Jim-Bob points at me, and then my Mustang. 'You got a lotta nerve showing your face here. Get back in your car and beat it 'fore you get yo'self hurt real bad.'

'Not so fast.' Butch tosses a contempt-laden glance at his brother. 'I want to know why he's here.'

I keep my gaze steady when returning his. Well, as steady as anyone can when a still-drunk youth with too few live cells is pointing a shotgun at them. 'I'm helping my friend investigate some murders. Was hoping you guys could answer a few questions, maybe help me identify a killer.'

'Why'd we want to help you?' Jim-Bob pushes past Butch and squares up to me. 'You beat up on us and then come a-crawlin' 'specting we'll help you out. You must be outta your mind, Mister.'

'Shut up numbnuts. He didn't beat up on us. If you remember what happened last night, you'll perhaps recall it was you who started throwing punches around. He defended himself, nothing more, nothing less. You were wasted and picked a fight. When you lost, I stepped in and lost too. He coulda pounded on us a lot more, state we were in, but he didn't. I'm interested in knowing why.'

'I ain't wasted now and neither are you.'

Jim-Bob's hands curl into fists. He's too close to me for Freddie to even consider pulling the trigger. It's the one time I've been pleased to be close to him.

'You heard your brother. Shut. Up.' Maisie-Rae's voice is laced with menace. 'I saw what happened last night. Ain't no difference if you're wasted or not; he'll kick your ass again. Don't your face hurt enough already?'

Butch fixes me with a stare. 'Say what you gotta say, Boulder.'

I let out a long sigh, relieved the conversation has got back on track. All the time Jim-Bob has been talking about fighting, young Freddie has been shuffling his feet while raising and lowering the shotgun.

I'm not used to having people aim guns at me. It's an unnerving experience. Doubly so when the person holding the gun is a hungover halfwit.

I give them the background on the Fournier's deaths and how I'm helping Alfonse investigate them.

Their reactions are telling. Freddie blanches and gives a little gag. The brothers remain implacable, bar the faintest trace of revulsion.

Maisie-Rae is the odd one; her face shows nothing but disinterest. 'You come up here askin' 'bout some niggers who got themselves killed. You're wasting your time, Mister. Ain't nuthin' to do with me, nor anyone else up here.'

The scorn and casual racism in her diatribe is lost on Jim-Bob and Freddie. Butch notices it though. He even goes so far as to wince.

'I'll deal with this. You get back to work.' Butch points at the house and the shack.

There are grumbles, but the other three do as he says. Freddie's offer of the shotgun is refused with a snarl accompanied by a violent push.

He leads me away from the house and we sit on the stump of a felled oak. His eyes hold intelligence and understanding.

It doesn't take much to imagine him in a better setting, surrounded by people who are his equal. Instead, he's scratching out a living while looking after his less intelligent family members.

As I watch his face, waiting for him to speak, I can almost see the cogs of his brain turning. He'll be trying to work out how to neutralise his mother's racist words, his nephew's threatening behaviour and whether to tell me anything he may know.

'She's from a different time. Doesn't know words like nigger are no longer deemed acceptable. I'll be honest, I don't know any well enough to form an opinion. I keep myself to myself and my family with me.'

I get his meaning. The unspoken words.

He's living out here for the benefit of his family. With their attitudes and limited intelligence, they'll end up incarcerated, or dead, if he doesn't keep them in check.

Trouble attracts people like the Augiers, and Jim-Bob and Freddie are dumb enough to go looking for it on the occasions when it decides to leave them alone. Smarter guys higher up the food chain will rope them into stuff beyond their means and use them as fall guys.

Butch doesn't let that happen. Keeps them out here, out of the way. Keeps them in a place where they're no danger to others and therefore not to themselves. Once in a while a marriage to someone from a similar family will dilute the blood or offer an avenue of escape.

The Augiers' lifestyle is one canoe and a banjo away from being a scene in *Deliverance*. It's no wonder they go overboard when they do come into town. With little schooling and even less social skills, there isn't one of them other than Butch who knows how to treat others with any glimmer of respect.

Compared to his family he's a prince among men, yet I'm not convinced he's going to win a Noble Peace Prize anytime soon.

'These murders. You said they were crucified, then burned. Bad way to go that.'

I nod. 'Let's be clear. I'm not accusing you or any of your family. I'm here because you know people I don't. You may know the kind of people who would commit a crime like this.' I hold his gaze. 'Do you know anyone who'd do such a thing?'

His jaw sets as he thinks. I have no idea whether he's giving my question serious thought, or concocting a lie.

When he speaks his tone is measured. His eyes make contact with mine and don't keep looking to the left or overdoing the looking at mine.

All of these are signs of lies being told. His voice is without stress. Lying increases stress levels.

The right side of the brain is both the creative side and the one which controls the left side of the body. Liars keep looking to their left when fabricating their stories. When they're not doing that, they overcompensate eye contact and give themselves away.

'My mother may use out-dated terms, but we don't hate those folk enough to kill 'em.' He shrugs. 'I can see why you came here – after all the spouting off when they get drunk. You're wasting your time though. We sure as hell didn't do it and I don't know anyone dumb enough to start killing black folks.'

I press a little harder. 'You sure? Seems like your brother was in the wars before you all came to the Tree. What happened to him?'

'I punched him for talking back.' There's no guilt or pride or shame on his face or in his tone. He's just matter of fact. As if hitting your brother is an everyday occurrence which bears no comment. I suppose in his world it is.

We talk for a while and then I leave.

As I drive back, I can't help but think about Butch and the sacrifice he's made for his family. He maybe wouldn't have made Senator if he'd left his family to look after themselves, but he'd have a better life than he does scratching a living out here.

I realise what had struck me as being odd about the Augiers last night. They'd sat at their table, ordered meals and then eaten and drank while talking to each other. Sure, the conversation hadn't been scintillating but it had been actual conversation rather than a group of people staring at their phones and communicating with strangers via Twitter or Facebook. Maybe they know something I don't.

Come to think of it, I hadn't seen one member of the family carrying or using a cell phone. In today's world the lack of a cell is a sign of poverty. Still, what use would cells be where they live? Mine had lost its signal halfway from Casperton.

As if by psychic methods, mine starts to beep. I must be back within range of a mast.

I glance at the screen. There are two missed calls from Alfonse and three from Chief Watson.

Chapter 29

The chief meets me outside the station. He comes out of the door as I'm climbing the four steps into the building. I'm no expert on the subject of body language, but I don't need to be. His stress-filled scowl tells me everything I need to know.

'Boulder, with me.' The order is barked at me as if I'm a new recruit.

I let it slide. He won't be asking me to accompany him for any other reason than he needs my help or wants to share information with me.

He reaches his truck in six brisk steps. I run around to the passenger side and clamber in as he's twisting the key with enough force to break it.

His manner suggests either major developments in the case or none at all.

'You know all that bull your friend was spouting about his cousin and the cousin's wife being deeply in love?' It's a rhetorical question as he doesn't pause long enough for me to gather my thoughts and formulate an answer. 'Well let me tell you, bull is exactly what it is.'

My instinct is to defend Alfonse, yet the chief is obviously in possession of information I don't yet have. A situation that needs to change.

'Why is it bull, Chief? What do you know that I don't?'

The Chief realises I'm in the dark and some of his pressure-fuelled anger dissipates. 'The coroner's report came in. Darryl Fournier has syphilis and his wife doesn't. Only one explanation for that.'

I don't even attempt to answer him. My mind is whirling at this latest development and the questions it has generated.

'So, where are you taking me, and have you identified who Darryl was sleeping with?'

'We're going to the coroner's office. I want to know more about this disease. Specifically, if it's an old infection which could have flared up again or if it had been caught recently.'

What he's saying makes sense. The fact that only Darryl had it speaks volumes.

Never having passed the three months' stage in a relationship, I have no idea how long a regular sex life carries on. For all I know, happily married couples make love twice a day or once a year. What goes on in other people's relationships is none of my business. The only person I can ask is Sharon and it's not an easy thing to discuss with your sister.

I'm tempted to ask Chief Watson but fear it may just tip him from irate to catatonic. Besides, he's a whole generation older than Darryl and Sherrelle. His is a generation that doesn't share discussions on their sex life with anyone.

At a guess, I'd say Darryl and Sherrelle would bump uglies once a month at best. Perhaps more if a special occasion or anniversary was marked on the calendar.

If I'm right, Darryl cheated on his wife in the last four weeks. Six at the most. A look at his movements should pinpoint the possible opportunities for indiscretion. Then it'll be a case of just asking the right questions of the right people.

Identifying the right questions will be the easy part.

The chief interrupts my thoughts. 'You up to speed yet?'

'I think so. I've no personal experience of syphilis, but I do know that with some strains, once you've had it, it's with you for life and can come back at any time. So I think we have to find out if it has come back or is a new infection. If it proves recent, we'll have to find out who passed on the disease. For all we know, he could have contracted the disease through some way other than sex and Sherrelle knew all about it.'

His lips purse in thought as he pulls into a parking bay outside the coroner's office. 'True.' He looks at me as he unbuckles his seatbelt. 'Homicide motives rarely extend beyond sex or money. Follow the dick and the wallet, they're what leads you to a killer.'

'I take it you're guessing their murders are a revenge attack?'

'What else could it be?'

'A hate group. Remember how they were killed? That's not the work of one man. It's the work of a group.'

I give him time to reconfigure his thoughts. It's too easy when following an investigation to get swept along by a new discovery. When that happens, key facts get overlooked as the evidence is made to fit the new theory. I was almost swept with him until I started questioning how his news fit with the known facts.

There's grudging respect in his voice when he speaks. 'You're right. It's still the best lead we've got though.'

'Perhaps. But what about the wife and kids? A vengeful husband or boyfriend wouldn't have killed them as well. He may have ruined their life by exposing Darryl's infidelity, but there's nothing to be gained by killing them. It's one thing to kill and a totally different thing to enlist help to commit multiple murders.'

'Dammit, Boulder. Do you always have to make such sense?'

He leads the way towards the entrance and crashes through the doors. His police issue boots squeak as I match his stride down the corridor.

He knocks on the pathologist's door and enters without waiting for an invitation.

There's a flash of irritation on the pathologist's face at the chief's rude behaviour. She is, however, wise enough to let it pass without comment.

Doctor Emily Green is pretty with auburn hair. She's intelligent, professional and has been dating Alfonse for a few weeks.

'How's Alfonse today?'

I make a non-committal noise, then add a few proper words. 'Busy. He's trying to find their killer.' I don't bother saying it's his way of managing his grief, she's smart enough to work that out for herself.

She accepts what I say, understanding that this kind of talk isn't what we're here for. Or good at, if I'm honest with myself.

I don't talk about my feelings with other guys and I don't expect them to talk about theirs. I have feelings and if they bother me, I deal with the root of the problem. If they still bother me after that, I tend to find myself waking up God knows where with the mother of all hangovers.

'Right then, Doctor. What can you tell us about Darryl and his syphilis?'

Emily turns her head so the chief can't see her rolling her eyes at the way he's given ownership of the disease to Darryl. 'When I ran the bloods as normal, we found traces of penicillin, and the natural antibodies which the body produces to fight syphilis, in Darryl. Sherrelle's tests showed the birth control pill. I'd also guess she was taking vitamin supplements as her levels are too good for her not to have taken them.'

'What about the kids?'

I don't like where Chief Watson may be going. I understand he has to go there, but I'm glad Alfonse isn't here to hear it.

'They were clean. No traces of anything.'

I throw a question at her. 'Was there any alcohol in Darryl's or Sherrelle's blood?'

'None.' She lets the information sink in. It doesn't take long. The single word is damning enough.

This is perhaps the most disturbing thing she's uncovered. All four of them were clean and straight when they were taken. None had drugs or alcohol in their systems. Nothing to dull the pain of nails being driven through flesh. Of flesh being ignited.

The chief lets out a long exasperated sigh. 'Is there anything else you found?'

'Just that...' Her eyes dart towards the exam room, then close for a brief second. 'Just that their lungs showed signs of scorching which are synonymous with inhaling a burning accelerant.'

I close my eyes while the chief lets out a string of curses.

My mind creates a distraction by focussing on the fact Sherrelle still used birth control. It shows she was still sexually active yet she hadn't caught her husband's syphilis. Therefore, the birth control was a years-long habit maintained for those times she and her husband made love, or she too was playing around outside the marriage.

Not knowing what goes on behind closed doors, I let flights of fancy have their moment and imagine the Fourniers wife swapping and attending swingers' parties.

Reality bites when I remember how devout they were. How they attended church every Sunday. Just because I don't practise religion myself, doesn't mean I don't recognise the good it can do for those who worship on a regular basis. My own issues with the church are aimed at the extreme groups who try to indoctrinate all others, or bend them to their way of thinking. Too often religion has been used as an excuse for war; not just in today's world, but right back through the annals of time.

I tune back into Emily and the chief's conversation. She's telling him she called Darryl's doctor and learned that the syphilis is something Darryl had contracted just three weeks ago.

The doctor hadn't been too forthcoming, but he'd said Darryl had suspected that he'd caught it on a recent trip to Las Vegas.

What happens in Vegas didn't quite stay in Vegas this time around. It never does.

Las Vegas didn't acquire the name Sin City for no reason. The identity of the person who passed the disease to Darryl is unimportant. Whether a bored housewife, cougar, hooker or male escort is responsible for the infection is irrelevant. A Vegas hook-up is the ultimate one-off experience. Names will have been optional or false; alcohol will have been consumed to the point of inebriation.

I've been there, done that. Somehow I've always dodged the bullet that'd have me visiting the clinic.

The chief scowls as I beat him to the obvious question. 'I don't suppose the doctor told you who Darryl went to Vegas with?'

'No.' Emily's head shakes. 'I'm sure his family will be able to tell you though.'

The chief's scowl is transformed into a questioning look.

I don't have to be a genius to know he wants me to ask the question of Alfonse and his family. It's not something I'm keen on broaching with him, but someone has to and the chief's heightened stress levels have made him gruffer than usual.

'I'll ask him. I was planning to see him anyway.'

'Good man.' His eyes turn back to Emily. 'Is there anything else we should know?'

She hesitates, but decides against whatever she was about to say. Either it isn't relevant or she's not convinced enough to put voice to her thoughts.

The chief's eyebrow raises and his eyes bore into hers. 'What is it, Doctor?' His tone has a sharp edge to it.

'The way you keep rubbing your temples – I'm guessing you suffer from stress headaches?'

'So? I'm trying to catch a killer. I wouldn't be normal if I didn't feel stressed.' The chief's voice is a growl but there's an admission in his words.

'Well you're not helping yourself kneading away at your temples like that.' Emily's tone matches the chief's for intensity. 'Give me your hands and I'll show you how to do it properly.'

Before the chief can protest, she rises from her chair and takes his hands in hers. I spend a surreal couple of minutes watching the pathologist give the chief of police a lesson in head massage. When he's not looking, I grab a quick picture with my cell.

As we leave he's still massaging away. A faint redness touching his cheeks. 'Don't you dare tell anyone about this, Boulder.'

'You're too late. I've already tweeted and Facebooked it.'

I let him curse and threaten me for a solid five minutes before telling him I haven't.

His final word on the subject questions my parentage.

Chapter 30

Noelle smiles at Oscar and slides onto the chair he's pulled out for her. Taking the other seats around the table are members of her family. Oscar's parents and sister are here too.

The rest of his family remain in Mexico, although she has travelled to Ciudad de Durango with him and met some of his many relatives.

Ciudad de Durango is the capital of the Durango municipality and Noelle had fallen in love with the city. The architecture reminding her of cities like Barcelona and Paris.

Oscar had given her a complete tour of the city, showing her the memorable landmarks and the unforgettable slums. So obvious was Cuidad de Durango ingrained into Oscar's blood, Noelle had suggested they leave Casperton and move there. He'd smiled, kissed her fingers, and told her he would never again live in Mexico.

Noelle's father raises his glass and starts another toast. His smile is wide and his words are nothing he hasn't already said in either of his first two toasts. Nobody minds, least of all Noelle and Oscar. Tonight is a celebration. Of love. Of new life. Of new beginnings.

Menus are distributed by the servers. A wine list is handed to Noelle's father. Tonight is his treat and he's intent on celebrating with style.

Gallo Vermiglio is the finest restaurant in Casperton. It's owned and run by a husband and wife team. She cooks while he runs the front of house. The business has been on sale for three years and isn't likely to be sold anytime soon. Every prospective buyer recognises the fact that Debora and Seppe are the business. The only people who could continue their success are those looking to build their own business, not pay the price of an established one.

Noelle runs her finger down the menu and tries to decide what to have. She fancies mussels but knows shellfish can be dangerous to pregnant women. Instead she opts for a steak: well done rather than her usual medium rare.

As the evening progresses, Noelle and Oscar bask in the celebrations. In the joy shared with those closest to them. Nothing is amiss. Everything is wonderful.

The one tiny issue is nothing more than a nagging doubt.

There's a man dining alone. He sits a couple of tables away and has a battered paperback in front of him. His face has a familiar look to it. Noelle doesn't know where she's seen him before, she just knows she has. She guesses he's just one of those people she sees once in a while, and when seen out of context is unrecognisable. Like a pharmacist without his white coat.

There's nothing remarkable or distinguishing about the guy. He's mid-forties with short greying hair. He's eating with one hand and his eyes are lifting from his book to make regular scans of the restaurant. There's nothing odd with that; she does the same herself when alone. She likes that he reads, tries to see the cover. Even in this moment of celebration, she wants to meet the stranger and talk books with him.

Chapter 31

Alfonse looks weary. It's not something that surprises me; he's spent all day staring at a computer screen and no sane gambler would bet on him having slept well last night.

Henry looks worse. He's not just tired, he's angry.

Not 'bad day at work' angry; 'someone's killed my brother and I want to kill them' angry. In someone with his energy and intellectual capacity it's a dangerous anger to have.

Assuming he gets his revenge without being killed himself. Aunt Nina has lost one son to a killer. She doesn't need to lose another to the prison system.

I can only hope Alfonse's calming influence rubs off on him long enough to prevent him doing something moronic.

Alfonse leads me through to the kitchen. Defeat fills the areas of his face untouched by exhaustion. 'I hope you've learned more than me. I've got the square root of diddly squat so far.'

I try not to grimace but he knows me well enough to spot a minor tell. It's a shock when the heel of his fist thumps the worktop. Perhaps Henry is rubbing off on him.

'I haven't got much. And what I do have is mostly negative.' I tell him of my conversation with Butch Augiers. He doesn't make any comment, but then again he doesn't need to. His face says enough.

'Anything else?'

'Yeah, but you're not going to like it.' I was going to try and break the news in a gentle fashion. His mood tells me that would be a mistake. He needs straight talking from me, not a pair of unfamiliar kid gloves. 'When Emily ran the bloods she found Darryl had syphilis but Sherrelle didn't.'

A curse escapes his lips. In all the years I've known him, it's only the second time I've heard him use a four letter expression of such powerful emotion.

I keep my mouth closed. He needs to work this out for himself. Reach the same conclusions and questions I did a couple of hours ago.

Give him his due, he doesn't pepper me with a dozen variations of the same question, nor does he doubt the results.

When he does speak, his words echo those of anyone who cares about their family's public image. 'Who knows?'

I know he's not worrying about himself. His concern is for Aunt Nina, Henry and Sherrelle's side of the family. About their shame and anger if Darryl's infidelity becomes public knowledge.

'As far as I know, it's just us, Emily and Chief Watson. Perhaps a couple of others at the coroner's office will know.'

'It's not going to stay that way for long is it?'

I don't answer him. His question is at least three parts rhetorical. All investigating officers will find out and, regardless of how slim the chances of their killer being someone connected to Darryl's indiscretion are, it's still a line of enquiry they'll have to follow.

Farrage and his cronies will ask their questions. Sooner or later one of them will say the wrong thing to someone they shouldn't. Word will spread from person to person. The news will move with stealth and subtlety at first, but will gather momentum and embellishment with every re-telling. Rumour will become fact and in a few short hours Darryl will be accused of having long-term affairs with every woman he's ever spoken to.

Alfonse sticks his head into the hallway. 'Henry. You better come through.'

Henry repeats Alfonse's curse and adds a few of his own when Alfonse finishes bringing him up to speed. His long legs propel him across the kitchen in three strides before he changes direction.

'Are you sure? Who knows about this? Why are they trying to destroy my brother's memory? They've got it wrong, haven't they?' His eyes bore into mine with such intensity I shift my feet so I'm better balanced if I need to defend myself. 'Tell me they've got it wrong.'

Alfonse lays a hand on his shoulder. 'They haven't got it wrong. Nobody is trying to destroy Darryl's memory. It's just a crap fact that's been found in the search for his killer.'

I have an idea which may help appease their distress. 'Darryl told his doctor he thought he contracted syphilis on a trip to Vegas. If we can find out more about this trip, and who Darryl had slept with, then perhaps we can contain this information.'

'How?' Alfonse and Henry speak as one person. That is, one person with two different voices. Distress and fury separate their tones.

'We get the information first and present it to Chief Watson. If it's the dead end I think it is, he'll focus the investigation elsewhere.'

Henry's voice is laden with contempt. 'How does that help?'

'It keeps the information in the hands of as few people possible. Those who went to Vegas with Darryl will almost certainly know what he got up to there. I'll find out what happened and then ask them to keep that information to themselves.'

I don't mention that I intend to use threats of violence to keep Darryl's secret. Alfonse wouldn't approve and Henry may want to come along to emphasise my point.

'So, what do we do?'

I look at Alfonse as I answer Henry's question. 'You tell me who Darryl went to Vegas with and then you get back to work. That's where the key to the killers' identities lies. This syphilis thing is nothing more than a side-line. If this were a movie, or a book, it'd be nothing more than a red herring. The sooner I can draw a line through it, the sooner we can all focus on the real leads.'

Alfonse looks at Henry with a raised eyebrow. 'Who'd he go with?'

'He went with one of his bosses and another lawyer.' A shrug. 'I didn't listen too close when he was telling me about it. He was more interested in the conference than anything else.'

This is good news from my point of view. Lawyers understand the need for discretion better than most. Businessmen who rely on a good reputation are easy to threaten. Violence isn't always the answer; though when it is I'm seldom found lacking a decent response.

Alfonse spends a minute telling me about his lack of progress, but after a few words he starts using technical terms which move the conversation several feet above my head. I glean enough to know he's got a lot of data still to process, and he's trying to narrow things down to people who live in the local area to minimise the number of potential suspects.

I'm about to leave when my cell beeps.

It's a message from Taylor. If the number of exclamation points after the three words are anything to go by, there's every chance I'm going to be single again before the night ends.

The realisation that I'm bothered surprises me.

Before I deal with that, I need to find out why Taylor is asking where I am. And where she expects I should be.

I scroll past the message she's just sent. What I find neither impresses me nor fills me with any confidence. The chain of messages shows me arranging a date for tonight. I'm supposed to have met her for dinner an hour ago.

Armed with this information I can at least reply to her.

On my way. Long story.

I have the five minutes it'll take to travel across town to work out why I'd poured my heart out to her in a message.

Sure, the time and date against the message shows it was sent on Tuesday night. The lack of grammar, decent punctuation, and the terrible misspellings attest to how drunk I was at the time of typing.

None of this changes the fact that I've opened up to a girl I am dating. Told her my innermost feelings.

I could blame the drink, but I've been drunker without doing this before. They say a drunk man speaks the truth. If this is true, I've been lying to myself about my lack of feelings for Taylor.

She's good company, intelligent, and has cheekbones higher than a seventies rock star. Her manner is easy-going and I can relax with her. She doesn't try to change me or feed me quinoa at every opportunity. I enjoy her company, want to keep on enjoying it.

I stop thinking about my feelings for Taylor and concentrate on getting across town.

Chapter 32

Taylor is sat in an alcove when I arrive at the restaurant. Even when she's pissed she's beautiful. Her blonde hair and blue eyes hint at a Scandinavian heritage, but there's no trace of an accent when she speaks.

'What kept you? I've been here an hour.' Her tone is cool. Not quite glacial, more like the first frosts of winter.

I take a seat opposite her without trying to offer a kiss. She's not in the mood for pleasantries. 'Sorry I'm late. I've been helping Alfonse look into his cousin's death.'

Her eyes widen with understanding, the coolness gone from her voice. 'You mean those poor people who were found up in Ashley?'

'I'm afraid so.'

Concern fills her face as tears touch the corners of her eyes. She stands and reaches for her purse. 'You should have blown me off. We can have dinner anytime. Alfonse needs you more than I do.'

Three sentences containing just eighteen words make my heart somersault. Taylor understands the way things are. The way things have to be.

'I have to eat sometime. May as well be in a swanky restaurant with a beautiful girl.'

'That is so, like, totally, corrrrrrrny.' Taylor's mocking of my compliment is softened by a melodic giggle.

The waiter comes and offers menus. I suspect from the way he's eyeing Taylor, he's a little bit in love with her.

After our order is taken, I give Taylor the broad outlines of the case. The only key fact omitted is the syphilis. It's not that I don't trust her, it's just not something I want to speak about in a public place.

As she listens her face depicts her horror.

I like that she's outraged. That she wants their killers locked away on death row. It shows Taylor shares my morals, my principles and my belief that perpetrators of criminal acts deserve to be punished.

A group of happy people brush past us. They're all toothy smiles and glassy eyes. I give a smiling nod to the blonde holding hands with a Mexican. Noelle is a nice lady – we'd dated. The relationship ran its course and we split by mutual consent.

Noelle looks sober compared to the rest of her group, she also looks happier. I guess it's her occasion and broaden my smile.

A pungent aroma makes my eyes water. There's puzzlement on Taylor's face as she looks over my shoulder.

I turn and find myself just three inches from Ms Rosenberg's chest. The power of her perfume is enough to make my eyes water as she moves round me and dumps herself into a chair without waiting for an invitation. A click of her fingers alerts a waiter who does well to hide his irritation at her lack of manners. 'You. Scotch on the rocks. Pronto.' Despite her size, she manages to overfill every room she enters.

'Good evening.' Taylor is polite although I can tell she's not pleased at the way Ms Rosenberg has gate-crashed our evening.

A fake smile is tossed her way. 'Hello, doll. I need to talk to Boulder. He's a hero you know. Treat him like one.'

'What do you want?' I've learned that Ms Rosenberg has no social skills. The only way to communicate with her is to be as blunt as she is.

'Have you learned anything useful yet?'

'No comment.'

Her eyes narrow as they examine my face. 'You're not saying that because I'm a journalist and you're working a case. You're saying it because you have nothing to say but don't want me to know it.' The waiter places a Scotch on the rocks in front of her. 'About time. Bring me another.'

However brief, the interruption has given me a moment's thinking time. She's on a fishing trip and is trying to get me to confirm something. I need to find out what.

'You can believe what you want. I have no comment to make because I have no information to give. And I know from past experience how dangerous information can be when it gets into the wrong hands.'

She ignores my barb and twirls a fork between nicotine-stained fingers. 'I need something from you, Boulder. All I got so far is the husband was definitely playing away. I don't for one moment think that's why they were all killed, but I need a story and that would be a good one. I'd sooner write about what's really happening, than follow that idiot Farrage around chronicling his mistakes.'

'You're obviously not after job security. Farrage could keep you in stories as long as he has a badge.'

Her laugh is an ass's bray. Heads at nearby tables rotate to look but she is uncaring. Half her Scotch disappears in one slug.

'I don't know what leads you're working on, but if I was you I'd be looking at money not sex. One drunken Vegas fumble does not a hate crime make.'

It takes me a second to reorganise her words into a coherent sentence. She uses the second to drain her glass and send a hurrying scowl towards the waiter.

'Why do you say that?'

'I've been around stories all my life. Ain't much I haven't seen, heard or written about. Murder is about money and sex. I figure sex is pretty much off the table so it's about money. Sure it may be about race as well, but there has to be a selection process. Find the reason they were chosen as the victims and that will lead you to their killer.'

She's right. While it is the line we've been pursuing, we've also had an open mind with regards to the fact it smacks of racial hatred. Instead of focussing all of our resources on the why, we've split ourselves so Alfonse is looking for a fictional who.

I need to return the favour she's just done me. 'Instead of writing about the investigation, why don't you write about the reaction to the crime? Get some quotes from a couple of churches, some community leaders and so on.'

'Boring. Predictable.' A half inch of Scotch is poured between bright pink lips.

'Perhaps.' I play my ace. 'But are you aware there's a Klan Chapter operating out of Salt Lake City? They have a website that gives the contact details of their spokesman, and also their grand panjandrum or whatever they call him. Get a quote from one of them and your piece will be neither boring nor predictable.'

A notepad has appeared from nowhere. She's filling it with indecipherable squiggles as I speak.

'Boulder, you're a star.' She rises from her chair, draining her glass as she stands. A turn of her head gives her eye contact with Taylor. 'You're lucky, doll. If I was twenty years younger you'd have yourself some serious competition.'

Somehow, Taylor and I manage to contain our laughter until Ms Rosenberg moves out of earshot.

Chapter 33

I slip out of bed and tiptoe into the lounge without waking Taylor. Sleep is eluding me so I figure it's kinder of me to leave her in peace while I go through some mental gymnastics.

The thing bothering me most, is Ms Rosenberg's insistence that money is the reason the Fourniers were selected. I know she's right but I can't see how.

Alfonse has been through their bank accounts looking for anything amiss. He found nothing. Their regular expenditure was around eighty percent of their income. They had no debts, no expensive bad habits and no secret funds. As an experienced detective and successful hacker, these were the first things Alfonse looked for. The reason he didn't find them is because they didn't exist.

Other than a night of passion in Vegas, the Fourniers were squeaky clean. Tomorrow's first task will be to find out about Darryl's Vegas trip. Second up will be another visit to the bank to dig a bit deeper into Sherrelle's work life.

I'm also concerned about the amount of time Alfonse is spending chasing after shadows. While his probing may give us a number of suspects, it won't do anything beyond identifying a number of people who happen to be racist. There will be no evidence to link them to the crime we're investigating.

Either Alfonse has to give up his search for the time being, or I have to find some suspects of my own so his findings corroborate my suspicions.

Running the Vegas angle seems like a waste of time but Alfonse and Henry are relying on me to keep the news contained. Ms Rosenberg's comments earlier, proved the news is already out there. To be fair to her, she's not talking about printing the story. Her threat no more than a bluff to get information from me.

Through Taylor, I've learned that Dr Edwards has a free space around lunchtime. I plan to take the appointment. I want to know more about the mind-set of the people we're looking for and the kind of people they might be. In its own way this may be as vague as what Alfonse is doing, but the more I know about the kind of person I'm looking for, the better equipped I'll be to spot them.

I remember about the missing girl. Nobody's updated me on her status so I assume there's no news.

To make sure, I call the station. It's Farrage who answers the phone. He's not happy I'm asking him questions but he gives me the answer I need, even if it's not the one I want.

I realise I've been hoping the girl would turn up somewhere unharmed and surprised at the fuss. A moment of impulse causing an unnecessary panic.

She hasn't turned up yet and the family have contacted every known friend. A social media campaign has been started. So far there have been no sightings. Farrage admitted that Chief Watson has called in a couple of retired cops to look into her disappearance.

This last piece of news is both reassuring and worrying. The chief bringing someone in is a good thing because every minute counts in cases like this. His doing so before the girl is officially missing means he believes she's been abducted.

The more crimes committed, the more chances there are of criminals making mistakes. I hope Gazala is returned safe and well but, if she isn't, her death may prove useful in the most awful way. It's crass and thoughtless of me I know. But if she is the next victim of whoever killed the Fourniers, her death may give us the clues we require to catch the killers. Having a second victim allows cross-referencing.

I want to add investigating the missing girl to my list of things to do, but I can't gamble on allocating the time until it's known if she's alive or dead.

Sleep is starting to beckon me. I need it; my mind is travelling in circles and until I have more information I won't be able to make sense of anything.

Chapter 34

Noelle caresses her bump as she walks along the bank of the stream. Little Eduardo, or 'Eddie', is holding both her and Oscar's hands. The sun is shining and the grass underfoot is lush and green. Oscar has proven to be a wonderful husband and father. Caring, devoted and selfless, he puts her and Eddie first every time. Life just couldn't be any better. The one blot on the landscape is a barking dog. It's not a welcoming bark, it's one of protest. Of indignation.

Her eyes snap open. She's wide awake at once. The barking wasn't in her dream. It's Buster who's barking. She suspects next door's cat is sitting on the window ledge again.

Oscar is dead to the world. He's a heavy sleeper at the best of times, and the wine and beers her father kept pressing on him have taken their toll.

Her feet grope for the slippers she keeps beside the bed. Buster's barking ends with a strangled yelp.

Her ears pick out heavy footsteps on the stairs. The noise is too great for it to be just one person. There are a few of them.

Terrified, she leans across the bed and shakes Oscar but he's too near unconsciousness to wake. For the first time in her life she wishes she owned a gun. She clenches a fist and punches his arm.

He doesn't react.

A creak on the stairs tells her they're near the top.

She hasn't time to start questioning who has invaded her home, or worry about what they're after. Just so long as they take it and go without harming either her or Oscar she doesn't care.

A scream pierces the night air, startling her until she realises she's the one who's screaming. The volume and shrillness combine to raise Oscar from his slumber.

'Huh. Wass goin' on?' Even as he's speaking, Oscar snuggles himself comfortable.

'We're being burgled.'

Her eyes search the starlit room for a weapon. Any weapon at all will do but the best she can find is Oscar's tin of deodorant. If she can spray it in their eyes she may be able to fend them off while they take what they've come for.

The bedroom door bursts open and a pair of flashlights shine right into her face. She turns away from the blinding lights. 'Take whatever you want. Just please don't hurt us.'

She feels rough work gloves on her bare skin. Her arms are pinioned behind her back and fastened with tape. Another length of tape is used as a gag. She wants to fight back, to kick and thrash against her captors. Thoughts of the baby in her belly stop her.

More than anything, she wishes she'd had the sense to shout that she had a gun. That would have stopped them. Kept her and Oscar safe.

One man holds her while three others bind a still groggy Oscar with tape. The room isn't dark enough for her to see the men properly. All she can tell is that they're wearing ski masks.

Their smell has invaded her home. It's a pungent odour borne of unwashed bodies, stale smoke and a bad diet.

Once they've bound Oscar, two of the men pick him up and head for the door. It's at this point she realises what the men have come for.

They're not here to steal. They're here to kidnap her and Oscar.

She feels the prick of a knife in her back and hot breath at her ear. 'Follow them. Be a good girl and don't try to escape. If you do, it will go worse for your beaner lover. Do you understand me, bitch?' The voice is muffled, as if there's a hand over the speaker's mouth.

Noelle nods. Her brain is turning somersaults as it tries to work out what is happening. Why they've been kidnapped. Who the kidnappers are. Whether their families will be able to pay a ransom.

Chapter 35

Eddy Hall ushers me into the boardroom of LH Associates. He's too polite to show his displeasure at me interrupting the start of his day, yet I can tell I'm an inconvenience. Perhaps my standing outside the door with a cup of take-out coffee is too public for his sensibilities. Too bad.

'What can I help you with?' There's a subtle edge to his voice. He's saying one thing with his words and another with his tone. His glances towards the clock and his wristwatch are designed to let me know he's a busy man.

His workload or schedule isn't my greatest concern. I'm trying to catch a gang of killers. Somehow I stop myself from pointing this out.

'Darryl took a business trip to Vegas a few weeks ago. I'm told he went with some colleagues. I'd like to speak to them and find out why they went to Vegas.'

Hall stops looking at the clock. He takes a seat and gestures I should too. 'Ursula and I went to Vegas with him. There was a conference about employment law which is an area we're considering branching into.'

That he went has taken me by surprise but it shouldn't have. Bosses are always the first to get the perks. 'Who's the Ursula, and can you ask her to join us?'

'Ursula Clague. She's the head of our acquisitions department.' He uses the desk phone to summon her. His telephone voice shows deference.

I wonder if she's the one who Darryl caught syphilis from. Two co-workers on a junket to the most sinful of cities. It's the oldest story in the book. A few drinks are consumed and they start to see each other in a different light. Before either realises what's happening, they're all hot and sweaty and naked together.

One look at Ursula Clague kills this theory. She has a certain look of intolerance about her. Her eyes are small, beady and critical. When they flick over me they show disapproval.

Ursula's posture is statuesque in its rigidity. All things considered, Ms Rosenberg has the personality of a Playboy Bunny when compared to the stern features of Ursula Clague.

'You asked to see me, Mr Hall.' She keeps her eyes on me. Perhaps she's trying to work out why I'm here. Her expression suggests she expects me to steal something.

'I'm not going to insult either of you by asking you to keep what I say to yourselves. You're both lawyers and understand the need for discretion. Blood from Darryl's body was tested as a matter of course. It was found he'd contracted syphilis. A conversation with his doctor informed us Darryl had suspected he'd caught the disease in Vegas.'

Ursula Clague gives a snort. 'Well that doesn't surprise me. That place is like a modern day Gomorrah. The only surprise is that Mr Fournier was fool enough to be seduced.'

Her defence of Darryl makes me warm to her a little. She's portraying him as a victim. As if no seductress can be refused. It's unfair to speculate that nobody has ever tried to seduce her, but life is unfair and she comes across as a harridan. Besides, Gomorrah was nothing more than the blueprint for Las Vegas.

Hall looks uneasy. He's licking his lips and a sheen of sweat covers his brow. If he doesn't look like a man with a guilty secret, no-one does. 'Are you sure he caught syphilis in Vegas? Are you even sure it was on the trip with us?'

'The dates match up.' I look at them in turn. 'Can either of you identify who he may have slept with?'

I'm hoping it was another lawyer. Someone they'd met at the conference. Someone easy to trace. Both shake their heads and give negative answers.

Hall is lying and he can tell I know it. His eyes flick at Ursula Clague and the door.

He's asking me not to push it until she's left.

Whatever he's hiding will be told if I play the game.

'Thank you very much for your time, Ms Clague.' I rise and offer my hand. 'I'm sorry to have disturbed your day.'

She retains her position a heartbeat too long before making for the door. It's obvious she knows she's been dismissed so the boys can talk. Her sensibilities are not my concern as she won't be the hardest person in the world to offend.

'Spill it.' My words follow the click of the door catch by a fraction of a second. Eddy Hall isn't the only one who needs to be somewhere else. I also want to let him know who's in charge of the conversation.

He glances at the seat his colleague has just vacated. 'As you can imagine, Ms Clague isn't the type of person who enjoys a trip to Las Vegas.'

I nod agreement and gesture for him to continue.

'On the last night, Darryl and I went to the Bellagio for a few games of roulette.' He shrugs. 'I hit a lucky streak and won a couple of grand. I had enough sense to cash it in and walk away before I lost it all again.'

Despite being able to see where this is going, I roll my hand a second time.

'One of the managers came over and congratulated me. Took us to the bar and comped us a couple of drinks. As we were drinking them, two women came over.' Another shrug. 'They were all over us. I can't speak for Darryl, but I felt like a god. I'd just won two grand and a pair of beautiful young women were practically launching themselves at us.'

'What happened next?' I can guess, but I want him to put it in his own words.

He mops his brow with a handkerchief. 'I took one of the girls back to my room and left Darryl with the other. Until you started asking questions today, I wasn't even sure if he'd slept with her.'

The handkerchief takes another pass. 'When I woke up she was gone and so were all my winnings.'

'Thank you for your honesty.' I mean it too. He's given me a lot of information with very little persuasion. 'And don't worry. I won't tell anyone about what happened there.'

Chapter 36

The chief is silent as he drives. It's part concentration on the road and part thinking time. His knuckles form white hillocks as he grasps the wheel. There are no lights or sirens on his pickup but that doesn't slow his progress.

Gazala has been found. Or rather her body has. The chief has told me she's been murdered but he hasn't said how. I'm guessing the how is either unknown or something we have to see for ourselves.

The crime scene tape beside a forest ranger's hut is a surprise, as is the crime scene tent. I've been expecting another charred body on a burned cross in a woody glade.

A team of white suited crime scene workers are milling around, their eyes above the protective masks grim. The customary black humour used as a coping mechanism is missing. More than anything else, it tells me that whatever is in the tent is horrific.

The chief pulls two forensic oversuits from his trunk. He curses as he struggles into his. I stay quiet.

This second death has far-reaching implications. If it's another racially motivated murder, the focus of the investigation into the Fourniers' deaths has to change. If unconnected, the chief has two big problems instead of one huge one.

The chief retrieves a picture of the missing girl from a folder and nods at me. 'You ready for this?'

'Yeah.' It's all I can say. I'd rather go anywhere but in that tent. I need to though. Need to experience the horror for myself and make my own judgements. It's not that I don't trust other people's accounts. I just trust my own more.

The chief approaches the fluttering tape and steps over it. A path of foot pads have been laid by the CSI team. We follow them. I'm happy for the chief to lead.

A man with a camera emerges from the tent. We perform an awkward shuffle to let him past without anyone stepping off the foot pads.

I don't mind the delay, but the chief's growl indicates he does. He pushes the flapping canvas aside and enters the tent. I take a deep breath and a hearty swallow then follow him in.

What greets me is a medieval torture scene. Gazala Kulkarni would have been pretty in life. In death, pain has transformed her into a hideous grotesque creature.

The cause of her death is obvious. That she suffered unimaginable pain in her last moments more so.

She's naked. The blunt end of a thick iron rod protrudes from her vagina. The other pointed end has come out of her neck, pushing her head to one side.

My teeth grind as I concentrate on not losing the contents of my stomach. The stench of voided bowels is bad, but not as bad as the trail of destruction on Gazala's corpse.

There are bite marks on her body where wild animals have feasted on a free meal. Her nose is missing and so is most of her right breast. I'm guessing foxes or maybe a bobcat. The damage speaks of small solitary animals. Had she been discovered by a bear, wolves or other pack animals there would be a lot more of her missing.

A stream of blood has passed from her vagina. None is evident at her neck which means she died as the iron bar was forced through her body. I can't stop the shudder that runs up my spine.

I have an idea and it's not a welcome one. I check my cell and find I have no signal; confirmation of my idea will have to wait until I can speak to Alfonse, or at least use my phone to search the internet.

The chief touches my arm and points to the exit from the tent. I don't need told twice.

We walk back to his pickup in silence. I strip off the protective suit while he starts issuing orders to his men and making requests of the CSI team.

My mind is chewing over the various aspects of my idea. If I'm right with my suspicions this death is linked to the others, and will without doubt be classed as a hate crime.

If, however, I'm wrong, there are two groups of killers out there. Killers who don't just kill, but who use horrific methods.

Dead may be dead, but there are good and bad ways to die. None of these deaths could ever be described as good ways.

I daren't voice my suspicions to the chief until I have confirmed them as accurate in case I steer his investigation the wrong way. I'm lucky to be here and that's not something I want to change.

Chapter 37

The chief is talkative on the way back to Casperton. He's bouncing ideas off me and looking for my take on the body we've just viewed. I don't have a lot to offer him but I do share his belief that a gang of racists are behind these killings.

The big question is how we're going to identify the group. So far we have no leads worth following and can't make anything except wild guesses at who may be potential suspects.

As soon as my cell shows a solitary bar on the signal icon I call Alfonse. 'Drop whatever you're doing and have a look at Google for me. I want to know ten methods historically used for punishment or ritualistic killings in Asia. Let me know as soon as you have them.'

Alfonse hangs up before I do. He'll know from my tone and lack of salutation I'm in a hurry for the information.

'What you thinking, Boulder?'

'She was impaled. The Fourniers were crucified then burned alive. I'm wondering if they're being executed in a way that's relevant to their heritage or nationality.'

He takes his eyes off the road to look at me. 'That's a good shout. I hope to God you're wrong though. Because if you're right, this is only the beginning.'

'If I am, you'll be able to call in the FBI.'

'Doesn't matter if you're right or not. It's a call I'll be making as soon as I get back from informing the family. You know what that means for you though, don't you?'

He's meaning my involvement will become limited at best. While he can flaunt the rules, and consult a civilian when he's nobody to answer to, the FBI agent or special agent who gets sent to investigate will want me kept out of sight and mind.

'I'm not bothered about being involved if the FBI come. I just want those killers found and locked up.'

It's the truth. Or at least it's the truth if the FBI are quick about their job. I sure don't want to face off against any more killers. Once is more than enough. I don't need any more fights to the death. Or nightmares.

Anyway, just because the FBI roll into town, it doesn't mean Alfonse and I have to stop our enquiries. It'd be easier to stop the proverbial runaway train than get Alfonse to drop this case. Anything we learn will be fed straight to Chief Watson.

A beep from my cell indicates an email has landed from Alfonse. I send the acknowledgement of receipt he's requested and scan my eyes down the screen as I scroll. He knows I understand the things I read better than those I hear.

The third one down is what I'm looking for. He hasn't just given me the requested information, he's also included a few brief details about each one.

Impalement is an historical execution method used in several Asian countries dating back to the fifth century BC.

This information is all I need to know. Twice now, killers have struck against the residents of Casperton.

The victims have been innocent people. Their only crime being the colour of their skin.

I tell the chief about Alfonse's email. He curses for a whole mile without repetition.

When he stops cursing he looks at me with a heavy expression. 'What kind of monsters are we up against? It's bad enough killing people of a different creed, but to make them suffer like this…'

He tails off his sentence, unable to find the right words to describe what he's feeling. As far as I'm concerned, curse words are the best fit.

'Are you going to alert the public?'

'You've got to be kidding me. What the hell do you want me to say? That there's a gang of murderous psychos who are targeting people of colour, or that all blacks should stay home?' There's enough scorn and incredulity in his voice to strip paint.

'Of course not.' I match his tone as my own frustrations pour out. 'You're the chief of police and you have a responsibility to protect the citizens of Casperton.'

'Who the hell do you think you are, telling me about my responsibilities?' The chief takes a corner too fast and has to swerve to avoid a truck coming the other way. Lights flash and a horn sounds. I have just enough time to see the truck driver flip off the chief.

The near collision gives us both a chance to take a deep breath and calm down.

'My point is that it's better you put out a warning of some sorts, than the public reading about it in the Casperton Gazette.'

'Dammit, Boulder, why do you always see things before I do?'

I don't answer him. The truth will do neither of us any favours. I'm a cynical pessimist by nature. I expect the worst and prepare methods to combat it.

Trust isn't something I give away easily. Not to people I don't know well, or to the government and certainly not the press. Even a free-speaking crusader like Ms Rosenberg puts her own spin on things. Her exposés may keep local government in line, but Ms Rosenberg is a journalist which means she's a sensationalist. Whatever life event moved her from New York to Casperton may just be reversed if she's the one to break the news of a hate group escalating from preaching to heinous murders.

The chief, by contrast, is an accepting man. For a police chief, he's too keen to see the best in people. By now he should have replaced Lieutenant Farrage and all his deadweight cronies. I suspect he hasn't because he feels he can train them into becoming good detectives. Perhaps they've got down on their knees and begged him with tears in their eyes. He'd fall for that. He doesn't possess the cynical nature of a hard-bitten detective who's met so many kinds of liar he doesn't even trust himself.

I respect him for not being like me. He's a good man. If I'm honest with myself, a better man than I.

Chapter 38

Noelle cradles Oscar's head in her lap. He's done little but groan in pain since they were pushed into this shack.

Upon leaving their house, she'd been pushed into the back of a van. Oscar had been tossed in to land at her feet. Two of their captors had joined them. They'd been silent and still. Their only movement had been kicks aimed at Oscar whenever he rolled near them.

Once the van had stopped, Oscar had been dragged out, the back of his head bouncing off the tow-hitch as he fell to the ground.

The masked men had laid into his body with their heavy work boots. She'd yelled at them to stop but they'd ignored her. If her hands hadn't been bound she'd have tried to intervene; to shield him.

They'd concentrated their kicks on his body. From his chest down the blows rained, but never above the line from his nipples. With hands and feet bound he'd been unable to defend himself.

The one saving grace was the fact they'd removed his gag prior to their attack. Coupled with the excessive alcohol intake the previous night, the kicks to his stomach, ribs and kidneys had sent violent streams of vomit from Oscar's mouth.

As a final insult, to add to the multiple injuries, one of the men had the others hold Oscar in place while he delivered a serious of vicious kicks to Oscar's groin.

They'd cut Noelle's bonds free and had pushed her into this rough shack. Oscar had been dragged in after her. His bruised body too damaged for him to offer any resistance.

For some reason she'd looked at her watch then. That had been five hours ago.

It's now twenty after eleven and Oscar still hasn't regained any strength or reasonable degree of consciousness.

The knot in her stomach could be there for a dozen various reasons. Hunger, revulsion, a desire to go to the bathroom, or just plain fear are her best guesses. Any one of these would explain it but she knows fear is the greatest contributor.

Not fear for herself – while they'd been rough with her, the men hadn't gone so far as to strike her. She was afraid for Oscar, the beating he'd taken must have caused some internal damage and the Lord alone knows what may be ruptured inside him.

There's also fear for their baby. There's no way the variety of hormones her body is dumping at the moment can be good for a baby.

It's bad enough she may lose Oscar. The added horror of potentially losing his baby as well is more than she can take.

She digs a nail into the soft skin between her left thumb and forefinger. The pain serves its intended purpose. It focuses her.

A few cracks between the boards forming the walls allow slivers of light into the shack. It looks bare in the dimness.

Noelle uses gentle movements to lower Oscar's head to the dirt floor and tries the door.

It's locked.

A search of the shack's walls reveals one boarded-over window and no weak spots. The dirt floor offers the possibility of tunnelling under the walls. Or at least it would if the dirt wasn't so hard packed.

Five minutes spent pawing and scratching earns her two torn nails and a hole the size of a soup bowl.

She looks round for a tool of some kind. Her eyes find nothing but dirt on the floor.

The walls are bare timber. There are no shelves or anything that can be pried loose to aid her digging or use as a weapon. The men will have to open the door at some point.

It's better if they don't. If they open the door it will mean more pain for Oscar. She'd face the pain herself if it wasn't for the baby.

She has another, more terrifying thought. *What if they never come back? What then?*

She knows Oscar will die from his injuries and she'll starve. As her body starts to devour its fatty tissues, the baby will suffer from malnutrition first.

The dryness of her mouth gives her another, greater fear.

Starvation won't be what kills them. Dehydration will.

She's aware the human body can survive three weeks without food, but only three days without water. Oscar's alcohol intake last night will have put him at a minus to start with.

Noelle presses her ear against the door but hears nothing.

Her eyes peek through the one crack she's tall enough to reach. She sees brushwood and scrubland surrounded by hills. Her best guess is they're in a valley somewhere.

With nothing left to gain by stealth, Noelle resorts to desperation.

She yells for help. None comes.

She screams, hoping the shrillness will carry further. Nothing changes.

With no reaction to her yelling and screaming, Noelle figures the men have abandoned her and Oscar to die.

Noelle reasons that the door is the weak point and backs herself against the opposite wall. She runs the four paces and throws her shoulder against the lock side of the door.

This time her scream is fuelled by pain rather than fear. The shack's door stands firm against her assault, making her shoulder numb with the impact.

If there'd been the slightest hint of give in the door, she'd try again regardless of the pain. She's about to try kicking out at the boards forming the wall when a voice interrupts her. 'Hey, bitch. Stop your hollerin'. From now on, every time you make a noise or try and escape, we'll come in there and beat your beaner lover some more.' Just like the previous night, the voice is muffled by a hand.

Noelle sinks to the floor and goes back to cradling Oscar.

Tears run down her face and fall from her jaw as she wonders why they've been kidnapped, and what the men plan to do to them.

Chapter 39

I can tell the chief is close to losing his patience and unless the person he's speaking to is an imbecile, they'll know it too.

He's spent the last five minutes getting the run-around from someone I presume is a junior desk clerk at the FBI office in Salt Lake City.

While he drums frustrated fingers on his desk, I read through the file he handed me after glancing at it himself.

The file is an initial report from the CSI team detailing the items found in the immediate vicinity of where the Fourniers were discovered.

I ignore the technical jargon and look for the salient facts.

The crosses were three by six-inch pine – available from any lumber yard. They'd been jointed with a half lap joint. I don't know a lot about carpentry, but I do know that a half lap joint doesn't require a cabinetmaker. Despite this, the report says the joints were well made and showed a degree of skill.

The nails used to affix the Fourniers were standard six-inch nails which could be purchased at most hardware stores or builders' merchants.

There's nothing enlightening in the report until I reach the pages concerning the items found on the track. Various candy wrappers and so on are all discounted due to them being aged by weeks, or months, on the forest floor.

The cigar butt offers more. It's a rare brand called a *Royal Jamaica Extrafinos No. 4.*

A quick search on my phone shows them to be retailing at over ninety bucks for three. The fact I can source them on the internet with less than a minute's searching says more about their retailer's marketing expertise than the actual rarity of the cigars. Tracking down local retailers – and purchasers – of the cigars is a job best left for Alfonse.

The next page is about the paint left on a tree by the vehicle that left the track. Chemical analysis shows it to have come from a Ford E250 panel van. The problem is that the paint is white, and therefore the van must be too. White Ford vans are commonplace.

I'm familiar with the model, having driven one in a previous job. They're workhorses for builders of all trades, delivery firms and a thousand other drivers. Even when I lived in Glasgow, the most common van on the road was a Ford.

What helps is that the few tracks they found were made by off-road tyres. This means the van has been modified to some degree. It's not much of a clue, but it's a clue if it helps to narrow the list of suspects.

I keep turning the pages, but find nothing more of any possible use.

All we need to do is find someone who drives the right kind of vehicle, smokes the correct brand of cigar, and has a history of racial violence or hatred and we're home and hosed.

If only it were that easy.

The chief's tone has changed. He's now talking to someone with a bit of authority. The report he's giving is brief and to the point. Key facts are covered and questions fielded with straight answers.

He thanks the person and ends the call.

'FBI are sending over a half-dozen agents. I spoke to the SAC at Amelia Earhart.' He waves a dismissive hand. 'I didn't get his name.'

Amelia Earhart Drive is in Salt Lake City. I look at my watch. 'Supposing they leave in half an hour and don't worry about the speed limits too much. It's still going to be three when they get here.'

'Your point?'

'We've got almost three hours to run down some leads before they take over. The more we can give them, the sooner these killers can be stopped.'

'Agreed. I'll get my boys to do a door-to-door where the girl was taken. What are you going to do?'

'I'm going to get Alfonse to chase down people who've bought those cigars. I'll also get him to find out who owns a white Ford E250 in this area. Once I've spoken to him, I'm going to find out what I can about the second victim.'

Even as I say it, I feel as if I'm betraying Alfonse. I know it's not true, but I can't help the pang of guilt. My aim is to get as much information as possible so the lives of the Fourniers can be cross-referenced against Gazala's. The points where their lives intersect may just give us the break we need.

'Me too.' His voice trips with foreboding. 'Except I have to get my information from the family. I sent Farrage over to do the death knock.'

I'm not sure how to answer him; the thought of Lieutenant Farrage breaking bad news to a distraught family is an uncomfortable one, so I ask a question. 'What do you know about her?'

He gives me a few bare facts. Other than her age, address and where she worked there's not much to go on.

It's her place of work that strikes a chord.

Chapter 40

C-Dude is just as I remember it. I buy clothes here on occasion. Not the high-fashion stuff – the end-of-season lines suit me best. They're cheaper and I've never been worried about staying close to the latest trends.

There's a young woman with a deep tan working behind the sales counter. She looks close to tears as she bags something for a guy in his early twenties. He's trying to flirt with her, but she's not interested. While I can tell she's struggling to hold it together, the guy is oblivious.

It doesn't take much effort to work out why a colleague of Gazala's is upset. News travels fast in a place like Casperton. Bad news travels faster.

At the back of the room a woman wears a disapproving look as she hangs suits on racks.

I wander round until the unsuccessful Romeo realises he's fighting a losing battle, and leaves.

The tanned woman is wiping her eyes when I approach.

'Sorry. Must have an allergy to something. How can I help you?'

The lie is unconvincing. I don't challenge it though. Instead, I nod at her and lean on the counter.

I keep my tone as casual as I can. 'I'm here for some information. About Gazala.'

'So it's true, she's dead?'

She crumples when I give her confirmation.

Brisk clacks forewarn the older woman's arrival. She comforts her younger colleague in a way that's not natural to either. There's too much stiffness from both of them. 'I'm sorry but I'm going to have to ask you to leave.' Her free arm points at the door.

I don't move.

She points again. This time she accompanies the gesture with a stamp of her heel. 'Sir, did you not hear me ask you to leave?'

The stamp itself is enough to make me dig my own heels in. I do, however, recognise this isn't a fight I should have – let alone try and win. Finesse is called for here.

'I did indeed hear you, Ma'am, I'm investigating Gazala's murder and just wondered if your colleague could answer a few questions.' I almost say daughter instead of colleague as a way to emphasise the woman's age.

The older woman is pushed away. 'It's okay, Marjorie. I'll be okay. If this man wants to ask me some questions; it's the least I can do for Gazala.'

I give the girl a mental round of applause for her strength and moral fortitude. 'Is there somewhere we can talk in private?' I look around the store.

Marjorie points towards a door in a far corner. The girl leads the way, telling me her name is Jenny and she's worked with Gazala for almost a year.

Jenny's face isn't familiar, but I wouldn't expect it to be. She's too young to be part of the regular crowd at the Tree and, if her appearance is anything to go by, there's no way she's a classic rock fan.

The door opens into a stockroom. There are piles of boxes stacked in neat rows. Rails are laden with unpacked clothes and covered with clear sheets. A coffee machine sits atop a small fridge in one corner.

Jenny leans her butt against the fridge. Her eyes are red and she looks as if tears are never going to be far away. 'What do you want to know?'

I throw a few questions her way. She bats the answers back. There's nothing untoward or interesting about her answers.

She and Gazala were colleagues for the eleven months she's worked here. They get on well and share a dislike of Marjorie. That's not a big surprise; two young women are always going to make friends with each other rather than a grumpy older woman in a position of authority.

They may be friends at work but they don't socialise together. Jenny admits she's out most nights while Gazala chooses to stay in.

I move the conversation onto life in the store, ask about customers falling out with Gazala or giving her a hard time.

She rubbishes the idea. 'Gazala is loved by the customers. She never has any problems or issues with them. Most times she manages to upsell to them as well.'

'What about boyfriends, do you know if she was seeing anyone?'

'Nobody that I know of.' Jenny picks at her top lip, glances towards the door. 'She is all about getting her own store. She doesn't seem interested in meeting a guy.'

'Surely she had guys chasing her? She was pretty enough.'

A sob catches in her throat making me wonder if my use of the past tense is causing unnecessary distress.

'She flirted a little to make a sale but never accepted any of the dates they offered her.' Jenny switches to past tense now that realisation and acceptance have arrived.

'Have you heard about the family that was murdered?'

'Yeeesss.' Confusion spreads on Jenny's face as she stretches the word.

I show her a picture on my cell. It's one Alfonse sent me of the Fourniers. 'This is them. Do any of them look familiar?'

'The girl does.' She points at the screen. 'Most weekends she hung outside with a couple other girls.'

This puzzles me until I remember that the adjacent store sells video games. Where better for a bunch of teen girls to hang out, giggling about boys and hopefully meeting some, than here?

'Did Gazala ever talk with her?' I have to fight to keep the excitement from my voice. This may be the connection I'm looking for.

'Yeah a few times. The girls can be pests at times, but Gazala would always chat to them when Marjorie wasn't about.'

'Do you know what they talked about?'

A shake of the head. 'I never asked.'

The cynic in me says Jenny would only be interested in a bunch of young girls if they had older brothers or perhaps a single father. Even in her state of grief I've caught her giving me the once over.

'Do you know who the other girls are?'

'I don't, sorry.'

The rap of knuckles on wood makes us both look to the door. Marjorie walks in followed by Lieutenant Farrage. Both fix me with a glare although Marjorie is the one to speak; her voice full of accusation. 'I thought you were the police.'

Farrage answers her. 'He's not the police, he's not even a private detective.'

I look directly at Marjorie. 'He's right, I'm not a trained detective. But I'm more of a detective than he'll ever be. And what's more, unlike him and his buddies, I'm not getting paid by the state to let you all down with my incompetence.'

Her lips purse tighter than usual. I think it may be my disregard for Farrage's authority. She's the type who feeds off the class system. Competence is not a necessary qualification in her world. The existence of a badge enough to ordain a higher communal standing.

She'll no doubt be aware of who his father is. This will further elevate him when compared to me.

I'm wearing jeans, heavy boots and a plain shirt. Farrage is wearing a tailored suit with polished shoes and a tie. His accent is local, mine foreign. In a mind as narrow as hers it's no contest.

For once, Farrage has enough about him to know when to keep his big yap shut. He wants to reply, to put me down with a sharp witticism, but he knows he's out-classed. His sole response is to point at the door.

'Thank you detective.' I toss him a sweet smile and a patronising look. 'That's a door. Spelled d-o-o-r.'

Marjorie's admonishments, on the subject of disrespect as I leave the store, are wonderful in their primness.

Chapter 41

Noelle starts as the door opens and daylight floods the shack. She's been lost in a world of self-pity, her mind worrying at possible reasons for their kidnap.

She knows the chances of them being rescued are slim. At Oscar's suggestion, they'd both taken the day off work to look at potential wedding venues. Nobody except a couple of wedding planners will be missing them, and they'll be used to broken appointments.

The men who come through the door are again wearing masks. They grab her, drag a hood over her head and lead her outside. Oscar is left lying on the floor, still on the point of unconsciousness.

She feels the men guide her around the shack. When they reach what she assumes is the far side, they push her backwards until her shoulders touch rough wood.

The hood is pulled off and one of the men thrusts a sheet of paper at her. Another is holding a cell phone. She recognises the pink case as hers.

Noelle looks down at the paper. At the top of the page is a terse instruction to read the page aloud. As her eyes flit down the page she recoils in horror. The hand clutching the paper moves away from her body, as if distancing it will make her feel safer.

It doesn't.

The third of her captors steps out from behind the one with her cell. He's holding a shotgun. He points it at her with a lack of urgency. The end of the barrel bounces twice; its meaning unmissable.

She starts to read the words on the paper. Every one of them is an affront to her. Even saying them under duress is an effort. She expects to die when she reaches the end. Her voice falters but she does not allow it to fail. As she resigns herself to death, her resolve grows stronger.

The man with her cell phone is holding it up. She guesses he's recording her.

As Noelle speaks, her eyes flit between the paper and the masks hiding the men from her view. She finishes the message with her head up and her voice strong.

'So, what now? Are you going to kill me?'

Another piece of paper is produced and handed to her.

She reads the instructions with dread, tears pouring down her cheeks as she realises what they mean for Oscar.

Chapter 42

I knock on the door and try my best to look respectable and unthreatening. A grown man asking to speak with a teenage girl is sure to raise any parent's suspicions.

The street where Ashlyn Sampson lives is a good one. The cars on the driveways are new models, the lawns are well kept and there's a general air of respectability. It doesn't surprise me; Robyn was a good girl from a decent family, it stands to reason her friends will be similar people.

The woman who answers the door is mid-thirties and mumsy in every way possible. Her blonde hair is in an unkempt ponytail and her clothes are stained with the detritus of child-rearing. A meaty smell fills the air with a promise of sustenance.

I explain why I'm here. Her initial friendliness turns to suspicion until I request that she sits with Ashlyn while I ask my questions.

She invites me in and calls out for her daughter as she leads me to her lounge.

Two toddlers are playing on the carpet, both pulling on a ratty doll. From their comparative sizes, I guess they're twins.

'Tyson, let Anna have Dolly.' The boy lets go of the doll and starts pulling at the nose on a stuffed bear.

A girl with a shock of frizzy hair and too much make-up enters the room.

'This man is here to ask you a few questions about Robyn. Okay?'

Ashlyn rejects the mother's patted cushion next to her and stands by the fireplace in a show of independence.

'Hi, Ashlyn. I'm told you were one of Robyn Fournier's best friends.' I want to ask what they did together, but can't think of a way of asking without it sounding creepy. 'You used to hang around outside C-Dude, didn't you?'

'Not, like, very often.' The glance at her mother tells me lies have been told regarding her whereabouts.

'That's fair enough. I believe Robyn was friends with one of the staff there. A woman called Gazala. What did they talk about?'

'School and stuff. I think, like, Gazala used to, like, sit Robyn when she was younger.' The unnecessary 'likes' in her speech pattern are irritating but irrelevant. She's giving me a genuine connection between the victims.

'Were they friends? Did they see each other anywhere else?'

Her face twists in disgust. 'They weren't, like, BFFs or anything. She was, like, way old. She was just, like, kind to us and knew Robyn best. Not like that Marjorie. She was a... cow.'

I hide the smile I can feel coming. Ashlyn was about to swear and just remembered in time that her mother was in the room. The mother is worldly enough to have a tinge of a smile in her eyes.

'So, you never saw Gazala anywhere else?'

'Once or twice at the mall, or by the park. Mostly at C-Dude though.'

I repeat the questions in different ways but don't learn anything beyond the fact Gazala had been polite to a kid she used to sit for.

Chapter 43

Noelle trembles as she waits in the back of the van. The hood is back over her head but she estimates there's at least one of her captors in here with her.

For the first time since being snatched she fears rape. When she was loaded into the van after making the video, a gloved hand cupped her left breast through the flimsy material of her chemise. It had lingered and given a firm squeeze before being removed.

Every part of her wants to do whatever she can to learn the identity of her captors but the risk of them hurting her as punishment is too great. If it was just her she had to care for then it would be different. With a baby growing inside her there is no way she can take the chance.

It feels as if she's abandoning Oscar. That she's leaving him to his fate without a fight.

The pragmatic side of her recognises there's little a pregnant woman can do against four men. Especially when one of them has a shotgun.

She feels the van draw to a stop.

Remembers her instructions.

Wonders if she's about to die. Thinks about the life forming inside her.

Rough gloves filled with strong fingers grasp her right arm.

She's lead out of the van.

Footsteps sound.

Another set of gloves take her left arm.

More footsteps.

A punch hits her square in the gut.

The gloved hands on her arms hold her upright; prevent her from doubling over.

Another punch lands. Then a third, fourth and fifth. Each one a little lower than the previous.

The final punch lands at the top of her pubic bone.

The gloved hands lower her to the ground. Through the pain she feels rough tarmac beneath her butt.

Somehow she remembers her instructions.

The racking of a shotgun fills the quiet as her count reaches three.

Tyres screech as metallic doors slam.

Noelle reaches fifty and pulls the hood off.

The first thing she does is lift her chemise and look down. She'd felt her panties filling with moisture and she can now see it's the blood she'd feared.

Sobs wrack her body as she howls in pain and anger.

It's a full ten minutes before she collects herself enough to think about finding help, when she does, she starts clinging to the faintest of hopes the baby has somehow survived the assault.

Her eyes blink away the tears and find a focal point in the distance. She looks around and finds she's on a deserted road.

Her cell is four feet in front of her. She groans in pain as she crawls towards it.

911 is the first number she calls. The need to get help for Oscar is an equal priority with summoning an ambulance for the baby.

The voice at the other end of the line goes through the usual routine in calm, measured tones: identifies the caller, asks which service and wants to know what has happened.

Noelle can't answer the question about her location. Frantic, she looks around to try and find a landmark she recognises.

As she turns to look along the road, she screams and drops the cell.

Chapter 44

I'm sitting in Miss Oliver's office. The atmosphere is, as my grandpa would say, 'colder than a polar bear's left bollock'. She's not trying to be frosty, she just doesn't know how to be anything else.

Every question I'm putting to her is being deflected. It's as if I'm prying into her personal life or asking for state secrets. I suppose to one as career-minded as her, it will seem as if I am.

'I'm sorry, but I cannot disclose that information.' She has the poor grace to look self-satisfied at her thwarting of my enquiry. 'We pride ourselves on our client confidentiality.'

'I'm sure you do. Perhaps it'd be better for all concerned if you wait for the FBI to arrive with a warrant.'

Her eyes narrow at my bluff. I can see her trying to work out why I'm doing an about-turn. 'What do you mean?'

'Well, if you wait until the warrant comes you'll be standing by the bank's principles. I guess someone in your marketing team may even use a strapline such as – "your privacy means so much to us, we'll obstruct homicide investigations". Your head office and regional manager will be proud of you. I bet you'll get a promotion out of this.' I turn the screw a little tighter. 'I'm certain Ms Rosenberg will give you a good write-up in the Gazette. Not sure how that'll play out with the families of the deceased though. You may lose a few customers until the marketing bods get the new slogan out there.'

'Why should I give this information to you rather than the police? You're not even licensed as a detective.'

We both know she's going to cave and this is her last act of defiance. It's one thing to protect your clients, another to hold up a major investigation. It would be career suicide.

164

There's no way she wants to attract the kind of public attention I'm suggesting she'll get, not when the FBI will force her to give them the information I'm after. I'm just here a couple of days ahead of them with less to lose by making threats.

'Any information you give me will only be shared with the police and my partner. I have no interest in breaching your bank's ethics. I'm just trying to identify some possible suspects.'

She's too young to purse her lips, but she does it anyway. 'It'll take time to get the information you need. It's not something I can do at the push of a button.'

'Poppycock. You should be able to have that information within five minutes.' I point to the computer on her desk. 'Are you telling me that you can't log in as Sherrelle and do a search for loan applications?' She doesn't answer me. Or meet my eye. 'That you can't segregate those approved and those denied? In this day and age I find that totally unbelievable.'

She blusters for a moment or two but my patience has worn through. I stand and move towards the door. 'Forget it. I'll just call Ms Rosenberg. I'm sure she'll be fascinated at the lack of functionality of the computer system in a bank that sells "digital banking for the digital age".'

My use of the bank's current advertising slogan breaks her.

'Sit down, Mr Boulder. I'll get you your information.'

Her face twists into a scowl as she stabs at the keyboard, muttering un-bank-manager-like curses under her breath, but she's getting me what I want.

Her printer spits out a sheaf of papers.

She hands them to me without a smile. 'This is everyone Sherrelle turned down in the last five years. They're listed by the value of the loan request. It should make your search quicker.'

She's come through in spades so I resist adding, 'it wasn't that hard, was it?' when I give her my thanks.

Chapter 45

I pull into the lot and find a space to park. There's a young couple holding hands as they push a buggy; a mother of three is yelling at her kids to watch where they're going.

Taylor rearranged my appointment with Dr Edwards when I called earlier. He agreed to hang back and see me after his last patient. Before I even get in there, I know he's going to exact a heavy price for this favour. My being five minutes late will only raise the cost.

As I stride in, Taylor is waiting for me. 'Go right in. And mind what you say, he's in a funny mood today.'

His door is open so I enter and take my usual seat as I apologise for being late.

He looks at me over steepled fingers. He has a way of looking at me that makes me feel like I'm a specimen in a lab.

'Let's not waste each other's time. You want answers for the case you're investigating and I want to know how you feel about killing a man. Shall we start with you telling me what you felt the moment you knew he was dead?'

His directness is unusual. I know he'll be expecting the same from me. I also know he's wily enough to use it, and rapid-fire questions, as a way to unsettle me and get quick answers, rather than considered, more ambiguous ones.

'I was glad I'd killed him. It was me or him and I didn't want to die.' I see no harm in giving him an honest answer. 'There's been a second murder and it's got loads of racial symbolism attached to it too.'

'Tell me more about this murder. Just the key facts though.' I like that he uses my word for the deed and doesn't correct me.

I've been in Casperton a long time, but I often find myself still thinking in Scottish terms rather than American ones. What I don't like is him limiting me to key facts. It's his way of controlling the conversation.

When I'm finished, he leans back in his chair and looks at the ceiling. It's a new gesture.

He sits back upright and scribbles a note or two onto his pad. 'A message is being sent. Not only are they targeting black people, they're attacking all non-whites. Their motives are unknown at this time, but I'd speculate they're waging some kind of racial war based on the principles of terrorism.'

'Why do you say terrorism when they're racially motivated hate crimes?' My thinking has been along clearly defined racial hatred lines.

'Terrorism is defined as an unofficial or unauthorised use of violence and intimidation in the pursuit of political aims.' He lays down his pen. 'How do you think the black and other minority communities are feeling right now? It's only a matter of time before they either start leaving town, or lashing out at those they deem responsible. These are the kind of things which instigate race-riots. You may have killed in self-defence, but now, weeks after the event in the cold light of day, how do you feel about the fact you took another man's life?'

'I'm comfortable with it for the reasons I already explained. He picked the fight with me. He lost. I'd rather not have sunk to his level but he took the decision out of my hands.'

'Interesting that you use the word "sunk". You've told me previously that you can't swim, and are in fact afraid of water.' Another note gets added to my file. 'The message being sent out is that people of colour are unwelcome – that they should leave. The methods of execution are symbolic as well as barbaric. Everyone fears death to some degree. We all hope we'll die in our old age after a long life. Most people's preference is to slip away in the middle of the night in their own bed. You've faced death a lot more closely than most. What's worse for you, is that you faced dying in an environment you feared. You've been there. Can you imagine the terror of the black community; they'll all be worrying that they'll be the next ones to be nailed to a cross and incinerated. How did you feel when you were dumped into the water and left to drown?'

I take a moment to digest his words. I'm focussing on the statements rather than the question.

'I'd be lying to you if I said I wasn't scared. There's no shame in that. Anyone would have been scared in that situation. What do you think is next for this group of killers?'

'I don't know what they'll do next, I suspect it'll be bad though. Whether they attack a different ethnic group or revisit one of those already targeted, I think their next strike will come soon. The chief of police will be calling in the FBI and will, I'm sure, be reassuring a scared public while also giving them advice on how to stay safe. Their mission will become harder with every passing day. It's also a basic principle of terrorism to keep the pressure on. As you say, there's no shame in being scared. I'm sure drowning was the subject of your worst nightmares. I would imagine you were angry as well. Am I right?'

'Yeah. I was angry. Furious in fact. With him, with myself for being captured. I used that anger to survive. To do what needed to be done.'

Fingers get steepled. The ceiling gets another examination. 'Tell me, Jake, how are you sleeping?'

He's done it again. He's steered me one way with his answer only to ambush me with a perceptive question. This is the one I've been dreading. I know how much emphasis psychologists and their ilk place on the power of dreams. My options are either lying, or admitting I suffer from terror-inducing nightmares. I choose to do both.

'I have the odd bad dream, that's all. I expect it's to be expected really.' His face remains blank at my blasé response. 'Can you give me any pointers towards identifying these killers?'

'I've told you before, Jake. I'm not a criminal psychologist. I'm an everyday psychologist. I can only give you guesses based on the information you give me.'

'Then guess.' The desperate anger in my voice catches us both by surprise.

'Okay then.' There's no resentment in his voice. 'My best guess is that they are a tightly knit group – family or co-workers kind of thing. Their education levels will not be as high as ours. They'll have police records for violence and petty thefts. Most will be single men.'

He doesn't know it but he's describing the Augiers. Or at least people like them.

'Thank you, Doctor. You've been very helpful.'

I stand to leave, but as always Dr Edwards has a cautionary word for me. 'You may try and pass them off as bad dreams, Jake. We both know they're more than that. Next time we speak, I want to discuss them further.'

We both know he means I have to tell him everything about the dreams. I thought I was tenacious until I met him.

Chapter 46

I'm a quarter of a mile from Alfonse's place when my cell rings. I answer it without looking, only to be met by the gruff tones of Chief Watson. From the stress in his voice I get a mental picture him of kneading his temples.

He tells me about a call that came in via 911. A woman had been dumped on a back road off the 191. They'd lost the connection with her but had put a trace on her cell as a matter of routine. The responding patrolman had found her.

Before getting the woman into the patrol car, she'd led the patrolman off the road and into the scrub. Had shown him a tethered wild goat with a human head tied between its horns.

I ask who the woman was; if the patrolman recognised either her or the head.

The chief says no to both questions and tells me to get my ass to the station as quick as I can.

I call Alfonse. 'Put your shoes on and meet me on the sidewalk.' I hang up before he has time to ask questions.

As I turn the corner he's locking his door.

I'm at the sidewalk a second before he is. Two seconds later I'm accelerating away.

He tells me of his day in six succinct words. 'I got nothing. Waste of time.'

I tell him about my day and the latest developments. He gasps as I tell him about the goat with its gruesome burden.

The whole scenario echoes the words of the Doctor. Another statement.

It's also another different racial group to be targeted. A new section of the community struck with terror.

Casperton is set to become famous for all the wrong reasons. It's nothing more than a matter of time before the news of these killings goes national, or global. I might not own a TV, but I spend enough time online to know how things can go viral. Social media sites will throb and hum as the public have their say. I just hope things don't get so bad that it's discussed in congress.

As a tactic to raise the profile of the killings, it's a brilliant one. The more I think about it, the better it seems.

I don't envy the chief his job at the best of times. Now it must be a torturous world of high stress and higher stakes.

The FBI coming to take over will ease a lot of the burden. Fingers will still be pointed at the chief though. Columnists with vitriol-filled pens and empty heads will file copy laden with criticism of a man who deserves better.

When we enter the station, Farrage is leading three of his sidekicks from the chief's office. To say they look chastened would be an understatement. Each carries an air of humble determination.

I poke my head around the chief's door. He's got the phone to his ear but he waves us in.

Alfonse and I sit in silence, like obedient children, until the chief crashes the phone into its cradle.

'You got the drift of this?' The chief's words come out as a scowl.

The pressure is taking its toll on him. His knuckles are kneading his temples in the familiar gesture. The newer technique, demonstrated by Emily Green, has been forgotten and he's back to using brute force.

'We're up to speed, but only as far as you've told us.' I hold his gaze. 'I take it you realise how big this is going to become when word gets out?'

He nods. His face etched with consternation. 'Yeah. I've threatened the jobs of everyone who knows, to try and keep it contained for now.' He makes a helpless gesture.

Someone will leak the news. The woman herself, a nurse or a patrolman struggling to pay their mortgage may take a few bucks for a newsworthy tip.

'Where is the woman now, is she hurt?'

'The patrolman who found her radioed for help before bringing her back. She's just been admitted to the hospital and is currently under evaluation. Both psychiatric and physical.' He looks at his watch. 'I've been told I should be able to see her in an hour or so. According to the patrolman, she's in an extreme state of shock and was just babbling. She kept pushing her cell to him but when he tried to take it she wouldn't let him.'

'Do you know her name yet, or whose head it is ?'

'Not yet. The head is still out there on that damned goat.'

'Why? Surely the patrolman brought it in?' I can't keep the incredulity from my voice. The police around here might be rubbish, but they should at least know better than to leave a goat wandering around with a human head between its horns.

'It's not that simple, Jake.'

I turn to face Chief Watson. 'What do you mean, not that simple? It's obvious that you retrieve the animal and the head for evidence.'

"You Can't just go interfering with a crime scene like that. It needs to be done by a specialist forensic team"

My eyes fall to the floor as I realise my mistake. "Tell me you've got someone capable on their way"

'Of course.'

'What about the FBI? Are they here yet, and have you updated them?'

'I spoke to the special agent in charge and he's been held up with car trouble. He said he'll get here in an hour, so I told him to go to the hospital.'

'So, we've got an hour before anything happens.' I stand up and make for the door. 'I suggest we use that time wisely.'

'What you sayin', Boulder?'

'I'm saying you'll have things to organise. A press conference for one. A higher police presence for another. While you're doing that, Alfonse and I will make ourselves useful. Can we use the other office?'

'You do what you gotta do. Just stop tellin' me how to do my goddamn job.'

'Chief?' Alfonse receives an enquiring glare. 'What was the colour of the skin on the head?'

'Brown. Marcus reckoned the guy looked Mexican.'

I'd never asked the question myself because I knew what the answer would be. There's no satisfaction in being right though.

Chapter 47

I park beside the chief's pickup and follow him into the hospital. I've left Alfonse working his way through the list of people Sherrelle had turned down for loans.

The chief marches to the Emergency Room counter and growls his query to the receptionist. She gives him the information he needs and points the way.

A minute later we're standing outside a cubicle while the chief argues with a nurse. It's a fierce argument which neither participant shows any desire to lose.

Neither party should lose either. Both are doing their jobs. The nurse is protecting her patient; the chief the townsfolk.

A doctor steps out from the cubicle and I get a look at the woman. Not a proper look, just enough of a split-second glimpse for me to recognise the fact that I know her. Try as I might, I can't put a name to her.

In the woman's dishevelled, grief-stricken state, her appearance will be a far cry from her usual look.

I need to see her again, for longer, to put a name to her. Her voice may be the better trigger.

The doctor is responding to the chief's demands. The nurse wears the smug look of a child whose parent has just told off another child. 'Chief. I fully understand your position, but there's no way you're going to be able to interview her. Her emotional state is too fragile for her to be able to answer your questions. She's also incredibly lucky not to have lost the baby she's carrying. I've given her a sedative to help her rest. She needs to rest. Not just for her own sake but for the baby's too.'

I step in front of the chief. Him snapping and growling threats isn't what's needed here. The doctor is using calm measured tones, so I do too.

'We appreciate your position, Doctor, and of course your patient's health is a priority for everyone. Do you know who your patient is yet?'

'No, I'm afraid I don't. Once she wakes up, we'll have her talk to a psychologist. Perhaps the news of her baby's survival will help her emotional state. All she's doing now is babbling incoherently.'

'I'll be honest with you. When you came out, I got a glimpse of her. I think I may have recognised her.'

'Who is she? Dammit, Boulder, you tell me who she is right now.' The chief steps forward. For a moment, I expect him to grab fistfuls of my shirt.

Even the sullen nurse is looking at me with expectation.

'I think she's Lydia Young.' It's a lie. I'm still not sure who it is but I'm trying to buy us enough of an audience with the woman to make a positive ID.

'Who's Lydia Young?'

It's the doctor who answers the chief. 'She's the administrator's daughter.' It's not the strip lighting which makes his face looks pale.

I take a tentative half-step towards the cubicle. 'Can I have a minute to see her, check I'm right?'

He steps aside and follows me in.

The figure on the bed is curled into a ball. I keep my distance so as not to alarm her, and bend down so my face is on the same level as hers. I take in every detail of her face: the pointed chin, high cheekbones, and opal eyes that pour tears. The woman's mouth is pulled wide as sob after sob wracks her body.

Crouching here looking at this wreck of a human being, I can feel the MacDonald blood in my veins boil. Not just for her, but for all those whose lives have been shattered by the killers' actions.

It isn't just the victims who have suffered. Their loved ones will be torturing themselves, imagining their pain and fear.

I keep my voice as soft and gentle as possible. It's almost a burr when I address the woman I suspect is Noelle Holten. 'Hello, I'm Jake. We used to date. Do you remember me?'

The tiniest of nods interrupts her sobbing.

Now I know she remembers me, I need her to confirm who she is. 'The doctor needs you to say your name, can you do that for me?' He doesn't, but she won't know that.

She moves her head off her chest and looks at me with unseeing, tear-filled eyes. I last saw her less than twenty-four hours ago, but she's aged at least a decade since then. Her voice when she speaks is faint, and slurred by whatever sedative the doctor has given her. 'No... No... Noelle.'

'Do you know who did this to you?' I hear the doctor tutting but ignore him.

Noelle's hands force their way free of the thin hospital sheet covering them. Clutched between white knuckled fingers is a cell phone with a pink cover. She slides it towards me. 'Vi... Vi... Videos.'

I take the cell from her fingers and give her hand a gentle squeeze as I push the cell into my pocket. She doesn't return the squeeze.

The doctor isn't stupid but you don't get to be a doctor by flunking out. 'You tricked me.' Curiosity sits where anger should.

I wait until we've left the cubicle before answering him. It'll save me repeating myself to Chief Watson. 'She's Noelle Holten, she's in her late thirties and lives on the other side of town.'

'And the other guy?' I pick up the chief's meaning. 'I'm guessing he's her boyfriend, and father of her baby. I saw them at Gallo Vermiglio last night with a bunch of folks that looked like family. They were all celebrating. Noelle was radiating happiness.'

A burly man in a dark suit strides towards us. He's almost a poster boy for the FBI with his upright posture and implacable face. He jerks his head to one side whilst looking at the chief. 'A word.'

I guess he's called Special Agent Doenig for information on Casperton and the law enforcers he's likely to encounter. Even forgetting the uniform, Chief Watson's iron grey hair and world-weary face are distinctive.

His lack of manners grates, but there are bigger issues at hand so I don't call him on it. The dark hue of his skin combined with the brusque voice are good indicators of how seriously he'll be taking this case.

He remains silent until we're alone in a corridor. When he does speak, his eyes are on Chief Watson.

'I'm Special Agent Gaertner. I'm guessing you're the chief of police.' He throws a disdainful glance my way. 'This one of your detectives?'

I'm not insulted by his pre-formed opinion. If he thinks I'm one of the local detectives, it's no surprise he's classing me as a moron.

'He's Jake Boulder, a private detective who's helping me out.'

Gaertner looks me head to toe as he reassesses. 'I've heard about him. Report I got was of a bright fellow who got lucky.'

I wonder what else Doenig has said about me. The FBI may be a bureaucratic organisation at heart but it's still staffed by human beings. Away from the public they'll have the same water-cooler gossips as every office in the world. There will be friendships, rivalries and a general sharing of experiences relevant to the areas they work in.

The chief springs to my defence. 'He's a good man to have around. He's been helping me on this case and I value his opinion.'

It's the nicest thing the chief has said about me but it doesn't have any effect on Gaertner.

'I'm sure you do. The FBI however, does not work with civilians.' Gaertner turns to me. 'Thank you for everything you've done so far. You can go home now. My colleagues and I will take it from here.'

The chief bristles and is about to respond to Gaertner's flat monotone with one of his rants, when a pair of orderlies wheel a gurney past us. The patient on the gurney is either asleep or unconscious. If the orderlies' expressions are any indication, his chances aren't good.

I hold up a hand to silence the chief. 'You know you can't stop me running my own investigation don't you? Four of the six victims are known to me and so is the survivor in there.' I jerk a thumb towards the cubicle.

'I don't want you interfering in the case, speaking to witnesses or running your own investigation. If necessary, I'll arrest you.' Gaertner's tone and face don't alter as he speaks. All human emotion is missing from his personality, it's as if he's a trained robot. 'And don't expect the chief to deputise you again. I will not allow that.'

I walk away without arguing with him. I'd sooner disobey him than wheedle and beg for him to feed me scraps. Behind me, I can hear the chief's remonstrations about this being his territory.

The inter-departmental pissing contest was always going to happen. I don't need to hear it though.

Chapter 48

Noelle's eyes flicker open. Everything she sees is a blur. The drugs given by the doctor are stealing her consciousness. They've lessened the pain in her belly, but done nothing to end the agony in her heart.

Antiseptic smells and the beep of machines give constant reminders of where she is. Not that she needs reminders. She remembers everything, but wishes she didn't.

The doctors have told her the baby is still alive but she doesn't believe them. She remembers the measured punches working their way down her belly, the pain, and most of all the blood pouring from her vagina. The baby can't have survived that.

Deep inside her, Noelle feels she could have coped with losing the baby if Oscar had been by her side. Together they could have managed the grief, healed each other and tried again. Many women miscarry. Few lose a baby to malicious violence; fewer still witness the horror she has.

In her bereft mind, the future looks bleak, unwelcoming. Everything she was looking forward to yesterday has gone. Stolen by maliciousness.

She can almost hear the platitudes friends and family will offer her. They'll talk about time being a great healer, about God's grand design. In time they'll insist Oscar would want her to move on, find someone else and be happy again.

That's not a future she can even hope for, let alone imagine.

Seared into her eyeballs is the image of Oscar's decapitated head. Try as she might, she can't picture his face any other way.

Not only has the love of her life been taken from her, the memories of him have been eradicated. How he looked when happy, angry, sad or a thousand other emotions, has been erased. Over-written by his face in death.

Every time she tries to think of him, his gentle touch and ready smile, her mind shows her the horror of his death.

She'd known, when she was reading out the men's words, that Oscar was going to be killed. It was only when she'd been given the sheet with her instructions, that she'd realised she was to be spared. The cruel way she'd been punched had stolen their baby. Robbed her of the life growing inside her. Never would she look at the child he'd fathered and see his face again.

The one thing stopping her from wanting to end it all, is a desire to see the masked men face justice for their crimes. That's why she held onto her phone until she saw Jake. She knows she can trust him to investigate the video she made. Her instructions from the men had told her there'd be another one on there. That she was to show both to the police.

Jake would make sure the videos are seen by the right people. She had feared the patrolmen would pass her cell to Farrage or one of the other detectives. Even in the depths of her grief she had known they shouldn't be the first to see them.

Noelle's eyes close as the medication takes full control of her body.

Chapter 49

I feel something dig into my butt when I climb behind the wheel. Reaching round, I pull Noelle's cell from my pocket.

I'd forgotten she'd given me it. I ought to go back and give it to the chief or Gaertner. Curiosity gets the better of me.

The engine burbles as I drive across town. I call Alfonse and we arrange to meet at my place. It's closer than his.

I want to see what's on the cell before I hand it over. Now I know the FBI's stance, I need to keep ahead of the game. Gaertner can arrest me if he wants, but I'm not giving up because of a threat that is three parts bluff. There are no laws against asking people questions. He can arrest me all he likes; I don't plan on doing anything that'll give him grounds to charge me. The best he can do is delay me.

Right now I could use some thinking time. Events are moving so fast I haven't been able to arrange my thoughts.

I expect the chief to realise that I walked away too easy. He knows me better. Once he calms down and manages to get away from Gaertner he'll be in touch. While the FBI will now bear the public responsibility for the case, like Alfonse and I, he'll still want to solve it himself.

With luck, the chief will keep us in the loop in exchange for first dibs on anything we learn. If not, we'll just have to manage.

Before I give Noelle's cell to the chief, I want Alfonse to have a look at it.

He's waiting at the door for me, his feet marching him back and forth. Restless energy is driving his limbs despite the fatigue on his face.

I don't recognise the set of his jaw or the growl in his eyes. He's not just angry, he's murderous. He wants blood and he doesn't care who knows it.

He speaks as I'm climbing out of the car. 'This better be good. I have too much to do to waste time yakking with you.'

I let the jibe slide over me as I put my key in the door. He'll apologise when he calms down. 'The FBI have stamped their foot and want us cut out.'

'So you're quitting. Is that it?'

Alfonse's hand lifts by way of an apology when he sees my face.

'This has gotten bigger than just being about your cousin and his family. It stands to reason the FBI don't want what they see as "a couple of amateurs" getting in their way. We'll do our thing and let them do theirs.' I hold up Noelle's cell phone. 'This might just give us the inside track.'

'Whose is it?'

'Noelle Holten's. She's the woman the patrolman picked up. When she handed it to me, she kept saying video.'

I hand it to him and he fiddles with it. He shows me the screen and there's an image of Noelle's head. She's speaking but we can't hear her words. Alfonse finds the button to turn it up.

We listen and watch together. His mouth hangs opens. Mine might be too but the words I'm hearing are too destructive for me to care about anything else.

When the video ends I get up and go for a pen and paper.

Alfonse replays the video in short segments while I jot down the words. In stark black and white they look innocuous until they're read.

My name is Noelle Holten and I've been chosen to read out this statement because I fell in love with a beaner.

The Christians of America have had enough. For too many years our proud heritage and gene pool has been diluted by niggers, Jews, beaners, and a thousand other inferior races. We, The Christian Knights of America are declaring war on all lesser species. Our aim is to rid the country we love of all impurities.

What is happening in Casperton is just the start. We have chapters in every state, every city. The white Christian population is what made America great. We built this country and now we're taking it back. We shall not surrender. We shall not be defeated. If you're not a white Christian you're going to die. Die horribly screaming in agony. Leave our wonderful country now and we'll spare you.

Offensive as the message is, I can't stop reading and re-reading it. I hear Alfonse's teeth grind as he does the same. He's the first to speak. 'This has to go to the FBI as soon as I've cloned it.'

He pulls his laptop from the case he always carries. He plugs in a USB lead and selects one of the multiple heads at the other end, and connects it to Noelle's phone.

I go to my PC, type out the message and print six copies.

'Shit.'

The intensity of Alfonse's curse makes my head snap round. Alfonse is looking at his laptop. 'What's up?'

'The video has been uploaded to her Facebook page.' He grimaces. 'It's not the only one.'

I stand behind him as he shows me the other video.

A Mexican man is being held down by two men wearing Klan robes. His neck is placed across a post and a woodsman's axe swings down. It takes three attempts to sever the head. A gloved hand grabs the head by the hair and carries it towards a tethered goat . The head is wedged between the goat's horns and bound into place with a rough twine . The video ends.

I'm reaching for my cell to call the chief when it starts to ring.

'What can I do for you, Kenneth?' He must sense something in my tone as he says what he needs to say before ending the call without any greetings or salutations.

'Don't tell me he wants you to work tonight?'

'No. It's something else. Remember he said someone had been asking for me? Well Kenneth said the guy was there again today. Said the guy was gonna come back tonight around nine.'

'You planning to meet him?' Alfonse's tone is sharp, but I ignore it.

'Yeah. If I'm back in time.'

'Back from where?'

'Seeing Butch Augiers. Apparently he went there looking for me too. Left a message with Kenneth saying I should go see him.'

'So, you're going to go running, are you? I need you here, with me, working the angles. I'm good at running down the obvious and getting into online places where I shouldn't be. You're better at coming up with ideas, theories and lines to pursue.'

I wave away his compliment. 'I'll only be gone a few hours. I'll drop Noelle's cell at the station, go see what Butch wants, and meet you at the Tree around nine. You run a trace on the cell movement and get everything you can from it. Then carry on with looking into the people on the list. I'm convinced Darryl and Sherrelle were chosen for a reason other than their skin colour.'

'Fair enough.' He points at his laptop, his face full of anger and frustration. 'They haven't just posted to her Facebook. They've put it up on YouTube, Vimeo, Twitter, Google+ and LinkedIn. They're telling the world, Jake. Trying to instil fear and cause trouble where there isn't any.'

'Are you able to take them down?' The sooner they're off the internet, the less potential they have to cause further trouble.

'Of course I can.' There's professional affront in his voice. 'You'd better check with Chief Watson and the FBI first though.'

He's right. Interfering with evidence is a serious crime.

I'm reaching for Noelle's phone as I dial Chief Watson on mine.

Alfonse is right about what they're doing. Their stating that they're not alone is the biggest worry. The only saving grace, if it can be called that, is there aren't huge swathes of under-privileged areas filled with ethnic minorities. If this had happened in certain parts of New York or Los Angeles there would be race riots to contend with. Tensions will still rise when the news of this breaks, but at least it's not happening in a place where racial unrest is already an issue.

Chapter 50

A reception committee is waiting for me at the steps of the station. It's safe to say they're not impressed with me. Even Gaertner's implacable face is covered with a scowl as I screech to a halt.

His hand extends without a word. He takes the cell from me and hands it to one of the two subordinates standing at his shoulder.

The subordinate wheels away and heads inside. I don't need a Harvard degree to work out he's Gaertner's techie guy.

'Listen to me, Boulder.' Gaertner's nose is a quarter inch from mine. If anyone else invaded my personal space this way, I'd spread their nose across their face with my forehead. However, FBI special agents get a free pass when I'm in the wrong. 'I don't buy your tale about forgetting you had that cell. I think you kept it back so you could continue your own investigation.'

His eyes bore into mine, defying me to deny his charge. I can't. I've been busted and we all know it.

I hold up my cell. 'It was a half-hour delay at most once I realised I had it, and it was a genuine mistake. Do you want me to get Alfonse to remove the videos?'

His temper drops from incandescent to furious as he sees the sense in what I'm saying. However good his man is, he's still going to be a few steps behind Alfonse. 'Do it.'

I make the call. I look at both Chief Watson and Gaertner as I add my own little request. They both nod approval.

The chief rounds on me as soon as the station door shuts behind Gaertner. 'You are a prize idiot, Boulder. And what's worse is you're making me look like one too. Here I am trying to fight

185

your corner and you're running off like some damn renegade. This isn't like TV, or the movies, where the hero finds clues by good luck. This is real life where processes have to be followed. You're a smart man, Boulder. Stop acting like a wise ass and start thinking about the big picture. Your selfish actions have set the FBI investigation back.' His finger jabs into my chest. 'I can't protect you much longer, and if you do something else like this I won't even bother trying.'

I find myself looking at my feet as I mumble an apology. I hadn't considered the chief going to bat for me. Hadn't thought how I was making a fool of him. Just because catching the killers is the most important thing to all of us, it doesn't give me the right to act like an ass.

'So, what are you going to do now?' The question is part a request for information, and part a demand for my good behaviour.

When I tell him, his eyebrows lift a full inch.

The Augiers live a few miles from where Noelle was picked up. He tells me to make sure he's kept updated and turns away. I can tell from his body language he thinks I'm wasting my time.

He may be right. The Augiers are just a couple of steps above the Amish in their lack of understanding modern devices like cell phones.

Chapter 51

Will Pederson pays his check and leaves a decent tip. The server is a cutie, but the attraction only flows one way. His batting average has dropped since passing his sixtieth birthday a couple of years back.

There was a time he could bank on hooking up with someone every week. Now he is lucky if it is once a month.

He knows age is a big part of it. While his body is still trim, despite his bulky frame, he is starting to look every minute of his age. It doesn't help there are younger, tauter men competing with him. His natural charm can only mask so many of his age-induced deficiencies.

As he stands, the room takes a wobble. He hopes it's the drink rather than his lack of youth. As a precaution he takes shorter, more considered steps than usual.

The lights flash on his car when he presses the blipper. He's got the door open when someone speaks to him.

'You off home, buddy?'

Pederson turns and sees a guy who had also been eating solo. They'd exchanged polite nods across the barroom but that was as far as things had gone.

'Yeah. Unless I get a better offer that is.' Pederson widens his smile.

Nothing about the man suggests to Pederson that he's gay. Yet he was dining alone in a bar where the majority of patrons are.

Pederson figures the man to be bi-curious. There's a hesitancy to his movements and a certain shyness. The guy had made the first move though, so he sticks out a hand. 'I'm Will. You are?'

'Brian.'

Pederson suspects the name to be an alias. It came after a moment's thought in which the eyes flicked left. A sure sign of a lie being concocted. The lie doesn't bother him. It just tells him the so-called 'Brian' has something he wants to keep hidden. Or private.

It also informs him that whatever happens will be a one-time affair. A situation which suits Pederson just fine.

The hand is rough and callused which contradicts the tailored suit and silk tie. Pederson guesses that Brian has chosen to wear his best clothes to try to satisfy a curiosity.

It's a familiar scenario. Some go for Sunday best while others dress like the TV stereotypes they've seen. Neither get it right. Gay people wear the same clothes everyone else does.

'Do you, uh, fancy a nightcap?' Brian flashes a wide smile. 'I've a bottle of eighteen-year-old scotch I've been waiting to try.'

Pederson gives his lips a mental lick. Malt whisky and a handsome man in his early forties. The evening ahead has just gotten a whole lot better.

Pederson drives as Brian gives directions from the passenger seat.

Brian is aware a panel van is following them.

Pederson isn't.

Chapter 52

The light is starting to fade as Butch Augiers walks towards me. His face is grim but there's no animosity on it.

None of his family can be seen. It doesn't matter. It's him I'm here to see.

A suspicious part of my brain makes me check out the landscape in case he's got a nasty surprise waiting for me by way of retribution.

He hasn't.

Instead he's appraising me. His eyes travel over every inch of my body as if I'm an animal to be observed. I find it unnerving, but keep my face straight.

He gestures to a tree stump where we sit.

I want to ask why he's asked me to come out here, yet a sixth sense holds me back. Whatever he's got to tell me has to come forth without pressure.

As I wait for him to speak, my eyes follow the silhouette of the hills against the night sky. It's picturesque out here, peaceful. I could live in a place like this – provided I got a cell signal and a decent internet connection.

'What I'm about to tell you goes no further. If you take it to the cops and they come looking, I'll deny everything. Then we'll come for you.'

I detect fear, worry and hesitation in him. Whatever is coming next is a big thing for him. He feels as if he's betraying someone by telling me. Or worse, putting his family at risk. Yet, he's still asked for me to come and see him. This tells me he knows something worth knowing. Or at least suspects he does.

He takes my silence as agreement of his terms. 'I spoke to the family' bout what you were asking. To cut a long story

189

short, Freddie has a buddy who's trouble. I don't mean gettin' inta fights or stealin'. Real trouble. The kid has gotten himself mixed up with somethin' real bad and he's trying to drag Freddie in.'

'Into what?'

'Freddie said the kid wouldn't tell him details. He'd just said he was doin' real work. Makin' a difference.'

My pulse quickens and I have to suppress the excitement in my voice. 'Who is this kid?'

'David Jones.' Butch shrugs. 'Known as "Young David" because he got his grandpappy's name.'

'Where does he live? The police need to speak to him.'

'Him getting hauled off by the police won't do no good. Boy's dumber than a fence post.' He scratches his chin. 'If he's mixed up in anything his family will be too. Ain't no way they'd allow him to work for someone else.'

'Then the police can round them all up.'

'What good do you think that'll do?' Butch shakes his head at me. 'They'll deny everything then start wonderin' why the police came a knocking on their door. Ain't no evidence the cops can use, is there?'

'So how do we get some evidence?'

'That's your problem. They're organising some fights. Running a book on them.'

'You mean they're fixing boxing matches?'

He chuckles at my question. 'Ain't no ring or a referee. These are real fights.'

I get what he means now. Bare knuckle bouts where the winner is the one left standing. They'll take place at some isolated location. Attendance will be by invitation only. Bets will be made; money won and lost.

The combatants will be tough grizzled men with few teeth and fewer brain cells. Their punishment nothing more than entertainment for a baying crowd. Each spill of their blood greeted with enthusiastic roars.

It's not a world I know or care about. 'So how does this turn into something the police can use?'

'Freddie says Young David has told him about a big fight happening tomorrow night. Says there's also supposed to be a fight to the death.' He spreads his hands wide. 'I don't know how much of this is true and how much is the kid running his mouth to impress Freddie. Could all be bullshit.'

'What does your gut tell you?' Men like Butch are all about instinct. Their primal senses more attuned than their brain.

He wipes a hand over his face. 'It tells me not to trust the kid as far as I can kick him. On the other hand, I know the family has a history of fighting. Fought quite a few of them over the years.'

'You were a bare knuckle boxer?'

He gives another chuckle as he gestures to his property. 'How do you think I got this place? When my great-grandpappy came over from France he had nothin' but the clothes on his back and the strength of his character. He, my grandpappy and my father all worked for someone else. I wasn't prepared to do that, so I found a way of making some money. I fought twice a month for two years to get enough money to buy this place. Didn't get much for the fights but I had some friends who laid bets for me.'

I look at him with different eyes. Ten or twenty years ago he must have been one hell of a fighter. His face doesn't bear the scars of defeat. His nose is straight and unflattened; his teeth aren't the best, but the fact they're there pays testament to his fighting ability.

I've never thought about it until hearing his story; his surname speaks of a non-American heritage. It's something I should have realised a long time ago. His family will have grown up with tales of the hardships faced by an immigrant family settling in a new land. They should never have been suspects.

'Maybe I should go visit them myself.' Unlike the police and the FBI, there's very little to stop me extracting information with violence if necessary.

'That's not a good idea. There's a whole bunch of them and if they don't like the look of you they'll run you off their land quick as look at you. And, if you got any sense, you'll go without a protest. With your accent you'll be lucky to say more'n three words before they want you gone.'

Interesting. They sound like a bunch of racists who're used to violence. Just what I'm trying to find.

After my suspicions of the Augiers, I'm wary of jumping to conclusions again. The Jones family seem like perfect suspects but perhaps they're too perfect. There's also the question of evidence. At least some will be needed to convince the chief and Gaertner of the family's involvement, let alone guilt.

I figure Butch already has a solution worked out. I'm just not sure I'll like it. 'So, how do I find out what I need to know?'

'You go up there and impress them. This fight tomorrow night is your chance. Old Man Jones was round here askin' if I wanted to make a comeback. I told him I'd think on it and let him know later.'

'You're proposing I enter one of these fights?' The idea is ludicrous. 'I fight when I need to – when the situation is forced upon me. I don't fight for other people's sport so they can make money off me.'

'It's the only way you'll get close to them. They're a fighter short for tomorrow night, they wouldn't have asked me otherwise. They're desperate. It's your best chance.' He strikes a match and lights his smoke. 'Once they accept you as a fighter you'll just have to keep your eyes and ears open. Make your own judgements.'

'Why are they a fighter short at this late stage?'

'Young David's father went and got himself into something he couldn't handle. Took enough of a beating to stop him taking part.'

I don't care for what he's saying. It's making the wrong kind of sense. I'll be better accepted by them if my presence helps them out of a hole. Their natural suspicions of a stranger dissipated by their gratitude to me for completing their bill.

Going back on my principles is my biggest problem. I don't fight at the request of other people. I don't take orders on who to beat up and when. I use my own judgement and hit only those who either deserve it, or those who try and hit me.

In the greater scheme of things, such concerns are of little importance. It's better to compromise my principles for the greater good, than to stand by them and wonder if I'm in any way responsible for further deaths.

I'm still cagey though. 'So what do I have to do, turn up and fight whoever is in front of me?'

'Pretty much. Either the fights will be pre-arranged or they'll be drawn on the night. Depends on how they're plannin' to run the book. Knowing Dave's grandfather, my guess is it'll be pre-arranged. He likes to control things and I'm sure whoever is runnin' the book will be givin' him a sizeable cut.'

'Will they accept me as an unknown, give me a chance at a fair fight?' The last thing I want is to find myself becoming cannon-fodder for one of their champions.

He gives a knowing smile. Now he's broken his silence, he's enjoying my discomfort. 'They'll not throw you to the wolves. There's no money to be made from a mismatch.'

There's no avoiding this. If I'm to find out if the Jones family are involved, I'm going to have to go undercover as a fighter. I give a sigh before answering him. 'I'm in. What rules are there, if any?'

'Only rules is you don't pound on a man who can't fight back and you don't go gouging no eyes. Other'n that, there ain't no rules. Be here for seven and I'll take you up there.'

Chapter 53

Alfonse is waiting for me in a quiet booth at the Tree. He wears the look of a man carrying several times his own bodyweight in stress. As ever, his laptop is open in front of him.

I point at him. 'You first.' I'm still not sure if I should tell him, the chief or Gaertner about tomorrow night.

'I deleted the posts after adding a searchbot to them like you asked. They'd been shared or downloaded by two hundred and seventy-two people by the time I took them down. Noelle's post by a hundred and five, and the other one by the rest.' His fingers hover over the keys. 'Say the word and I can trash every one of those computers.'

'Don't do it.' The words pour out in a hurry. Alfonse's finger is too close to the button for comfort. 'Some of those computers will be at the police station. If you trash those, all hell will break loose.'

'Well, duh.' It's nice to see his natural sarcasm has replaced the earlier anger. 'I know their IP address and have removed it from the trash list.'

'What about the FBI, do you know their IP addresses? What about the other agencies they're bound to have alerted over this? They're sure to have downloaded the videos for analysis.'

He looks shame-faced.

'Don't sweat it. You're too close to this – too angry and upset to see beyond your immediate focus.'

'Are you saying I'm useless?'

'Don't talk nonsense.' A passing waitress pauses in surprise at my raised voice. I take the heat out of my next words. 'You're angry because you're grieving. It's natural you want to trash those computers. It's a way you can take revenge, fight back. Your thinking is clouded because you're a decent, caring human who's suffered a personal tragedy.'

Alfonse gives me a tight grin. 'Aren't I the one who usually has to calm you down?'

'What did you find in the cell records?' I want to move the conversation away from thinking of his errors, to something he's good at. 'I'm sure you've got something from them.'

If anything, his mood darkens.

'The videos were both shot around noon today. Noelle's being the first. They were uploaded to the social media and sharing sites from her cell and left to go viral.' He grimaces. 'When I checked her email logs, I saw the videos were sent to CNN, the Washington Post, New York Times and several other major news outlets. And before you ask, as soon as I saw that, I let the chief know.'

I shudder to think of the conversations taking place at the station. Gaertner will be reporting back to various superiors and mobilising a small army of agents with the goal of neutralising the news carriers. The chief will be pacing like a caged beast, pausing only to spit orders at his men.

Stress levels will be through the roof; tempers frayed and arguments breaking out over the smallest things. Sure, they're all professionals, but they're also humans. Never before has a mess like this erupted. The power of social media and smartphones mean news travels faster than ever.

'Have you run a trace on the cell's movement?' It's a formality the FBI will have replicated, but every piece of information tells us a little bit more. 'Can you tell where it was when the videos were sent and uploaded?'

'The cell's trace disappeared at 2.15am which coincides with a battery failure log. The logs show it was switched on at 12.13pm and 1.05pm but never picked up a signal. The signal and battery returned at 2.56pm. A quick run of the co-ordinates show it was more or less where Noelle was picked up. That's also pretty much when the videos were sent.'

Everything slots into place. They took her cell when they abducted her. To prevent the cell giving away their location or movement they removed its battery. When they knew it would have no signal, they switched it on long enough to make the necessary videos then pulled the battery again. They re-inserted it to send the emails and post the videos at the drop off point.

'There are clues in there. There is an almost two hour gap between the last video being made and the phone being switched on at the drop off point. They're not going to have done what they did anywhere public, so I'd say they'd be lucky to do more than fifty miles an hour on the back roads. That gives us a hundred mile radius.'

Alfonse beats me to the math. 'Which means we're looking at a search grid of thirty-one and a half thousand miles. We've practically found their doorstep.'

I ignore his sarcasm. 'I reckon I can get it down to about a fifth of that, a quarter tops.'

'How do you plan to do that?'

I point at his laptop. 'Bring up Google Maps and centre it on the area Noelle was dumped.'

When he does, I use a straw as a pointer and indicate the area a half-hour north east of Casperton where Noelle was released. 'Think of a circle two hours from this point. To the west and south there's Indian reservations which means a lack of privacy. To the east is the dinosaur monument which always has tourists around. Going north there's Rock Springs and that's without discounting the forested areas. If you remember the video with Noelle, she was standing with her back against a wooden shack.'

'So, how does that help us?'

'The skyline behind the shack showed a bare ridge. That tells me she was in the wilderness somewhere rather than a forested area.' I point at the map again. 'My guess is that shack is only about fifty miles from where she was found. It'll be in the north east quadrant, away from busier roads, respectable farmers, and places where hikers or rangers frequent.'

'Makes sense.'

'They've also shown they understand technology and how best to wage a terror campaign.'

Alfonse makes a connection. 'It must have been planned in advance. They pulled the battery from her cell before they even left the house. That speaks of preparation.'

'So does the goat.. They're not something you find lying about. Especially ones that size.'

'True.' I'm about to suggest we leave the resources of the FBI to try and trace the animal's origin, when someone approaches our table.

I look up into the face of a familiar stranger. It's like looking into a mirror and seeing a younger version of myself.

The stranger is hesitant. He too must be unnerved by our similarity.

I'm glad of the moment – it gives me a chance to unscramble my brain. Or at least try to.

Alfonse pushes the lid of his laptop down and shifts round in his seat. 'I'll give you guys a minute.'

I reach for his arm. 'It's fine. Stay where you are.' The stranger still hasn't spoken. A closer examination reveals he's got a pallor about him. Not just the usual Scottish whiteness, but the grey skin symptomatic of illness.

The stranger points at his face and then me. 'There's no point in asking if you're Jake Boulder. It's pretty obvious you are.'

His accent is Scottish. Not the Glasgow one that comes from my mouth; his is a softer rolling burr, the kind I'd associate with the better areas of Edinburgh or perhaps the Borders.

'I am. And you are?'

'John…John MacDonald…I'm your brother.'

Chapter 54

Alfonse puts a coffee in front of me and opens his laptop. He's aware that John's appearance isn't something I'm ready to discuss yet, and has re-directed us back to mine so we can discuss our next moves.

'Did you get anything on the paint sample or the cigar butt?'

I expect the FBI to run these angles as well, but the more information we have the better. There's also a chance the FBI are focussing on the other end of the investigation as well as trying to protect the public.

Like me, Alfonse doesn't believe the Fourniers were chosen at random. This belief is what we're basing our investigation on.

He consults his laptop. 'There are eighty-six Ford E250s, with white paint, registered within fifty miles of here. A hundred and fifty-two within seventy-five.'

The numbers are higher than I expected but not by much. Those vans are popular and, since hearing of their involvement, I seem to have seen them everywhere.

'And the cigar?'

'I've checked the ten biggest internet sellers. In the last six months only two boxes have been sold to people in this area.' I feel a buzz of excitement. The lower the number, the better the chance of a decent lead. 'They were bought by Mayor Farrage and Darryl's boss, George Ligotti.'

He lets the sentence hang. Those two names are big ones. While nobody should be above suspicion, those names are tough to point a finger at. Mayor Farrage might be pretty useless, but he's backed every programme going for the betterment of the poorer areas of society. Areas which are predominantly filled with a hodgepodge of racial mixes.

A big cigar is part of his image. Like Groucho Marx and Winston Churchill, Mayor Farrage is rarely seen without a huge stogie.

Ligotti, on the other hand, has obvious Italian descent. He employs people of various races and, while a businessman at heart, he showed genuine compassion when learning of Darryl's brutal death.

Both men have too much to lose by resorting to murder. While it's an accepted fact that psychopaths often succeed in business and political ventures, they tend to achieve more than either Farrage or Ligotti have. Whichever way I analyse my thoughts, or examine their possible motives, I just can't see them being involved.

'What about local stores, does the place in the mall sell them?' Another thought strikes me. 'How many places on the internet sell them?'

The keys of his laptop chatter as he searches for the answers. He looks up after less than a minute. 'The place in the mall doesn't list them on their website. As for the internet, I'm getting dozens of possible retailers.'

'You'll need to trace as many of them as you can. See if you can widen the search. I'll speak to Ligotti and the Mayor tomorrow.'

We chase around one or two theories without creating anything tangible. After a while, we're both out of ideas so we fall silent rather than repeat ourselves.

There's an elephant in the room and its name is John. Neither of us approaches the subject, but we both know it can't be ignored forever.

'What did Butch want?'

I've been hoping Alfonse wasn't going to ask this question. I still haven't decided how much to tell him.

'He's got a suspicion about who might be involved.'

'Who is it? Why haven't you mentioned it until now?'

I bring him up to speed and watch the fire in his eyes dim.

'You're not going to go through with it, are you?'

'Of course I am.'

He scowls at me, his face twisting into unfamiliar viciousness. 'Then you're a fool. You're not going to be fighting six-beer heroes who know your reputation and quit at the first sign of retaliation. You'll be fighting real fighters who'll know how to punch without getting hit themselves. Stop trying to be the hero and start using your head. It's brain we need right now not brawn.' He throws his hands up. 'All that's going to happen is you're going to waste an evening getting your ass kicked in some bullshit machismo display. You're a good fighter, Jake, but you're not that good.'

'I've always been good enough to protect you.' I'm on my feet now, full of anger and bitterness at his words. 'Or have you forgotten that?'

He leaves without saying another word.

It's for the best. Both of us are too angry for each other's company right now.

I shouldn't have said what I did, but his lack of faith in my fighting skills hit me harder than any punch ever has.

Now I'm alone, I let my thoughts focus on John.

His resemblance to me is strong enough for any instinctive denials to be quelled before they gain any traction.

It stands to reason my father had found love again after walking out on us. It's just not something I've given any consideration. Any thoughts I've had of him, or discussions with Sharon about him, have all been focussed on why he left. As we got older and learned more about the world, we hypothesised he'd left mother for another woman. We just didn't envision it working out for him.

Him settling with another woman long enough to have children, isn't something we've ever discussed. I expect our subconscious minds were protecting us, shielding us, from the despair of supplication. The alternative is that neither of us wished him any happiness, and therefore didn't ever raise the possibility of him finding some.

My father had stayed true to form. He'd walked out on John's mother three weeks after John's fifth birthday.

Like the strangers we are, we talked round the edges of things and passed on general information. He's married with two daughters, and his younger sister Sarah is a single mother with one son.

All of a sudden I have two half-siblings, a brace of nieces and a nephew.

What Mother will make of all this is beyond me, I'm an uncle, but she still isn't a grandmother. I suspect that, when she gets over the initial shock, she'll try to use John's proven fertility as a way to goad me into giving her the grandchildren she so craves.

I'm not yet ready for her to find out about John. I need to get the case out of the way first.

My thoughts wander their own sweet way.

It's a beep from my cell that brings me back to reality. Taylor has messaged asking why I've just rang her and not spoken.

I call her back, and this time I do speak. My subconscious has betrayed me by selecting the one person I want to discuss this with, and making contact.

As I open up to Taylor, I start to accept I'm developing real feelings for her. A situation I find more concerning than tomorrow night's fight.

Chapter 55

I force my eyes open and look for my cell. Once again I've fallen asleep in my recliner rather than going to bed. I find the cell between my legs where it has slipped from my hand.

Chief Watson's gruff tones complete the job of waking me.

I listen to what he has to say and give him the answers I can. He's reluctant to return the favour when I put some questions to him, but I get most of what I ask for.

His calling me at six in the morning is a sign he still values my input, but is either unable or unwilling to contact me when Gaertner is around.

The most significant things about the call are him informing me that Will Pederson can't be traced, and that all the news outlets who've been sent videos, have discredited the footage and therefore will not be running the story.

At first I sense Gaertner's hand in the latter, but on reflection I realise any pressure or mention of the videos from a high-ranking FBI man would give the papers and news channels all the confirmation they need.

It's only a matter of time before the videos are reposted by those who downloaded them. Once that happens, and the media pick it up, they'll run the stories with added intensity.

I know Will Pederson. He spends a couple of hours drinking at the Tree every Saturday evening, before heading across to the Manhattan Bar on the other side of town. He's a decent guy and, as an ex-cop, has plenty of stories to tell. In his own way he's fought discrimination since coming out at his retirement party five years ago.

The chief had tried to raise him when rounding up all local law-enforcers – past and present. He'd been unable to contact Pederson and, while a player like him could be anywhere, it's unusual for an ex-cop to drop off the grid.

Pederson might well be a white Christian, but his sexuality could see him become a target. Without any of his own men to spare, the chief has asked me to check on Pederson's whereabouts.

Alfonse won't be happy to hear from me – especially at this time of the morning – but I select his number and make the call.

His cell rings out and goes to voicemail. I'm not sure whether he's blanking me or sleeping. Regardless, I leave a message suggesting that he traces everyone who's downloaded the videos. If the killers are as clever as they appear to be, there's a chance they've downloaded the videos to another computer so they can be re-shared in the event the cops or the FBI took them down.

Whoever is in charge of the killers possesses more than a little intelligence. The using of Noelle and her cell as conduits to social media proves as much.

Without any physical evidence, other than the bodies, there are few leads to follow. If there had been a note, the paper could have been analysed; the handwriting or printing used as factors to help secure a conviction, or possibly even give a firm lead.

I haul myself up and begin the process of making my first coffee of the day. While it's brewing I slump myself in front of my computer and start browsing Facebook. I'm not a big user of the site and for me it's nothing more than a way to connect with other keen readers and a few authors I admire.

I'm looking for something in particular and it doesn't take me long to find it. I check Twitter and discover #HeadOnAGoat is trending.

As ever with social media, there are some who endorse the actions of the killers. Others with a more sensible and decent nature, rage against the killers calling them worse than scum.

Arguments are breaking out between the two factions, and every thread I look at sees a rise in the aggression levels of those championing the racists' actions.

This is what everyone involved in the investigation has been dreading. The video has now become a recruitment poster for the Christian Knights of America. Once it got noticed on social media, it was always going to go viral.

While the social media sites will do everything they can to take it down, it will already have been seen and downloaded by many thousands of people. It'll feature on blogs and websites where opinions are given and rants made.

I curse myself for delaying until I was with Alfonse before viewing it. That extra half hour could have been the difference between the video being suppressed and it becoming the hottest topic in the world.

Gaertner won't be impressed when he learns how this has all blown up. He for one will be quick to point a finger in my direction. I wasn't to know its incendiary content, but that doesn't change the fact I made a conscious decision not to look at it at once.

Next I check the websites for the major newspapers. Every one of them is now running with the story. None have yet gone as far as writing an opinion piece, but that'll come along once the world wakes up.

So will responses from the so-called great and good. It's only a matter of time before statements are issued by the FBI director, the senator for Utah and various members of the political elite. With the president being black, there's every chance he'll want to have his say too. And that's before all the celebrities see voicing an opinion as an opportunity to get themselves in the limelight.

The only people to benefit from this sorry mess will be Casperton's hoteliers, as reporters are dispatched to the epicentre of the story.

I'm about to try Alfonse again when there's a knock at the door.

It's Taylor, and she's carrying takeout coffee and a baggie filled with donuts. 'Here. Since you're doing police work, I thought you'd like some police food to go with your coffee.'

'Thanks.' I take the baggie and put it on the counter without telling her I don't much care for donuts. She's trying to be kind and I don't want to hurt her feelings. I'll give them to Alfonse later, that is, if he's still speaking to me.

'I just wanted to drop by and see you're okay. You sounded really stressed last night.'

'Yeah, I'm fine. Just needed to talk it through with someone. Sorry to have bothered you.'

'Don't be silly. It's what you do when you love someone. Relationships aren't all hearts and flowers you know.'

That cherished little word has crept into the conversation between me and women before. Whenever I hear a woman say love, I feel myself clam up, my mouth goes dry and I start looking for a way to let the woman down gently. For some reason I'm not feeling that way today.

I pull Taylor into an embrace and kiss the top of her head. With so much going on in my mind right now, her arms offer a temporary respite to the horrors of the investigation.

In the last twelve hours, I've fallen out with my best friend, agreed to become a bare-knuckle boxer, and potentially worsened racial tensions across the whole of the United States through my pig-headed selfishness in wanting a first look at the videos on Noelle's phone. On top of all that, I've met a half-brother I didn't know I had.

Whatever the next twelve hours has in store for me, things can only get better.

Chapter 56

Will Pederson comes to with the slowness of someone awakening from an alcohol induced stupor. His mouth dry and tongue furry. There's a pounding in his head that's all too familiar and he's not sure how long he can go without hurling. His body is stiff and uncomfortable and when he tries to raise a hand to his face his arm won't move.

'Oh look, the faggot is awake.' The voice is unfamiliar. It's not the man who called himself Brian.

He remembers Brian pouring the whisky; an eighteen-year-old Glengoyne from the highlands of Scotland. Smooth and rich, Brian's generous measures had gone down a treat. Conversation had flowed around the usual topics of sport and, by following Brian's lead, he'd realised nothing was going to happen.

The last thing he recalls, from the night before, is sitting in a chair with a glass in one hand and his eyelids growing heavier by the second.

He forces his eyes open. Finds himself staring at a pair of scuffed work boots. Above the boots are a pair of worn jeans and a plaid shirt. The face above the shirt belongs to a stranger. A stranger who's been fighting. If the marks on his face are anything to go by, he didn't win.

They're outside somewhere. He can see rocks and scrub bushes. There's a gurgle of nearby running water but all he can smell is his own foul breath. He tries moving his arms a second time. Fails.

When he looks down he sees his hands are tied and his clothes have been removed.

'What's going on, who are you?' Pederson hates the fact his fear is showing.

The stranger looks at him with disgust. 'I am a Christian Knight of America. Along with my brethren, my purpose in life is to rid this fine country of ours from all the inferior races, and to cleanse society of its perversions. You are to be cleansed today.'

The words make no sense to Pederson's groggy mind. He feels rough hands grabbing at his naked body, hauling him to his feet. He's too weak with nausea to offer more than growled threats and weak kicks as resistance.

Once upright, the hands push him towards the watery sounds. A minute later he sees the narrow creek. At best it's six feet wide and three deep.

A violent shove propels him forward until he's at the edge of the water. Another sends him stumbling into the cold clear water. A gasp escapes his lips as he trips, and falls headlong into the water.

The shock of the cold water is enough to kick-start his body into a semblance of normality. His hands being tied make it hard work, but he manages to right himself and rise to his feet.

He sees them all now. The stranger, a bald man and a callow youth. Their faces are blank apart from looks of disdain. It's as if they'd rather eat their own shit than look at him. It's a look he's used to. While he'd made the step of coming out at his retirement party, he'd never hid his sexuality. For a man of his generation it had meant stares, pointed fingers and a barrage of homophobic comments.

Twice in his life he'd endured physical assaults. He guesses today is going to be the third. The guys in front of him are stupid; they're showing their faces. He uses his training to memorise the details – the shape of noses, eye and hair colour and everything else he can.

The stranger points at him and the bank of the creek. Pederson thinks about disobeying, but decides obedience is his best bet to minimise the forthcoming beating. Retaliation will do nothing but increase the levels of anger, therefore increasing the amount of punishment.

The idea of defending himself is discarded at once. Nothing will increase his suffering more than antagonising the men by hurting them. Three onto one is a tough proposition at the best of times, plus he's bound, hung over and years older than his adversaries. Not even the most optimistic gambler would bet a red cent on him winning.

He feels a tremor in his limbs as the men lead him towards a spruce tree. Whatever beating he's in for, will take place here. A rope hangs from a branch. He's delighted to note the end isn't tied into a noose.

The youth throws a punch into his stomach, doubling him over in pain. Before he can straighten up, the loose end of the rope is looped around the one binding his hands, pulled tight above his head and tied in a rough knot.

Pederson can move three or four feet in any direction before the rope prohibits him from travelling further.

The stranger approaches, malice written all over his face. 'Leviticus; chapter twenty; verse thirteen; states: "if a man lie with mankind, as with womankind, both of them have committed abomination: they shall surely be put to death; their blood shall be upon them".' Pederson's bowels empty as the stranger continues. 'In accordance with God's holy law, we, the Christian Knights of America, sentence you to death for the crime of lying with other men.'

Two of the men facing Pederson bend to the ground and pick up fist sized rocks. The youth holds a cell phone which Pederson recognises as his own.

The first rock misses. The second crashes into his left foot making him yelp as he hops on his one good foot.

Chapter 57

I look around the waiting room and find nothing of any interest – there are bland pictures and out of date magazines just as there are in waiting rooms the world over. Ligotti being with a client has me kicking my heels until I can speak to him.

Before coming here I'd swung by Will Pederson's place. It was deserted with no car on the drive. A peek through some of the windows had revealed nothing beyond a typical man's home. Tidy and minimal with no soft furnishings or floral touches. Pederson might be gay, but he isn't effeminate.

I'd tried a couple of Pederson's neighbours. They'd known nothing of his movements, but had said it wasn't unusual for him not to come home.

Whichever way up I stand it, Pederson is missing, but until we know whether he's alley-catting as Granny called it, or has been abducted, there's nothing we can do.

I've emailed Pederson's cell number to Alfonse with a request he run a trace on it.

A secretary or paralegal walks in. 'Mr Ligotti will see you now.'

Ligotti is pacing when I enter his office. Any thoughts that his last meeting is the source of his agitation are blown away when he opens his mouth. 'What is it this time? We're trying to run a business here and, as you well know, we're now short-staffed.'

His sarcasm is aimed towards the wrong target at the wrong time. I only hit him once. A short dig to the underside of his ribs. Just hard enough to knock the breath from his body and double him over.

While he's gasping for breath I explain some facts of life to him. Perhaps it's harsh of me to have lashed out, but his priorities are in dire need of re-calibration.

'Now that we're on the same page, Mr Ligotti, I want you to understand that I, my colleague and the police will come here as often as is necessary. And if I should hear another complaint from you about being short-staffed because of Darryl's murder, I will make a point of informing Ms Rosenberg, and all your staff, just what a callous piece of crap you are. Do you understand me?'

'Yes, damn you. There was no need to hit me.'

I disagree. Unlike him, I'm not going to waste time arguing semantics. We've established I'm the alpha male in the room. 'You bought some cigars. One was found on the trail leading to where Darryl and his family were found. Can you explain that, or should I call the police and have them arrest you?'

It's not often you see a face pale when it's gasping for breath. 'I don't know what you're talking about. There's no way I was involved in what happened to him and his family.'

I sit in Ligotti's chair and cross my feet on his desk. 'I didn't ask if you knew about it, I asked you to explain.'

'I don't smoke – cigarettes or cigars.'

'Then why did you buy them?'

'To use as gifts. From time to time we throw parties for our best clients. Sometimes I buy a box of cigars to hand out and other times I'll get a few bottles of cognac or malt whisky.'

What he's saying makes sense. He's not someone I suspect, but it doesn't hurt to make him think I do. 'The cigars I'm interested in are Royal Jamaica Extrafinos No. 4s. Can you remember who you gave them to?'

'Those are the ones I always buy.' He looks at the ceiling as he thinks. 'The Mayor, Eddy Hall, Darryl and—.'

I don't hear any more names after Darryl's. We know the killers help themselves to things from their victims' houses. Noelle's cell being grabbed has taught us as much. I've attended many parties where Darryl has been present. Cigars have been handed round and he's never accepted any. I figure he didn't want to refuse his boss's generosity, Ligotti doesn't seem like the kind of employer who'll tolerate a subordinate refusing a gift.

Give Ligotti his due, he's not just telling me who was at the party, he's scribbling their names down on a legal pad. He passes the sheet across when he finishes writing. 'I shudder to ask, but is there anything else I can help you with?'

Traces of sarcasm have returned, but he's smart enough to stay out of reach. It wouldn't be fair to hit him a second time just because a lead has turned into a dead end. He doesn't need to know it though.

I stand and move towards him. 'Next time I come here, you will drop whatever you're doing and offer me full co-operation, won't you?'

He gives a quick series of nods as he backs himself against a wall.

Chapter 58

Dr Edwards greets me with a quizzical look when I walk into his office and take my usual seat.

'Why is it that my receptionist gives you every free appointment I have?'

I don't bother answering his question, instead, I throw one of my own at him. 'Have you heard about the latest killing?'

'The last one I heard about was the Asian woman who was impaled. Has there been another?'

I bring him up to speed with a few short sentences. He makes notes as I speak and twists his lips at the more graphic details.

'You're not here because they've broken cover and escalated their profile. You're smart enough to recognise that yourself. I'm guessing the FBI are now involved and they've cut you out. They'll have their own psychologists and behavioural analysts who'll be far better suited to making speculative guesses than me. So, Jake, why are you here?'

It's a good question. One I'm not sure of the answer to. When Taylor had told me about the free appointment I'd jumped at it without thinking what I wanted to talk to the doctor about. Perhaps a latent part of my brain wants me to discuss the feelings I have for Taylor, or maybe I know I have to talk about the nightmares; a third option is John. It's not every day your family tree grows a new branch.

A thought strikes me and I use it to get myself out of the hole. 'I'm pretty sure that whoever is masterminding these crimes is a very intelligent man. He's smart, organised and, now they've broken cover, it's clear he knows how best to maximise their exposure. What's your take on him?'

'Like you say, he's clever. I'd guess he'd be accepted into any Ivy League College he applied to. He's also attuned to social media and is a manipulator.' The edges of the doctor's mouth twitch as he warms to his theme. 'It's a given that he or she is charismatic. To get others involved in homicides is one thing; to have them believe they can drive out what they deem as undesirable elements, with vicious executions, is another. There's also the name they've given themselves; Christian Knights of America has Klan connotations.'

'It's grandiose isn't it?'

'That, and pretentious. It's also a clarion call to the right wing elements of Klan memberships. In fact, it will appeal to racists and bigots worldwide.'

'You mean like David Koresh?'

'Similar, but his goals are more along the lines of ethnic cleansing than messianic. Think Hitler, not L. Ron Hubbard.'

It takes a conscious effort not to gape like an idiot. 'Seriously, you're comparing this guy to Hitler?'

'Absolutely. From what you've told me, I'd have to say this guy is a charismatic megalomaniac, who sees murder as a way to dispose of the elements of society he doesn't like. How have you been sleeping?'

His attempt to catch me off guard almost succeeds. 'Not too bad. So how are we supposed to figure out who this guy is?'

'You're the one assuming the role of detective. That's something I can't help you with. You say you're not sleeping too bad, would I be right in also interpreting that you're not sleeping too good either?'

'I killed a man. I wouldn't be normal if I didn't have the odd dream about it. Leaving the main man out of it for a while, what would his followers be like?'

'Good question. They'll be tough men who've had hard lives. They'll be nothing like as smart as their leader is, but they won't know it. He'll show just enough of his intelligence for them to be compliant. If they feel he's too smart, they'll figure he's using them. You say you lose the odd night's sleep. Not just a few hours here and there. Do you worry about the nightmares before you go to sleep?'

I don't know how to tell him that I'm terrified of my nightmares – I'm not even sure I want to. There's no way I'm prepared to tell him I'm reluctant to go to sleep in case the nightmares come. The physical experience was bad enough without reliving it on a nightly basis. 'What age will these men be?'

'Your failing to answer my question means I'm going to assume you do worry about the nightmares coming.' He adds another note to my file. 'The killers could be of any age. Or gender. Are you taking anything to help you sleep?'

'Nothing.' I don't mention the occasional gutful of alcohol. The less he knows about my drinking habits the better. 'You think women might be involved? That sounds like a bit of a stretch to me.'

'Perhaps, but look at the way sex is used as a sales tool. Sexual manipulation happens all the time. Who's to say the brains behind these crimes is male or female? While males are more commonly associated with these kinds of crimes, there are many women who have committed despicable acts.'

There's not a lot I can say to that, so I say nothing more than goodbye. I've learned a little and I'm sure he has too.

When I check my cell on the way out, I find an email from Alfonse telling me to get to his place as soon as I can.

There are no clues as to the reason, just a terse message.

He may still be pissed at me, but at least he's communicating.

Chapter 59

When I leave the office of Doctor Edwards, I find the ever pernicious Ms Rosenberg leaning against my car. A half dozen cigarette butts litter the ground at her feet. She's wearing her usual two-piece – today's is grey with irregular flecks. Perhaps they're not flecks but ash from the constant stream of cigarettes she devours.

As ever, her perfume reaches me before the cigarette smoke.

'Morning.'

'Yeah, yeah. Good morning and all that.' She talks round the cigarette which dangles from her mouth. 'You've got the inside track again, Boulder. Tell me, what's going on?'

'Bad people are killing good people in really bad ways.'

My flippant reply gets me a mouthful of second-hand smoke. 'Don't give me any sass, Boulder. I'm not in the mood.'

I'm not surprised. A whole media storm has erupted in her backyard and she wasn't invited to the party. Her omission from the killers' list of people to notify, will rankle on both a personal and professional level.

As a rule of thumb, major stories filter up from local to national level. The alteration to this status quo has left her floundering. The only way she can now compete with the big boys, is to use her local knowledge to get an inside scoop.

Having seen me with Chief Watson at two crime scenes, she's now looking for me to be the one to reinstate her edge.

'What do you want?'

'I want to know what the police are doing to protect the local citizens; what the FBI are doing to catch these killers; and what you yourself are doing.'

'I can't help you. The police and the FBI are the ones you need to ask the question of. Surely they've arranged a press conference?'

'Yeah. The director of the FBI is giving one right about now. In the J. Edgar Hoover building. In Washington.'

The way she's fragmenting her sentences doubles the frustration in her tone. It's no wonder she's annoyed – the biggest story of the year is happening on her doorstep and she's being kept inside.

'What about Mayor Farrage, isn't he going to say a few words, try and reassure the locals?'

'Pah. Any cub-reporter can take down what he says and write up his statement. I'm after a story not a script. Why are you seeing Dr Edwards, are you consulting him?'

I don't want her to know about my meetings with the doctor so I try a little deflection. 'I went in to see Taylor, his receptionist. She's the girl you saw me at dinner with the other night.'

'I know who she is. I've been watching her through the glass door for half an hour. I never saw you until a few minutes ago. You spent no more than a minute or two with her before coming out here. Now, are you going to tell me the truth, or have I got to make up a story about how the heroic Jake Boulder is so traumatised by his exploits he's now seeking counselling?'

'Your threats won't work on me.' They would if I wasn't so convinced they are an empty bluff. 'You don't want to write a speculative piece about something that's now a historical event. You want to be in at the heart of the story that's breaking. If it was any other way you wouldn't be talking to me in the hope of getting a scoop or an angle.'

'Touché.' She gives what she thinks is a smile. It's more of a pained grimace. 'So, what angles are you investigating?'

If it wasn't for the fact that my actions, since being chased off the investigation by Gaertner, have all been wrong, stupid or both, I'd give her something to work with. The last thing I need is for her to celebrate my involvement in print. Gaertner would use it as an excuse to imprison me for interfering in an FBI investigation.

'None. The FBI are in charge now. This is too big for me, they have all the resources and training.'

'You make a poor liar, Boulder. The family who were killed are related to your buddy. There's no way you're giving this one up. You just don't want me knowing. Or perhaps more pertinently, you don't want me mentioning it in print. Did the FBI toss you out on your ear and tell you to stay clear?'

I don't answer her. She drops her cigarette and pulls another from a pack in her purse. She waits until a young mother loads her children into the car parked next to mine before continuing. 'C'mon, Boulder, you're bound to have something you can give me.'

I'm not sure I have anything of any use to her, but I do have an idea she may find useful. 'You've railed on Lieutenant Farrage and his cronies often enough. Why not go the other way this time?'

'I can't praise them. Not after everything I've said in the past. I'd be contradicting myself.'

I shake my head. 'You misunderstand me. I mean you should say the task is beyond them, but that's okay, no small town police force is equipped or trained to deal with this kind of threat.'

'Why should I give them an easy ride this time? Lots of other journalists will be writing the same kind of thing. What'll make mine unique?'

'Your local knowledge. Leave the eulogies to someone else and write about the effect this is having on Casperton. Only a local can gauge the mood with any accuracy. Every other journalist will be getting soundbites from those brassy enough to speak to them. You know yourself, those who speak out rarely give a true feel for a community's mood. With your local knowledge and list of contacts, you can become both the barometer and voice of Casperton.'

'You make a good point, Boulder.' She drops her cigarette and marches off in her hurried style that's more movement than progress. As short as she is, she can't take big strides at the best of times, let alone when hampered by a tight skirt and four inch heels.

Chapter 60

I let myself into Alfonse's place. While we're still frosty to each other, I don't help myself to coffee or anything else.

He doesn't look as if he's slept. Bags hang under bloodshot eyes and his natural ebullience has all but vanished.

He needs a friend, and I need him to be my friend. Our spat has to be resolved before it becomes a rift.

'About last night, Alfonse. I shouldn't have said what I did.'

He doesn't answer me for a full minute. He just sits there, staring at me. 'No, you shouldn't, but you're not the only one who said the wrong thing. I just don't see how you going off and fighting for other people's sport can help catch whoever killed Darryl.' He flaps his hands. 'Now I've had time to think, I'm still not convinced, but I trust you know what you're doing. I should have trusted you last night.'

The more time I've had to consider it, the less sure I've become. I could be setting myself up for a beating or just wasting my time. I can live with the beating, if getting it progresses the case.

Wasting time isn't something I can countenance though. New victims are turning up every day. Each one killed in a horrific manner.

The publicity garnered by the videos has given the investigation a different dimension. We need to start closing in on the killers instead of reacting to their latest atrocity.

Alfonse hands me a sheet of paper with an address on it. 'This is where Pederson's cell was last sending out a signal.'

I fold the paper and stuff it into a pocket as he tells me about the traces he's run on the IP addresses that downloaded the original videos.

'Have any of them re-posted after they were taken down?'

'Six.' He rubs his nose. 'I'm running traces on them now.'

'Good. As soon as you have anything solid, let me know and also send it to Chief Watson.'

'Well, duh.'

Sarcasm may be the lowest form of wit, but it's how Alfonse and I communicate. The fact he's starting to use it again is encouraging. It gives me hope that his black mood will soon lift.

'I've also heard from Emily.' Again he passes me a sheet of paper. 'We're not supposed to have this. She called me late last night and told me her findings from the autopsy on Gazala Kulkarni. These are the details.'

I glance at the sheet. It's got a lot more information than the first sheet.

'Is she doing the other autopsy yet?'

'No. The FBI have brought in their own guy. She's mighty pissed at being kicked out of her own morgue. Hence the fact she's breaking rank and giving us information the FBI wants kept private.'

Emily is taking a risk and putting her career in our hands. If Gaertner finds out about this, he'll make sure she'll never again work as a coroner anywhere near Utah.

I let my eyes focus on the page. The details are all there, specific information lies in silent rows saying nothing. The entire page is mute.

Perhaps if I hadn't attended the scene with Chief Watson, the report would be more informative. All it does now is force my mind to revisit the horror.

I don't need the technical medical speak for the manner of her death. I saw how she died, the agony on her face and the brutality of her execution. What I want to know is if Emily found any clues when performing the autopsy.

Was there any foreign skin under her fingernails from where she'd scratched her attackers? Were any fingerprints found on her body? Had she been drugged? If so, what with? Were there other wounds or injuries to her body which may be used to identify a specific weapon, or location where she'd been held?

Only one of these questions is answered. Admittedly it's answered on multiple fronts. Traces of adhesive have been found on her wrists, ankles and feet. A spectrograph test of the adhesive shows it to be from a generic brand of duct tape; a killer's first choice of restraint.

What's odd is that it's been found in strips on the tops of both of her feet. She's also got torn and strained ligaments in one ankle.

I lay the paper down, and stare at the coffee machine for a moment as I process these details along with the other facts I know about her last day on earth.

Alfonse dumps a cup of coffee in front of me with enough force to slosh half a mouthful onto the table. 'You could have made it yourself, or even asked.'

His words jolt me back to the present.

I was imagining a young woman running for her life. Terrified that the chasing men would catch her. Arms and legs pumping like never before as her tape wrapped flats protected her feet. Breaths would be ragged as surges of adrenaline filled her mouth with a coppery taste.

She was young and fit. Her pursuers may not have been. Did she think she was getting away when her ankle twisted? I'll never know the answer to this question, but I'll always want to.

How she got the chance to wrap her feet and make a break for it will also nag, yet it's her state of mind that interests me most. I hope she had the euphoric feeling she was escaping, that some part of her ordeal let her have the tiniest glimmer of hope. She deserves that much and more for her guts and ingenuity. I never knew her in life, but I find myself respecting her in death.

I narrate the movie in my mind to Alfonse.

His jaw hardens and his breaths grow loud and deliberate.

'Stuff the police. Stuff the FBI. We've got to get these guys. They can't get away with this. With killing Darryl. With kill—.'

His vehemence ebbs away as sobs wrack his body. He sinks to the floor and cups his head in his hands as his shoulders heave.

I slip down beside him and rest a hand on his shin. There for him yet not intruding. He needs the release – for too long he's kept it together, been strong for others and not faced his own grief.

To my knowledge he hasn't cried since his father's funeral six years ago. Since then he's taken care of his mother and stepped into his father's role as head of the family. Even then his father had passed away after a lengthy battle with cancer; his death an escape from suffering, rather than a shocking act of violence.

I sit with him until he recovers his composure and stands. He doesn't say anything and neither do I. We've been friends for too long for words to be necessary.

He goes to the bathroom and I brew more coffee.

Alfonse returns and gives me a small nod. I respond by pointing at the coffee I've poured him. We might talk about this one day and we might not. It's his choice and I trust him to make the decision that's right for him.

'I'm going to head now. Can you cross-check the names on the list of people who Sherrelle refused loans to, and the owners of the vans?'

Chapter 61

I follow the coordinates on Alfonse's notes and park behind an aging station wagon. The house I'm looking for is at the end of what looks to be a good street. Lawns are trimmed and there are decent cars in most of the drives. The station wagon in front of me will be the oldest car on the street and if the jumble of tools in the back is anything to go by, it doesn't belong to one of the residents.

The low bungalows, and lack of children or toys, make me wonder if this area of town is a kind of retirement village. The one person I see on the sidewalk is walking with a cane in one hand and a hunch across his shoulders.

A car is parked on the driveway. It's the same make and model as Will Pederson's. A check of the notes Alfonse gave me verifies the licence plate as his.

This is the sticky part. The last thing I want to do is knock on the door and bother them if they're still in bed. It's bad enough Chief Watson jumping at shadows without me being guilty of coitus interruptus.

There's no sign of another car at the house so I take a walk around the garden wall and peer through the garage window. I see a lawnmower, various other gardening implements and a variety of hand tools. The space where a car would go is empty.

I switch my gaze to the house, specifically the windows. The drapes are all open and the longer I watch, the less I see. No shadows pass the windows as people in the house move around. There's no flicker from a TV or any other signs of life.

A mental image of the chief kneading his temples makes me circle back to the street and walk up the path. When I knock at the front door there's no answer.

With Pederson's car left here there are a dozen reasons why the house would be empty – them having gone out for breakfast being the most obvious.

I try again with the same result.

I'm at the point of giving up when a woman crosses the street. The pink tinge to her hair and velour sweats remind me of Mother.

'Can I help you, Son?'

It's well over a decade since I came of age, but I recognise her use of son is a generational thing. Her words are more polite than either her expression or tone.

I decide to bluff it out with an outrageous but heart-rending lie. 'Hi, I'm wondering if you can help me? I'm looking for my uncle. My mother has taken another turn for the worse. I've heard he'd be at that house over there but I can't find him. Please lady, my mother's real sick and she wants to say her goodbyes while she still can.'

Her face softens. 'Is that his car?'

'Yes. Have you seen him?'

'Not today I haven't. There was a stranger there yesterday. Said he was a nephew of the Nelsons and was spending the night there while he repainted his own bedroom. I didn't believe him, but he had a key so I went back to minding my own business.'

I have to bite down on a snort at the thought of a busybody minding her own business.

'Has everyone gone out then?'

'Who's the everyone? The Nelsons are away on a tour of Europe.'

'What about the nephew, have you seen him this morning?'

'I never saw nothing of him earlier, although I heard a noise around two this morning. When I got up, I saw a panel van pulling away from there.'

I can feel a sense of dread enveloping my body, only for a wave of excitement to wash it away. If this lady has spoken to the supposed nephew there's every chance that if Pederson has been snatched, we'll get the first positive ID on one of the killers.

'This nephew of the Nelsons, can you describe him for me?' I give a helpless shrug. 'I'm going to try a couple of places, see if they went out for breakfast.' I repeat the shrug. 'My uncle has a weak bladder and may well be in the bathroom so it'd be good if I know what his buddy looks like in case I miss him.'

She looks me up and down. 'He would be about your height, perhaps a few pounds heavier although he wasn't fat. His hair was dark, with some grey starting to show.'

'What age would you say he was?'

'I'm not much good at guessing people's ages. Never have been.'

'Go on take a guess.' I give a conspiratorial grin. 'He's not here to be offended if you get it wrong.'

She returns the smile. 'If I had to guess, I'd say he's about forty.'

'What about his clothes, how does he dress?'

'He dresses well, real well. But then again, he's a very handsome and charming man.'

'Did he give you his name?'

'He said it was Brian, but I've never heard them talk about a Brian.'

This is the kind of lady who gossips with her neighbours and pries into their family. Her not hearing of Brian speaks volumes. 'Did you notice anything else about him; eye colour, accent, anything like that?'

Her eyes narrow. I fear I've overstepped the mark.

'No. I only spoke to him for a moment.' She folds her arms together. 'I'm sorry I can't be of any more help. Good day to you.'

I have my cell in my hand as I stride towards the Nelson's front door. When I lift the fake brick from the porch I find it empty.

Perhaps the Nelsons removed the spare key before going to Europe. I'll bet they didn't though. This would explain why the man calling himself Brian has a key to their house.

The chief answers on the third ring. By my fourth sentence he's barking orders and demanding to speak with Gaertner.

I finish my report and end the call before Gaertner comes on the line to yell meaningless threats. When he's had a chance to digest this new information, he'll realise that, while I've gone behind his back and carried on with my investigation, I've also uncovered what may be the best lead yet.

She doesn't know it yet, but the pink-haired lady is going to be talking with a whole lot of special agents.

Chapter 62

The woman's eyes show hostility and mistrust, but those emotions are something Ms Rosenberg is used to. When you've earned a reputation for bringing errant politicians to account, you learn to grow a skin thick enough to cope with preconceived ideas about your motives.

Natural persistence helps, as does a dogged refusal not to accept anything but the truth.

'I just want to get your opinion on these killings. You're an important person in your community and as long as those heinous killers are at large, those you represent will turn to you for guidance.'

'I ain't no Martin Luther.'

Ms Rosenberg pounces on the softening of the woman's expression. 'Perhaps not, but you're the one they come to when they need help.'

'P'r'aps. It ain't right for me to speak for them unasked though.'

'I don't want specific names or instances. You're the only person whose name will appear in my column.' Ms Rosenberg gives what passes for her gentlest smile. 'Like it or not, you are the one who represents your community and, as such, your views and opinions are important. You won't just be speaking for the black community in Casperton. Everything you are thinking and feeling will be reflected across every state in the country.'

The woman's resistance breaks and she starts talking. Ms Rosenberg's pen scratches out her own bastardised version of shorthand as she listens to the stories of people afraid to go about their normal lives; of rosters being drawn up to share the burden of watchfulness as the community bands together to protect itself.

When she hears of parents refusing to let their children go to school unless armed guards are present she feels her heart race as she imagines headlines. School shootings are all too common in the US and, while Casperton is under siege from racial attacks, a school in the heart of the black and Mexican community makes an inviting target.

Everything she hears makes sense and ties with her own imaginings. The minority communities are working together in the right way to protect themselves. It's not that they don't trust the police, it's more them recognising how impossible their job is.

The police are doing their best to reassure the locals – she's seen more police cars patrolling the streets than ever before – and now the FBI are involved, the level of protection is bound to increase.

She's planning the column in her mind as her pen scratches out the woman's words. Even though it's only a first draft circulating in her brain, she knows it's going to be a powerful column.

Instead of her usual diatribe against an individual, she's planning a different tone: one of a community banding together in the face of adversity. She's still planning a certain amount of censure, but that will be aimed towards the racists behind these brutal killings.

She knows all too well about racial targeting. Her parents were smuggled, along with a dozen other children, from the village of Otterwisch, southeast of Leipzig, into Switzerland when the rounding up of Jews began.

They'd been relocated to an orphanage in Queens and had never parted until her father passed away.

She'd done everything she could to find out about her grandparents and other family members left behind. She'd taken a trip to Otterwisch after getting a tangible lead through the JewishGen website. The trip had been poignant but worthless. All traces of her family were gone. Lost as part of Hitler's pogroms. The Germans may have tattooed prisoners, and kept records towards the end, but in the early days of the Holocaust no records or identifications were made. Jews were simply executed.

Growing up, she heard countless tales of the hardships and bigotry her parents had faced as they forged a life for themselves and their only daughter.

Now she has the chance to kick back at bigots and racists, she plans to take it. The black community's plans for self-preservation will provide the meat of her column, but she intends to add her own fiery sauce to show defiance and revulsion.

This is no longer about reporting or getting a scoop before rivals, it's now become a personal crusade against oppression.

Chapter 63

I take a seat opposite Mother and wait for the usual bout of narcissism. She examines me from her chair. As ever, she sits bolt upright surrounded by the chintziest room imaginable.

'What brings you here today, why aren't you out risking your neck like before?' She fixes me with a glare. 'Are you trying to see me into an early grave, is that your aim?'

'Enough.' It's only one word but I say it in a way that silences her. 'We need to talk. About Dad.'

'That worthless piece of garbage. You haven't asked me about him for years. Why are you asking now?'

I'd believe the sneer in her voice if it wasn't for the uncertainty in her eyes.

'Are you sure you can't guess?'

'Why would I? I haven't heard anything of that scumbag for years.'

I pounce on her mistake. 'Don't you mean since he walked out on us?'

'Don't you be arguing semantics with me, Jacob Boulder.' The return of her Glasgow accent and use of my full name prove she's rattled. I'm not here to upset her, but I need to know the truth about my extended family. 'I can't tell you what I don't know.'

'I want to know what you do know, not what you don't.' I soften my tone and relax into the chair to remove some of the confrontation from my words. 'Like, if you knew Dad remarried. That he has two more children.'

I stop short of mentioning his grandchildren. She may be a domineering narcissist, but she's still my mother and I have no intention of causing her pain.

She looks away without giving one of her normal snarky retorts.

I wait five minutes for her to speak.

When she does, her voice is frail and laden with unresolved pain. 'I knew. I just didn't know how to tell you and Sharon. I haven't heard anything for years. I'm sorry but you and Sharon had a rough enough time without telling you that some other children got to grow up with the father who abandoned you.'

'They didn't though. He abandoned them too.'

'He did? What a douchebag.'

I smile at Mother's use of an American insult. When we'd moved here she used bawbag as her insult of choice. Now though, she does everything she can to Americanise herself.

'When did you divorce him?'

Since hearing John's mother was married to my father, I've realised Mother must have been aware. He couldn't remarry without first divorcing Mother. I've only just figured that she too needed to have gotten divorced so she could remarry.

'Three years after he left, I got a letter from a solicitor that said he wanted to divorce me. I spoke to your Grandpa and he told me your father was looking to marry some other woman. Trust me, Jake, signing those papers was the best thing I ever done.' She takes a slug from the ever-present glass of water at her side. 'What brought you here asking questions about him anyway?'

'My half-brother turned up.'

'He did, why?'

'I don't know. Curiosity I guess.' I make a dismissive gesture. 'I'll find out tomorrow night. I'm meeting with him then.'

Pain and longing lace her next question.

There's no way to soften the answer so I keep it as brief as possible. 'Two daughters. His sister has a son.'

'Does he look like you?'

'Yeah. Why do you ask?'

'Because you're the double of your father. Always have been. Stands to reason his other son—.'

My cell interrupts her. It's Chief Watson.

I walk into the kitchen and take the call. I listen to what he has to say and thank him for keeping me updated.

Returning to the lounge I catch Mother wiping tears from her eyes.

'Damn that man. I thought he'd hurt me for the last time.'

I'm not through with my questions. 'Tell me the truth. When did you last hear from him?'

She takes a few slow breaths to recover her composure. 'A month after our divorce was finalised, he sent me a letter apologising for walking out on us.'

'Have you heard much about him since?'

'Only that he married that other woman at Gretna Green. I didn't know he'd left her too. Serves her right anyway. She deserves to feel how I felt when she stole him from me.'

I recall Gretna Green being famous for weddings, but can't remember why.

It's hard to concentrate on the conversation with Mother when my thoughts are centred on what the chief has just told me about Will Pederson's murder.

In a moment of weakness, I decide to brighten her day. 'Keep next Friday night free will you? I'll take you and Neill to dinner. There's a girl I'd like you to meet.'

Her smile is wide as she walks me to the car. I've never done a 'meet the parents' dinner before and she'll be getting all the wrong ideas about me and Taylor.

I just hope Taylor recognises what I'm doing. The act of kindness to Mother may well turn out to be one of cruelty to Taylor.

Chapter 64

As I drive home, I call Alfonse to bring him up to date and request he grabs a copy of the latest video – if the feds haven't already taken it down. He tells me he'll email the coordinates for Pederson's cell movement.

The information swirling around my head is threatening to overwhelm me. Tonight's fight may turn out to be a good thing – I need a physical release from the contortions of my thoughts.

When I get back to my apartment I grab some energy bars and go back over what Chief Watson told me and try to work out how the details can be used.

Will Pederson's naked body has been found on the Eastern boundary of the Uintah and Ouray Reservation. He's been stoned to death: his entire body smashed with rocks.

Once again, the killers have used their victim's cell to make a video and post it online. Pederson's cell was left at his feet as was a message from the killers.

Spelled out in pebbles and small stones was the reference 'Leviticus 20:13'.

A Google search brings up the right passage. Cutting through the biblical speak, it basically advises that homosexuality is punishable by death.

Again, the chosen way to murder ties in with the perceived offence from the victim. Stoning is an ancient method of execution with many biblical connections.

Pederson has been killed because of something in his biological make-up; a thing as fundamental as the pigment in his eyes or the genes that govern height and weight.

The killers are setting out their stall and defining their targets with more than just words. Every death makes a statement.

Each victim highlights an element of society.

Now they're posting their kills online, their supporters will amass in every state. Decent people will of course decry them, but the potential victim groups will either live in fear or get angry and start fighting back.

The email from Alfonse comes in and I reference the location against Google Maps. It's pretty much where the chief told me Pederson was found.

When I read more of the email I kick myself as I realise the mistake Alfonse and I have made in not keeping a full trace on Pederson's cell.

If we'd done that, we'd have known the exact moment the cell came back online, and could have sent Chief Watson and the FBI towards the location.

Alfonse has included this data in his email. He's also included the video.

The video was sent to the press at 9.24am and uploaded to YouTube at 9.25am. He goes on to list all the other places the video was uploaded to.

I don't bother reading the list beyond a quick scan. There's nothing to be gained from knowing where it's gone and when. The FBI will chase all those leads down. We need to pursue something else. What the something else is, I have no idea at this moment.

Unable to delay the inevitable any longer, I click play and watch the video with a growing revulsion. I'm not the kind of morbid ghoul who delights in the suffering of others and this is a truly revolting spectacle. The video is fifteen minutes in length. I pause it after six.

It's bad enough watching a man die, without having to listen to him screaming in pain and begging for mercy. I know I need to watch the whole video in case there are any clues, but right now I don't have the stomach.

Time after time, fist-sized rocks were thrown at Pederson's feet and shins until they were too smashed and broken to support him. As Pederson hung by the rope binding his hands, the rocks moved upwards onto his thighs as the killers worked their way up his body.

When I pick up the video, the rocks are thudding into Pederson's waist. They move up to his chest, leaving behind a trail of bloody welts and torn skin from their rough corners. As they reach his chest there is enough focus on the video for me to see ribs being broken.

The step up to Pederson's head is sickening. His chin starts off resting on his chest, either his heart's given up or the pain has knocked him unconscious. With luck he won't awaken to suffer more.

A rock thrown to his forehead knocks his head back, exposing his throat. The killers adjust their aim.

The next missile smashes Pederson's jaw sideways. Others shatter his nose, cheeks and eye sockets with repeated dull thuds, transforming his face into a bloody pulp.

Rocks continue to be driven into his face with vicious malice until a smaller one buries itself into one of his eyeballs. A larger rock thumps into the smaller one, driving it into Pederson's skull, sending his body into a series of twitching convulsions.

The person recording the execution zooms in on what's left of Pederson's face and switches off the video.

I have to run to make it to the toilet before the heaves in my gut start ejecting the coffee, power bars and fruit I've consumed today.

Chapter 65

A check of the major news outlets shows they've received the new video. None go so far as to display all of the footage, but each has taken screenshots to use in their updates. Nothing they say is anything other than wild speculation, or evangelical criticism against the horror of the killing.

They've pixelated Pederson's face and privates in their copy. It doesn't work, the images are still repugnant. The news outlets all state the existence of a second statement from the killers – I don't want to think of them by their self-appointed moniker, to do so will legitimise their existence. The fact that none of them have printed, aired or even commented on its content tells me the latest communique has rhetoric nobody wants to broadcast.

I go back to the email from Alfonse and find he's included a copy of the statement. He's transcribed it from the video which he says is nothing more than a series of still photographs stitched together with online software; each still a photo of a typed sheet of paper.

A deep exhalation is necessary as soon as I click on the file:

Our beloved nation has become overrun with undesirables and it's time to fight back.

We, the Christian Knights of America, are calling for all true-blooded patriots to take up arms and help us eliminate the many scourges defiling our wonderful country.

White Christians are welcome to stay and live in safety. Others are not.

Niggers, beaners, Japs and all other non-whites should leave.

Jews, Muslims, Hindus and those who worship anyone other than the Lord should leave.

Our latest victim was a white Christian, an ex-cop. These facts were not sufficient to save him. The man was a homo. Homos, gays, lesbians, transgenders or whatever they call themselves should leave too. Their acts of coupling are nothing more than an abomination in the eyes of the Lord and they shall be punished for it.

All who stay shall be executed in a way relevant to their ancestry.

Those who choose to leave will survive.

We'd rather there were no more deaths, but we will not flinch from the unpalatable acts necessary to cleanse this great nation of its diversity.

Again, we urge the white Christians of America to join us in this war against those dragging our nation down. Our economy, heritage and racial superiority are all suffering because of these infiltrators of our lands.

God bless America and its rightful inhabitants.

It's no wonder this hasn't been broadcast to a wider audience. At best, it's propaganda. At worst, inflammatory rhetoric, designed to incite others to join their crusade and murder innocents in their name.

Any news outlet who published this in any context would find themselves the recipients of serious censure – not just from the public, but from the myriad of government agencies handed the task of extinguishing the fires their callousness has fanned the flames of.

I read the statement five times so I can absorb every nuance and shift in tone. With each reading I notice more and more amiss.

The rhetoric is both messianic and megalomaniac. While its message is clear, the writing is jumbled and repetitive. Too many specifics litter a document intended to be general.

No mention is made of Native Americans which is a contradiction to their message; surely no other group can have a higher claim to be the rightful inhabitants of the United States?

The killers can hardly claim superiority over the people who preceded them, but Native Americans are neither white nor Christian which means they fit into their target demographic.

As much as I'd like a philosophical debate about irony and hypocrisy with the person who wrote this statement, I'd much prefer we spend five minutes in a dim alley with no witnesses.

Another factor to strike me is the intellectual feel of this communication. It's not as polished or erudite as it should be, if the leader of this group is as intelligent as Dr Edwards suspects.

I wonder if the man is dumbing down on purpose so as not to alienate those in his target audience. If he is, he's cleverer than I've given him credit for.

Chapter 66

The keys chatter under Ms Rosenberg's nicotine stained fingertips. The column flows unbidden – the way all her best ones do. Whenever hands take over from brain, she knows what they produce will be some of her finest work.

She clucks her tongue as she reads what her hands are communicating from her subconscious. Her very soul is being laid bare on the screen before her, as the affront to her beliefs and heritage is given voice.

Her plan had been to create a column praising the stoicism and bravery of the ethnic groups targeted by the killers, but the column she's writing has a darker, more confrontational tone. Instead of decrying the killers for the heinous monsters they are, she finds herself crossing into more personal insults as the anger inside her spills onto the page.

In a brief crisis of confidence she wonders if she's just venting at them because they didn't include her, or the Casperton Gazette, in their first communique.

She shakes her doubts away. Her last column addressed that issue so well that the Gazette received the latest video, and a new statement from the Christian Knights of America.

The words keep coming and coming as her subconscious continues to pour forth with criticism and vitriol. She feels a paragraph about the newest statement may be too strong until the next one validates the anger with an eloquence she doesn't recognise.

When finished, she gives it a quick read, changing the odd word here and there, before emailing it to her editor.

She lifts her cigarettes from her pocket as she strides outside. The flame of her lighter kisses the tip of one as she passes through the doorway.

Not being able to smoke indoors is a constant irritation to her. When she cut her teeth on the Staten Island Advance, the room had a constant blue-grey fug hanging from the ceiling. Every person who worked there was a character with a thousand stories and a unique way of telling them. Desk drawers were filled with used notebooks and bottles of whisky.

The act of looking back with nostalgia makes her feel old, but those had been good days. Each one was filled with laughter and enthusiasm, where all she feels now is a wearying outrage at the injustices of life.

Few things worked out the way she'd planned. An unreliable source had made her dangerous enemies, forcing her to leave New York and find a new home. An editor had taken a chance and hired her after a telephone interview, so she'd packed what she could into two suitcases and left the vibrancy of New York for the sleepiness of Casperton.

New York she could live without. Halvard's refusal to come with her was what had broken her heart.

She's never given another man a serious look since leaving New York. After all the years that have passed, she knows he's never going to come for her, but if he does, she'll be ready.

The temptation to look him up never leaves, yet she knows doing so will only cause her pain. If they are ever to re-unite, it has to come from him.

She arcs the cigarette butt into a drain and lights another. When it joins its predecessor, she turns and marches back into the office ready for a fight.

'My office. Now!' The words greet her as soon as she walks through the door. Forest Clapperton is the editor who took a chance on her. They have aged and raged together in a dance familiar to newsrooms the world over. Star reporters and editors have different agendas, they may be friends, lovers even, but they'll argue at least three times a week as each battles for supremacy.

'Your column is likely to get us either killed or fired.' Clapperton runs a shaking hand over his liver-spotted head. 'Not only that, it's fifteen hundred words too long. What the hell were you thinking, woman?'

Ms Rosenberg straightens her back, to maximise her meagre height, as she stands her ground. She's known for twenty-five years how to win an argument with Clapperton, and only loses the odd one as a way to keep him thinking he's the boss. The fact he's already brought word count into play shows he doesn't expect to triumph.

'Are you white? Yes. Christian? Yes. Gay? With three failed marriages and countless affairs, I hardly think so. Tell me, Forest, what makes you think you're going to be killed? Your name isn't on the piece, mine is.'

'Good God woman, you can't antagonise killers like that. Calling them cowards, scum and what was it, oh yes, impotent weasels lacking the intellectual capacity to lead themselves out of a dead end, let alone lead a nation as great as the one they claim to love.'

Ms Rosenberg takes a seat and gestures for Clapperton to do the same. He does, oblivious to the fact it's his office and he's her boss. 'What, d'ya think they're going to target me because I call them a few names? Every sensible person in the world will be calling them worse than shit, and rightly so.'

'Perhaps they will. And perhaps they should. But they don't announce their Jewishness in a rant that practically throws down a gauntlet. Tell me, how many of these keyboard warriors live near where the killers are active? How many have newspaper columns?'

'I don't know and I don't care. You know as well as I do, what's in that column needs saying and I'm not afraid to say it, even if you are.'

Clapperton's smile makes Ms Rosenberg uneasy. For the first time since coming back into the office she feels she might not get her way. 'Don't try that old line on me. And don't ask for a box so you can clear your desk either. That article is as inflammatory as the killers' call for support and you know it.'

Ms Rosenberg rises from her chair and slaps both hands on his desk, her chin jutting forward as she breathes stale cigarette smoke at him. 'Where're your balls man?'

'In a security box where my ex-wives' lawyers can't get their hands on them.' His face softens. 'It's a great column, possibly the best ever written for the Gazette. Certainly the best in my time. If I could afford to hire a bodyguard for you, I'd print it like a shot.'

'Print it. I'll get my own bodyguard.'

'No way. I don't trust you. Besides, don't you spend all your money on cat food and cigarettes?'

Ms Rosenberg brandishes her cell at him for a moment then starts to scroll through her contacts list. When she finds Jake Boulder's name she first presses the call button and then selects the speaker option.

When it goes to answerphone she scowls until she hears the beep. 'Boulder, Rosenberg. I need a bodyguard and you're the only man I trust to protect me. The Gazette will pay your check. Call me when you get this.'

'I just told you the Gazette couldn't afford a bodyguard.'

'Boulder's not a bodyguard. He's smarter than anyone else who's trying to find out who those killers are. I'm going home to feed my cats and then I'm going to book a room at the Holiday Inn. They have night porters so there's no way anyone can get to me. Satisfied?'

Chapter 67

Butch Augiers is sitting on the hood of his truck when I arrive at his place. He's not alone. Jim-Bob and Freddie are loitering around him, as are a few more members of his family.

Most are holding beer cans and Freddie looks to be at least half-way into his cups.

I draw the Mustang alongside Butch's truck and kill the engine. 'Climb in, I'll drive.'

Butch spits out a gob of tobacco juice as he clambers down. His finger is pointing at my car. 'Ain't no way your fancy low-slung car's gonna git us where we're going.'

I don't like relying on him for a lift, but it doesn't look as if I have a lot of choice in the matter.

Jim-Bob gives me a thorough looking over as I walk across to Butch's truck. I'm not surprised he's looking at me with puzzlement. I'm wearing an old pair of paint-splattered jeans and a vest top that's seen better days. Win or lose tonight, there's going to be blood spilled and possibly a roll in the dirt depending upon the rules. I don't see the point in ruining decent clothes and, by looking more like a bum, I may just get my opponent to underestimate me. Every little advantage counts when fists are raised.

Butch twists a key in the ignition and the truck roars to life. Other family members pour into the other trucks and a small convoy forms with Butch in the lead.

As he navigates the back roads with care and familiarity, I ponder two things. Upmost in my mind is the fear I'm walking into a trap. Now I've been separated from my Mustang, I'm reliant on the Augiers for transport. Should they decide to exact a little payback for the other night, I'll have no option but to stand and fight them.

While retreat isn't a word or action I'm fond of, or use, it's nice to have the choice. This situation has all the hallmarks of a set-up. I'm being driven into the middle of nowhere by people I've established an uneasy alliance with after kicking their asses.

Less of a concern and more of a puzzle is the voicemail I'd gotten from Ms Rosenberg. Try as I might, I can't figure out why she thinks she needs a bodyguard. Regardless of her reasons, she'll have to look elsewhere. I don't fancy spending my days under siege from clouds of cigarette smoke and semi-toxic perfume.

I didn't bother returning her call. It's a task that can wait until I get home.

Butch slows to navigate a sharp corner. His truck may look like a beat up old wreck but the engine is sound and the suspension is doing an admirable job of coping with the rough tracks. The inside shows signs of wear and age but none of neglect.

'You nervous?'

'No.' It's a fib rather than a full-blown lie. I don't admit weaknesses to myself, let alone other men. 'Should I be?'

'Hell no. You get nervous, you'll get your ass whupped.'

My nerves are more about the possibility of a set-up than about the fight. I've fought too often to worry about catching a few blows. Adrenaline will get me through tonight and, if necessary, I'll take some painkillers tomorrow when the pain has had time to corral its forces.

Before leaving my apartment, I spent an hour stretching various muscles to improve blood flow and suppleness. I also rehearsed a few combinations in a spot of shadow boxing to sharpen both mind and body.

'So, what're the rules then? Is it fists only, or is it just a straight-up fight?'

'That depends on how Old Man Jones is feeling. He'll tell you any rules before your fight starts.'

'You're such a font of information. It's a wonder no one has asked you to become a teacher.'

Butch laughs at my sarcasm. 'You maybe ain't nervous, but you're plenty keyed up. Take my advice, listen to what you're told and make sure you hit first, hit hardest and hit most often. You do that, you'll be okay.'

His advice is good. If I'd been asked to pass on some fighting wisdom, I'd have said much the same thing.

Another issue on my mind are the odds on me learning what I want to know. It seems improbable I'll overhear a conversation where someone owns up to the murders. Those of us who are fighting may well be kept to one side.

On the other hand, knowing how men like to shake the hand of a winner, there's every chance we'll be feted and liquored up. If we are, I'm prepared to act the racist when I join conversations. I've been Alfonse's friend long enough to have heard plenty of racial slurs. The hard part will be not showing my revulsion.

A full hour after leaving the Augiers' place, we arrive at our destination. I can't guess the exact location as there have been too many turns, and changes of both direction and speed, since we crossed the 191 and turned west. I figure we're south of Ashley National Forest by about five to ten miles which means we're about forty miles north west of Casperton. The fact I could be out by five miles in any direction doesn't matter too much.

I'm here with no hope of back-up, no transport and a cell I've left charging in my car. Whatever happens tonight, I've got nothing but my wits and fists to get me out of tight spots.

I've faced worse situations. Those who can't be reasoned with can always be pummelled. The only variable to cause me concern are the numbers I may be up against and the possibility they'll be armed.

Chapter 68

The track rounds a bluff, and I see a collection of trucks, pickups and a few panel vans. Groups of men stand around chatting. Their hands clutch beers, cigarettes and in the odd case a bottle of liquor.

Off to the right someone is standing behind a portable barbecue. The smell of grilled meat elicits a growl from my stomach. If it wasn't for the impending fight and the fact I've retched up what little I've eaten today, I'd be over there like a shot.

'Stick with me and don't get smart with anyone. Let your fists do most of your talkin'. You're here on my recommendation 'cause I figure you might learn something that'll help you catch the men you're hunting. Don't go runnin' your mouth off with your educated talk, you might well be the smartest man here, but lettin' people know won't help you none.'

I'm comfortable with his suggestion. Playing dumb and keeping quiet is part of my plan anyway.

A man with a rugged face and no hair comes across. 'This your fighter, Butch?'

'Yeah. This is Jake. How ya doin' Connor, is your father here?'

Connor looks me over without speaking. I keep my features unconcerned and nonchalant. When the examination is over he points to a wizened old man.

'He's disappointed you're not fighting. Your man better be good value.' He jerks a thumb towards his father. 'Go let him know you're here.'

Neither of us speak as we walk over to the wizened man. He sees us coming and repeats his son's evaluation of me.

'Mr Jones, this is Jake. He's the guy who's takin' the place you offered to me.'

Jones doesn't speak. Perhaps he's afraid the cigar will fall from his lips if he does.

A guy with a battered face stands at his side like a lieutenant. With a face like his, he's more like the private who gets all the crappy jobs than someone of officer class. I guess he's Freddie's father: the man whose place I'm taking.

'Hi.' I offer a hand forward. 'Thanks for letting me take part.'

Old Man Jones squints at my accent as he ignores my hand. 'You English, boy?'

'Scottish.' I give him the benefit of the doubt. He has the look of a man who has never left the county, let alone the state. His face is etched with years of hard work and harder living. Despite this, his eyes are flint hard and brighter than the noon sun.

I reckon Old Man Jones is a tough, intelligent man who has battled all his life. The deference shown to him by Butch is part respect and part fear.

'Scottish eh? Just as well, Butch. If you'd brought me an English pussy, we'd've had a need to be having words.' He looks at me after glancing at his watch. 'You get a thousand bucks for takin' part. If you're confident, you can bet on yourself. First fight's at eight, rules'll be explained then.'

I spend twenty minutes walking around, doing a series of muscle loosening exercises and stretches as I go. The movement gives me the chance to move among the vehicles with impunity. Of the three white panel vans present, two have scratches on their sides. None of them look recent, but I memorise their licence plates all the same.

A foghorn sounds and everyone starts to assemble around the pickup Old Man Jones has clambered into the back of. Beside him stand Connor and the battered man with an easel bearing a chalkboard.

Old Man Jones removes the cigar from his mouth and slugs from a beer can. 'Gentlemen, you are here to see some fightin' and some fightin's what you're gonna see. We've got us eight brawlers and we're havin' us a tournament. You can bet on each fighter and ev'ry 'dividual fight. The rules is, fighters can't use no weapons. Fists, heads, elbows and feet is all they got. And that includes pounding another man's head against any rocks. Other'n that, anythin' goes. Only when a fighter concedes, or can't get back to his feet, is the fight over.'

I try not to act surprised as he starts drawing names from a hat. I now face having up to three fights instead of one. The possibility of me escaping with a few minor cuts and bruises has all but disappeared. A few minutes ago I had a fifty-fifty chance of victory, I now have one in eight.

My name is read out fourth which means I'll be able to at least watch one match before it's my turn. Every little scrap of information will help.

Connor produces a stick of chalk and starts marking up odds. Because I'm a stranger, the odds on me winning this tournament aren't what you'd call favourable. Again, me being an unknown quantity, they're not making me a rank outsider either.

I walk up to Connor and pull the ten c-notes from my pocket. 'Five hundred on me to win your tournament, and another five hundred on me in the first bout.'

He licks his lips as he scrawls out the bets on two slips of paper and throws a look to his father. Old Man Jones mumbles a few words and Connor halves the odds on me winning down to five-to-one.

Butch puts a couple hundred bucks on me to win the first fight but doesn't look at me when placing the wager. Whether he's backing me out of belief or a sense of duty isn't important, failing to do so would have lessened him in Old Man Jones's eyes.

I run myself through a few more stretches and out of interest check the odds for the guy I'm fighting. He's the second favourite.

Chapter 68

My opponent stands before me. And over me if the truth be told. He's a big guy known simply as Crusher. There's something about his bovine face which makes me suspect the nickname wasn't earned because of his crushing intelligence.

He gives me a toothless grin filled with confidence in his superior size and strength. If I'm supposed to be intimidated, it doesn't work. His downfall will be a lack of mobility and speed.

After watching the first bout I know what's expected. The first two fighters had flown at each other with a flurry of blows lacking in direction. Noses and lips were bloodied before a telling punch was landed. Even then, the eventual winner had taken four wild swings to finish his opponent when one should have sufficed.

Crusher advances with a huge blow. I dance to one side and throw a punch into his bulging gut as I duck under his arms.

He grunts, but wheels to face me undeterred by the blow. Again, he launches himself forward hoping I'm stupid enough to get ensnared by his arms.

I'm not.

This time I duck without throwing the punch to his gut. Instead I stay outside his arms and deliver a vicious elbow to his face when he wheels to face me. Before he can recover his wits, I whirl behind him and stamp on the back of his right knee.

Him going down to one knee gives me the opportunity to rain a few hard punches to the side of his head. I don't expect him to be beaten like this, but every punch I land weakens his spirit.

To escape my punches, he rolls himself forward and spins until he's crouched in the position of a linebacker. I wait for him to charge at me.

He doesn't. He's learned I'm too fast and too wise to get caught that way.

When I don't advance on him, he straightens and waves me forward.

I raise my hands and creep forward a pace or two. I'm up on my toes, ready to dance away from his longer reach.

Crusher apes me by raising his hands so we're matched like a couple of boxers. His left hand snakes out, but it's a range finder and falls short by a good foot. I bat it inwards and deliver a hard blow to his kidneys as I wheel behind him.

He spins faster and throws his right elbow at my face. My still raised left catches the blow, but there's enough force in it to send me staggering back.

I don't have time to recover my balance before Crusher swings a wild left at me. Rather than let it connect and do its intended damage, I throw myself to the ground. Even as I'm falling, I'm dropping my left hand into a position of support and lashing my right foot in a wide arc.

I connect with the side of Crusher's knee as planned. That's as far as the plan works though. The minimal time to build up speed or power, and the lack of rigidity from connecting with the top of my foot, rather than the toe of my boot which carries the support of the sole, means the kick's impact suffers a dramatic lessening.

Crusher stands over me and roars as he swings his foot back. With no time for defence, I roll away from him as quick as I can.

His toes catch my spinning body and deliver a hard kick to the side of my chest. The fact I'm moving away from him prevents any ribs from breaking, but I still yelp at the pain. Encouraged, he throws the other foot towards my head.

I block it with both hands, but the impact pushes me backwards. I feel the exposed skin on my back tearing on the coarse rocks beneath me.

My hands now grasp Crusher's ankle as he changes his tactics and tries to stamp on my head. The more weight he puts behind his foot, the harder it is to prevent him making contact.

With both hands occupied, the only weapon I have is my feet. He's too close to my head for me to reach him with my boots, so I shift the thrust in my hands from upwards to sideways forcing his foot past my head so he's momentarily off balance.

I release his foot and throw a punch upwards between his outstretched legs. While he's doubled over and cursing, I wriggle free and scramble to my feet.

We straighten at the same time. I'm less injured, fitter and quicker than he is. My uppercut hits his chin as his hands release his balls.

Crusher wobbles but doesn't go down. I repeat the blow with a little more venom. I've no problem with knocking him out, but I don't see the point in breaking his jaw. There's no glory for me in gratuitous brutality.

The second uppercut does its job. He topples forward into an untidy heap. His only movement the rise and fall of his back as he breathes.

Chapter 69

Connor scowls as he gives me a sheaf of notes. I've made a five grand profit which isn't bad for a few minutes work.

One grand goes back in my pocket to replace my original stake. The other four and a half I give back to Connor. The odds on me winning, either the tournament or my next bout, have shortened to three-to-one.

The extra money isn't something I'm interested in. The laying down of a challenge is my primary intent in gambling. I want them to know I intend to win. Sometimes you have to push a rock over to see what crawls out from underneath.

I watch the next two fights with Butch. One is a bloody, drawn out battle that leaves even the winner looking like he lost. The second is over in three seconds. The winner pulls off some weird handstand arrangement and delivers a roundhouse kick to the side of his opponent's head.

My next fight is against the guy who won the fight before mine. His face is swollen from the damage caused in his first bout, and his left eye is one decent punch from closing.

As tempting as it is to target the damaged eye, I don't want to risk blinding him. For me the point is to win, not maim. The crowd can get their kicks from the others; I've no intention of causing lasting damage.

We've both seen each other fight and know what to expect. He's a brawler whereas I'm a counter attacker. Or at least that's what he thinks.

To confound his expectations, I step forward and follow a left jab with a swinging right. He ducks back to avoid the jab which leaves his gut wide open. My fist connects with his solar plexus and removes every last trace of breath from his body.

He backs away, fighting to regain some air in his lungs. I follow him and wait for the moment when he recovers. As soon as his back starts to straighten, I throw a couple of combinations at his face.

He goes down but tries to get back up. I stand a pace away, then step forward when he makes it to one knee. My fists are ready but my heart isn't in it. 'Do you really want to get up just so I can put you down again?'

The fight goes out of his eyes as my words settle in his brain. His head shakes and he sits on his ass.

Nobody brought any water, so I pick a couple of ice cubes from a cooler and suck on them as I watch the next fight. The first cube hasn't melted before the dancing gymnast pulls off another feat of acrobatics and lays out his opponent with an elbow to the jaw.

Old Man Jones and the guy with the battered face are watching as I roll my winnings over a second time. I'm now betting eighteen grand at two-to-one. There's also the original bet of five hundred bucks at ten-to-one. If I win this next fight, I'll clear fifty-nine thousand five hundred bucks.

Winning may be something of an issue though. The dancing gymnast is fast and deadly. While my fights weren't long knock-down drag-out affairs, I still caught a hefty kick from Crusher which has made my ribs tender. As soon as I settle into one position, stiffness will arrive with a side order of pain.

During the fifteen minute lay off before the final, I walk around keeping muscles loose and eyes open. The real purpose of my being here isn't to fight, it's to investigate. The fighting nothing more than a key I'm using to enter a locked room.

As I make a circuit I notice another two white panel vans have arrived since I checked earlier. One has no scratches or anything remarkable about it. The other has a slight jacking to its suspension, off road tyres and a fresh scratch on the driver's side.

What I wouldn't give to have my cell in my hand right now so I could call in the police, FBI and any other government agency who wanted to come along. Out here it wouldn't pick up a signal and would amount to nothing more than a collection of useless microchips and plastic.

I memorise the licence plate and keep moving in case the van's owner notices the attention I'm giving his vehicle.

'Hey, Boulder. How you planning to not get your ass kicked in the final?'

It's a good question Jim-Bob has thrown at me. I'm not sure of the answer so I give him a flippant one. 'I'm going to pretend he's as slow and dumb as you are.'

I walk away leaving Butch laughing at his brother's consternation.

Freddie and another young lad are cavorting around trying to emulate the dancing gymnast's moves when Old Man Jones throws a handful of pebbles at them. 'Quit yer foolin', boy.'

They stop their antics and the stranger gives a shameful excuse for an apology. As they wander off, I hear Freddie call his buddy Dave. His name doesn't matter to me – other than it being a way to connect some more dots.

Like everyone else here, I disappear behind a parked vehicle to take a leak. When I return, I'm called forward for the final.

Old Man Jones gives the kind of introduction Liberace would consider over the top.

As I square off against the dancing gymnast, I realise I still haven't worked out a way to combat his athletic prowess. The mismatch in our sizes is similar to my first fight with Crusher, only this time I'm the bigger slower fighter.

He comes at me, bouncing on his toes. There's no way to predict how or where he'll attack. I feint left then step right hoping an opportunity will present itself.

It doesn't.

I don't want to go on the attack too much as he'll pick me off, but I've always rated attack as the best form of defence and so far his defence remains untested.

He shifts back as I push forward. I'd like to pressure him a little but don't want to make the mistake he's waiting for. I see a change in his eyes a millisecond before he drops into a crouch and tries a leg sweep.

I lift my right leg up, just enough for his leg to pass underneath, then flick my foot towards his head.

He's seen me counter a similar move and mimics me by grabbing my foot. Not being as reliant on brute strength as Crusher, I release the weight from my standing leg and drop my knee into his gut.

A grunt is all I get for my efforts, so I drive an elbow into his face. His lips split, but his exceptional agility comes into play as he wriggles himself around me.

Through some kind of wrestling move or other, he manages to roll us over so he's on top of me. My left arm is pinned beneath my back leaving only my right for defence.

I deflect some of his punches but most find their target. One breaks my nose and I feel at least two teeth loosen.

His weight on my chest prevents me from wriggling free so I grab a fistful of his collar and pull his head towards mine.

With my head on the ground I can't get any purchase on the headbutt, but I can direct him so his nose strikes my forehead. The buck from my hips adds to his momentum.

Instinct makes him rear backwards. As he does so, I hook a hand under his knee and help him on his way.

He gets to his feet before I do, but he wastes a second wiping blood off his face. I don't care whose blood it is, the action gives me time to brace for his next attack.

Now when we face off, I see fear and uncertainty in his eyes. I hope he sees triumph and confidence in mine.

He feints left then right before pulling one of his gymnastic moves. Instead of doing the expected, and trying to dodge or defend the coming blow, I ignore it and step forward throwing off his aim. Instead of his foot crashing into my head, his knee bounces off my shoulder.

I press home my advantage and nail him with a left right combination as he tries to recover his balance after the failed attack. He goes down but doesn't look as if he's staying there so I follow him.

His arms are covering his face, but his legs are free. I feel one snake its way around my neck and press me backwards. His other foot appears, but rather than join the first in an effort to push me back, the dancing gymnast throws his heel at my face.

I roll away before it connects and this time he's the slowest to regain his feet.

Next time when he throws a punch it's not a feint. His knuckles slam into my jaw, but it's not the hardest I've been hit.

With his high impact moves causing him more problems than successes, he's switching to more orthodox tactics. His greater hand speed will wear me down unless I manage to land enough decent punches of my own.

We trade punches like a couple of twelfth-round boxers, convinced we'll get the judges' decision.

I can see I'm wearing him down, but I can feel myself slowing too. Rather than wait to see who tires first, I decide to take a chance.

When his next punch comes at me, I deflect it and take a quick step forward, arching my back as I go. My headbutt slams into his nose and sends him reeling backwards. I follow him and throw several combinations until his knees give way.

I stagger away to a large rock and sit down to catch my breath. When I collect my winnings I want to be in the best possible shape – in case Connor or anyone else has any silly ideas about me not getting the money.

Chapter 70

Butch is the first person to come across to me. His face is beaming as he shakes my hand and claps me on the back.

Others follow him, and a bottle of beer is pressed into my hand. I want to drink it, but know I shouldn't. One beer has never been enough for me and I need my wits about me for whatever may come.

The dancing gymnast is picked up by his friends. He steadies himself and comes across to me. I clench my fists ready, but I've misread his intentions. He proffers a hand and gives me a bloody smile. 'Well done.'

I hand him the beer and head off to where Connor is handing out money to the few who'd betted on me.

He greets me with a smile. 'Hey, Boulder. That was a good show you put on. Anytime you want to come back, we'll be happy to see you.' As he speaks he pulls out a sheaf of notes and starts flicking through them.

Two minutes later I have my winnings and appearance fee in my pocket and no idea what to do with the money. The only thing I know is that I won't be keeping it. However the money has gotten into the hands of the Jones family, I'm positive it's not got there legally.

So far as I'm concerned, other than my initial stake money, every cent I'm carrying is tainted by a victim's misery. The sooner I can pass it on to a charity or two the better.

Butch comes back with some beers and frowns when I refuse one. I want to get back to civilisation, to call Alfonse and Chief Watson, tell them about the white van with the fresh scratch, but there's no way Butch is ready to move.

A group of shady looking characters come my way. The leader of the group stands in front of me. 'We lost a lot of money betting against you tonight. We'd like the chance to make some of it back.'

I don't say anything. I want to hear what they have to say before I tell them no.

'Y'see we know you earned big betting on yo'self. We can double or treble that money.'

'How?' My interest is now piqued. I've no intention of doing anything with the guy, but Chief Watson may be interested in hearing about his business proposition.

'You come and fight for me. Depending on the purse, you make up to a hundred grand a night. Plus you c'n bet on yourself. You interested?'

'Yeah.'

'Good.' He passes me a card with nothing but a cell number written on it. 'When you're ready to fight again, call me.'

I'm more likely to juggle rattlesnakes than call him, but I stuff the card into a pocket.

A foghorn blares and is followed by Old Man Jones's voice.

'Gentlemen, we got one more fight for you and it's gonna be a good un. We've seen some fine battles tonight, but what we're offering you now is gonna be somethin' real special.' My stomach flips as I wonder if he's about to drag my name into things. All of a sudden, my plan to challenge them by winning their money doesn't seem anything like as smart as I'd first thought.

'We got us two men, two knives, but we only gonna have us one survivor. I give you a fight to the death. In a moment you'll meet our fighters, but first I'd like you all to follow Connor and Kevin.' He points to a cleft in the rocky wall of the small valley we're in.

Unsure of what's about to happen, I hang back until I'm the last to pass through the cleft. We're in a kind of hollowed out basin whose walls are ten feet high.

Connor climbs a ladder at the far end and everyone clambers up after him. Being last doesn't seem such a good idea anymore, so I push my way past one or two guys who look at me in amusement.

Try as I might, I can't work out why anyone would agree to take part in a fight to the death. I'm interested in seeing the two modern-day gladiators on an anthropological level.

What I'm not wanting to witness is their fight. As much as I enjoy a punch-up myself, I get little pleasure from watching others do it.

Chapter 71

When the last person climbs the ladder out of the basin, Connor and Kevin climb back down and take the ladder back to the cleft.

A white panel van reverses into the opening. Connor opens the back door and hauls a black man into the centre of the basin. Kevin does the same.

They use the ladder to climb onto the van's roof. I check the licence plate. It's the jacked van with the scratch on the left side.

The driver is dressed in the same jeans and shirt as everyone else, but his look is better quality. He's a handsome man who is treated with respect and deference by the Jones brothers. I don't recall seeing his face, but there are others who're also unfamiliar. What is familiar, is the description given by Will Pederson's neighbour of the man calling himself Brian.

Everything I see leads me to think I've stumbled on the killers through dumb luck. Where the luck has run out, is the fact I'm in the middle of nowhere with no way of contacting the authorities, and no transport of my own.

I look at the two black men who are standing in the centre of the basin. There's fear on both their faces and their close proximity to each other speaks of comradeship rather than enmity. Their clothes are soiled with the detritus of rough living.

I figure that Brian has picked up a couple of street bums and plans to use them for sport. The colour of their skin the deciding factor in their selection.

A feeling of helplessness washes over me as Brian exits the back of the van, and walks towards the two fearful men with a pump action shotgun in his hands and a cigar in his mouth.

They shrink back from him, but he waves them forward. I see his lips move as he gives quiet instructions to his two latest victims.

They shake their heads at him. As he retreats, they try to follow him, their protests snatched away from my ears by the breeze. Brian answers their protests by aiming the shotgun at them as he backs away.

When he gets to the van he clambers up the ladder. Connor hands him two hunting knives, which he tosses to opposite sides of the basin, while Kevin pulls up the ladder.

The black men stay where they are so Brian lifts the shotgun to his shoulder. 'Begin.'

I pity the two men. They're in a situation neither has chosen. There is no escape for them. Brian's shotgun and the van block the cleft, while the rock walls of the basin form a natural arena for their bout. Even if they could climb out, without being stabbed by the other, the spectators at the top wouldn't let them leave. Their only hope is winning.

The two men split and run to the knife nearest them. As soon as they turn with the knives in their hands I know who the victor will be. The taller of the two waves his knife as if it's a sword, while the shorter man with the greying hair holds his blade steady in a backhand grip.

Neither advances too close to the other. The taller one is slashing a lot of air without ever threatening Grey Hair. A lunge from him sees an attempted stab miss by at least two feet.

I want to intervene, put a halt to the horror unfolding before me, but there's nothing I can do. Any attempted intervention will be ended by Brian's shotgun.

Grey Hair dances away from a slashing lunge. His counter splits open the taller guy's left bicep. The crowd roars in delight while Freddie and Dave do a happy jig.

The taller guy's left arm hangs loose by his side as he continues his wild slashes. A second counter-attack gashes his knife arm causing him to drop his weapon.

Grey Hair steps forward, preventing the taller guy from retrieving his knife. Without his given weapon, the taller guy shrinks to the back of the basin and lifts a fist sized rock. The way his arm is held, it's clear he plans to use it as a missile. He advances towards Grey Hair, who stands his ground.

When they're five feet apart, the rock is launched at Grey Hair. It smacks into the middle of his chest a split-second before the taller guy throws himself after it.

The two men land in a heap, each wrestling for control of Grey Hair's knife. The taller guy is on top of Grey Hair when a violent thrust sees him spasm in panic as the blade slices his throat.

Grey Hair rolls the dying man off his chest and crawls away. When he's three yards away he wipes the blood off his face, then hurls his guts up.

I know how he feels. I've only been watching and I feel sick. At least when I killed a man, I didn't end up covered in his blood.

Brian approaches Grey Hair and gestures for him to return to the van. Grey Hair seems to refuse. A lifting of the shotgun changes his mind.

The van moves away and Connor brings back the ladder. As we walk back towards the various trucks I touch Butch's elbow. 'You ready to get out of here?'

'Hell yeah. That ain't what I call entertainment.' His words are no more than a whisper but I catch the disdain in his voice.

He rounds up his family and tells Freddie to get in the back seat of his truck.

As we're climbing into the truck, a single blast of a shotgun rings out. I can only hope Grey Hair didn't see it coming.

Butch drives back with little regard for the punishment his truck is taking from the rough tracks. The main focus of his anger is young Freddie, who he berates with a constant stream of abuse and vilification for his actions and conduct.

He uses his superior intelligence to ask the idiotic boy a series of questions which cannot be answered without dropping himself deeper into trouble.

Chapter 72

The chief is waiting for me when I pass through the media scrummage and enter the station. My call on the way back from Butch's had been passed straight to Gaertner.

There's not a trace of the FBI anywhere in the station. Even Gaertner has scrambled to the Jones's place.

When he sees the cuts and bruises on my face, the chief hollers for Darla to bring the first aid kit.

As I give him a fuller account of my evening, Darla fusses round me wiping away blood and dirt from my face.

Resisting Darla is a waste of time. She just agrees with you and carries on doing what you've asked her not to. Her personality is louder than the Hawaiian blouses she wears and her rich booming tones are only ever one syllable away from calling people sugar or honey.

'The licence plate you gave us for that van is registered to an address in Salt Lake City. It's also registered to a twenty-twelve Chevrolet Spark. The owner of the Chevvy is in her eighties.'

'You got someone going to see her?'

'FBI have.'

We share a grimace. The licence plate on the van is so obviously false, it's not worth discussing. The little old lady will have to be interviewed, but as a formality rather than a serious line of enquiry.

'I presume you're on the lookout for it?'

'It's just as well you mentioned it. I never thought of that.' His scornful tone is powerful enough to shrivel rock. 'You're the amateur here, not me.'

I ignore his ire. I need to know what the police and FBI are doing so I don't waste time doing the same thing.

Chief Watson snatches up his phone before the first ring finishes. 'Yes?'

I watch his face as he listens to the caller. Whatever he's being told, isn't good news. The knuckles of his free hand are at their usual place, massaging his temple.

His end of the conversation doesn't give much away, but I can guess the general topic.

As soon as he hangs up I speak. 'Well?'

'None of them were there except David and the women.'

'Young David was there. Are they bringing him in?'

'Not the young David, his grandfather. Gaertner is bringing them all in, but David Jones is denying all knowledge of the fight tonight, and says he's never left the house. The women are all backing his story up. They're lying of course, but at the moment it's your word against his.'

'I'll take you up to where the fight was. Show you the blood.'

He raises a hand. 'I believe you, Boulder. We just need to get proof they were there.'

'What about Kevin and Connor, where does he say they are?'

'He claims they had a falling out and he hasn't seen them for two years. It's bull and we all know it, but if he and those women all stick to the story there's damn little we can do without proof.'

'What about this Brian guy, did Gaertner ask Jones about him?'

'He didn't say. They're bringing them back here and will sweat them, see if someone breaks rank.' His head shakes. 'If anyone does, it'll be one of the women. Can't see it myself though.'

I don't like his assessment, but I have to agree with it. While people like the Jones and Augiers family aren't what you'd call rednecks, they're only a half-step away. They have a natural distrust of what they think of as city folks. Authority figures like the police and FBI are viewed with suspicion. Gaertner and his men will have a tough job breaking their resistance. Threats of jail won't work. For people used to scratching a living from unforgiving territory, a vacation at the government's expense holds no threat.

The other overriding factors will be their fear of Old Man Jones and Brian; plus the fact that any admission they make could mean life imprisonment, or Death Row, for their loved ones.

'You say you saw this Brian guy?'

'That's right.' I give him the best description I can. The distance between us and the horror of the knife fight prevented me from getting as good a look at him as I had wanted.

He opens a file and passes me a sheet of paper. It's a computer generated picture of a man. It's a fair approximation of Brian, but I'm too sketchy on the details to point out the flaws that prevent it from being a perfect likeness.

'That's him. Have you run him through your computers?'

'Gaertner has. Says they didn't get any hits.'

That's telling in itself. If the guy isn't on the FBI's radar, or that of any other agency, there's little chance of getting his real identity without one of the Jones family spilling their guts.

If Connor, Kevin and Young David aren't at home, they must be with Brian. Which means they're either acting out their next atrocity, or they're planning it.

'You heard news bulletins today, Boulder?'

'No.' My answer is hesitant as a growing feeling of dread envelops me. 'Why?'

'The copycats have started. There have been three stonings and one beheading. There's also been a serious upsurge in Klan style activity all over the country.'

'I take it there's been an increased police presence in sensitive areas?'

'Hell yeah. The national guard has been called out in a lot of places.' He gives a scowl of annoyance. 'Domestic shootings have doubled in black households because they're so damned scared they're shooting at the slightest noise and killing their own family. Wouldn't be so bad if they were shooting burglars.'

When the wider media starts tracking back, and learns about the burning crosses and impalement, things will get worse in a hurry. I'm all for free speech and a free press, but there are times when they ought to display a better social conscience about what they publish. I'm not convinced their editors and shareholders will share my sentiments though.

He doesn't mention the pressure of having the world's eyes watching Casperton. He doesn't need to, it's evident on his face and in his every gesture. However he's feeling, Gaertner will have it double or treble. It's only a matter of time before the Special Agent in charge of Utah, or a bigwig from Washington, comes to take over from him. The second they arrive in Casperton, his career will be tarnished and he'll be forever thought of as the man who failed.

I leave before Gaertner returns with the Jones family. He'll want to bawl me out, and if Old Man Jones sees me he'll want to issue whatever the hillbilly equivalent of a fatwah is.

Chapter 73

Alfonse's face shows concern when he sees mine. I wave away his worries and change the subject to the matter at hand.

He's up to speed because, as soon as I'd finished speaking to Chief Watson on my frantic drive back to Casperton, I'd called him.

'Those names I got from the bank, how'd you get on with them?'

He smiles. 'Well. Working from your description of the guy calling himself Brian, I've pinned it down to three people.'

'Who are they?'

'Ian Lindstrom, Vern Tate and Penelope Anderson.'

'What you got on them?'

He gives me three sheets of paper, and time to read them. As ever, Alfonse has provided a detailed report on each person.

Ian Lindstrom's loan application was turned down because his business plan wasn't considered to be viable. Since being refused by Sherrelle, he's failed to secure funding elsewhere and his bakery store has closed.

To confound matters, his listed address has changed from an upscale location to an apartment in a block nicknamed the Lonely Hearts Club, due to the number of recently divorced people passing through its doors.

Alfonse's notes state that his Facebook pictures are all images of delicacies from his bakery. Dr Edwards would suggest he's living in the past. I'd agree with him.

It's almost too pat, how his life has nosedived since Sherrelle rejected his loan. A nagging doubt pulls at the back of my mind.

'Did you Google him, see what's in the local news items?'

He pulls a face. 'Nine out of ten times, doing that is a waste of time.'

'Humour me.'

He blows a raspberry as he reaches for his laptop.

I read the report on Vern Tate next. It's a similar tale with two key differences. Tate's business has survived, although it's only just breaking even. He's also still with his wife. A picture gleaned from his Twitter account shows a family portrait of them and their daughter. Without being judgemental about his wife, it's hard not to think Tate is punching above his weight.

'Dammit. Strike Lindstrom from the list, he's black.'

'Why dammit? Surely it's good to eliminate a suspect?'

He scowls at me. 'Of course it is. I just had him as my favourite.'

I hide my smile from him – aware of how much he hates it when his hunches are proven wrong.

I change the subject. 'What do you make of Tate?'

'Not a lot. He's not fared well since being turned down, but he's still got his business and his family. He's a possible. What about the woman?'

'Brian is a man.'

'Well duh. Read the report, Jake.'

For once in my life, I do as I'm told.

Penelope Anderson tried to borrow a hundred thousand bucks so she could open a health food shop. Her husband's name is also on the application: Richard B. Anderson. At this minute, I'd bet every one of the sixty thousand dollars in my pocket that the B stands for Brian.

Other than an address, there's no other information on either of them.

'What else you got on them?'

He shrugs. 'Nothing yet, but I'm working on it. I've programs running their details now.'

I'm about to call Chief Watson when Alfonse shakes his head. 'I Googled their address along with the other ones. Their house burned down two years ago. I've been through the postal service trying to find a forwarding address for them but I've come up blank.'

'We should still tell the chief. The FBI may know a way to find out where he lives now.'

'They might. I doubt it, but they might.'

I've hurt his professional pride as a hacker. Tough. There are bigger issues at stake than his feelings. I try another tack. 'Did you try the DMV to see if any vehicles are registered in his name?'

'Of course.' He's sullen now. 'He's got a white panel van registered to the house that burned down.'

'No other vehicles?'

'She has a Ford Taurus registered in her name.'

She has a nice car and he has a van. The set-up is quite typical for families where the husband works with his hands rather than his head. 'Do we know what the husband's occupation is?'

'It's listed on the application as construction worker.'

Which could mean he's anything between a manual labourer and a skilled tradesman with a decent income. If Brian is as clever as we think he is, my guess is he's an electrical engineer, or something equally requiring of intelligence. As much as the desire to work with your hands may steer your career path, intelligent human beings also need to challenge their brains, otherwise they soon become bored.

It's why I read so many crime novels. Working the door at the Tree doesn't require a great amount of thinking, so I read mysteries to give my brain a workout.

While waiting for his programs to finish their sweep, Alfonse tells me how he traced a reposting of the first two videos to a library in Rock Springs, and the second two to Casperton's library.

It's a smart move by Brian. Libraries offer free internet, and because it isn't sourced to his own address there's no way to trace anything he does back to him.

He passes on some more details that are nothing but background information.

'This is no use, Alfonse. We're being reactive here. Instead of following the snake's tail we should be trying to cut off its head. We need to find a way to find the man.'

'How?' Frustration adds a nasty layer to his tone. 'We can only work with the facts we've got.'

'We need to think about the ways those facts can be used proactively. Can you write a program you can lock onto any new videos posted, and have it notify you if they're reposted along with the location?'

'Yeah. It'll take a few hours though.'

I stand and move towards his kitchen. 'I'll get you a coffee and then leave you to it. If your searchbots produce anything let me know.'

'Gee, thanks buddy.'

I let his snarkiness wash over me. I'm going to head home and get some rest while he'll be working through the night.

Chapter 74

I groan at the stiffness in my body as I reach for my cell. For once my sleep has remained uninterrupted by nightmares of drowning. Instead it's lone blasts from a shotgun that have disturbed my slumber.

I look at the screen before answering. See Alfonse's name. 'Yeah?'

The excitement I'd felt at the call disappears as I listen to what he tells me. By the time he's finished speaking I have the shower running.

I spend five minutes longer than usual in the shower. I could kid myself I'm thinking about Ms Rosenberg's disappearance. The truth is, I'm trying to ease the pain from muscles that are all but seized up.

When she hadn't made a seven o'clock meeting with her editor he'd called her hotel. The member of staff who'd answered had refused to bother a guest, but he'd shown a journalist's persistence and had gotten a manager. After a month's free advertising had been discussed, the duty manager had used a passkey to check her room.

Her room was empty apart from a small case, her bag, two notepads and a dicta-phone. The bed was still made as per the hotel's style. A check of the car park had found her car.

The clincher had been a discussion with a night porter who'd seen her making frequent short trips in and out of the hotel. He'd seen her exit around eleven-thirty but hadn't noticed whether or not she'd returned due to dealing with other customers. The porter had figured he'd missed her and that she'd gone to bed.

Chief Watson has ignored the twenty-four hour rule and put out an APB on her.

I agree with his instinct. Her column, in a special late edition of the Gazette, was tantamount to a challenge. A beautifully eloquent piece of writing, it was laden with venomous barbs and even went so far as to question not just the motives, but the manhood of the person masterminding the killings.

It's little surprise she's been targeted – what makes less sense is the time frame. Brian had been out at the fight, as had Kevin and Connor. I don't see how they could have left there, read the article and located Ms Rosenberg in such a short time.

I wonder if I'm wrong about his involvement. That I'm not just barking up the wrong tree, I'm in the wrong forest.

The one tiny positive from this situation, is that we have a chance of doing something proactive now that we have a confirmed disappearance.

More than anything else, the dicta-phone and notepads being left in her room tells me she didn't run off after a story. Even when I'd seen her at dinner the other night, there had been notepads bulging from the bag slung over her shoulder.

I dismiss any ideas of a romantic tryst. She's not the type to engender amorous feelings, let alone run off with someone new at the drop of a hat. According to Alfonse, when Chief Watson had asked the question of the editor he'd been laughed at.

Chapter 75

Ms Rosenberg thrashes at her bindings for perhaps the hundredth time. Like the ninety-nine previous attempts she achieves nothing beyond chafed skin.

She has no idea where she is, other than the fact it's dark, cold and the floor is made of unforgiving concrete.

She moves herself around her tiny cell as best she can with bound hands and feet. It's about eight feet square. Not once does she feel anything that might be a door handle, a ladder or a trapdoor.

Unable to smoke in the hotel room, or open a window far enough to lean out, she'd gone downstairs every half hour to satisfy her craving. As a precaution against being seen, she'd exited a back door and smoked at the edge of the hotel's car park.

On the eleven-thirty visit she'd been approached by a man whose face had never been on the winning side of a fight. He'd smiled at her and glanced at the cigarettes they both held. 'Filthy habit.'

A scream had rang out from the other side of the car park. It had been a girl's voice. The man had run towards the scream and she'd done the same. When she'd rounded a white panel van the man and a bald guy had grabbed her.

They'd bound, gagged and thrown her into the van in less than a minute. As they'd driven off with her lying on the van floor, the bald man had mocked her by replaying the scream from his cell phone.

She's enough of a realist to know she's going to die. Even at her youthful best she'd attracted few admirers, so it's unlikely she's been snatched by rapists. Besides, after the column she had published, there could only be one group who'd choose to abduct her.

All she can hope for is a quick, painless death. She doesn't want to die but knows that, considering how many cigarettes she goes through, she's already cheated the Grim Reaper by making it to her early sixties.

The fact she may have brought on her abduction and eventual murder by writing the article doesn't worry her. Free speech always has a price. Over the years her articles have brought many threats of lawsuits and physical harm. That one will be responsible for her demise is something she's always known could happen. After all, she's spent the last thirty-nine years hiding from the New York mob.

While she doesn't expect to become a martyr, there will be a certain amount of backlash from the media at large when one of their own is targeted.

Nothing engenders communal feelings quite like a shared fear. She knows that, in death, she'll be clasped to industry bosoms in a way quite opposite to how she was treated in life.

With nothing to do but think, she tries to divert her thoughts away from how she'll be killed, to what she can do to assist in the catching of her killers.

Her hands are bound in front of her but she can still move her fingers. If she gets an opportunity, she plans to scratch any of her captors who come within reach. She doesn't expect to hurt them, her aim is to get something under her nails for the coroner to find.

She runs her hands over the floor until she finds a pebble.

It's not easy to write on a wall in the dark using a pebble, but she does what she can. Her words start off describing the two men who abducted her, before morphing into what will be her final article.

Chapter 76

I call Chief Watson as I drive to Alfonse's. He gives basic answers to my questions, making me suspect Gaertner is with him.

This is confirmed when the FBI man comes on the line. He gives me a hard time about the fight until I force a grudged admission from him that he at least now has some suspects to investigate.

He wants me to come in for a full debrief. I tell him that Chief Watson knows everything and hang up.

There's no point in wasting time repeating myself when there's a chance Ms Rosenberg may still be alive.

The coffee in Alfonse's pot is stewed to the consistency of treacle but delivers a welcome hit. I pour him one. His bloodshot eyes are a sure indication he needs the caffeine even more than I do.

'What you thinking, Jake?'

'Everything and nothing. I'm trying to think like the killers. Trying to figure out how they plan to kill her.'

'She's Jewish, right?' He slugs his coffee and pulls a face at the taste. 'They'll gas her.'

'I got that far. The question is how?'

'Simple. They'll bind her hands and feet, toss her in a car and run a hose from the exhaust.'

He's giving voice to thoughts I've already had and dismissed. 'I doubt it. Like you say, it's too simple. It's also not symbolic enough. Every death so far has been a statement. A direct affront to whichever racial or social group they're targeting.' I point to his laptop. 'What does Google have to say about methods used to execute Jews?'

His fingers dance across the keys. Where their usual pace would be a quick-step, exhaustion has slowed them to a waltz.

'There's stoning, burning, slaying and strangling on the first site.'

'We've had stoning and burning. What does it say about the other two?'

He rubs his eyes with the back of his hand. 'Slaying is what they call beheading, which is another we've had. The strangulation is done by burying a person shoulder deep in mud. Two handkerchiefs are tied together, wrapped around the victim's throat and pulled in opposite directions.'

Strangulation has a dramatic sound to it. The biggest flaw is the digging of a hole to put the victim in. Around here the ground is hard and unforgiving. Even a hole big enough to contain the diminutive Ms Rosenberg will entail a couple of hours hard work with a shovel.

'What else you got?'

'The burning is different to the way Darryl and the others were killed. It's much the same as strangulation except the cloths are on fire and, when the victim's mouth opens for air, molten metal is poured down their throat.'

'This sounds more like something Brian would do. It's not what you'd call synonymous with Jews though. We've had to do research to discover the method. Burning crosses, stoning and human heads affixed to wild animals are things most people would know about. As is gassing.' Unable to sit in one place, I pace around the room to help my muscles deal with the stiffness. 'However accurate its historical connections may be, it'll never carry the same association as gassing. I think that's what they'll do.'

'Thought you said a hosepipe through the window wasn't symbolic enough for them?'

I go to pour myself some more coffee then remember its taste and don't bother. 'It's not. But there is more than one way to skin a cat.'

He scowls at the Scottish phrase. 'What you on about?'

'I'm saying, the method the Nazi's used when they killed Jews, was to gas them when they thought they were taking a shower, right?'

'Yeah, but how does that transfer into what we're talking about?' He slaps his forehead in a mock Eureka moment. 'Of course. That's it. You know of some gas chamber the Nazis built. Next you'll be telling me it's only a mile along the road.'

My hand slamming down on the counter makes him jump. 'You're tired, I get that. But instead of ripping it, why don't you listen for a moment? You remember the local make-out places – specifically that place down the forty-five, across the river?'

His eyes widen. 'You mean the former military place?'

'Yeah. That's the one. We've got a Jewish person lined up as the next victim, an abandoned military bunker and some twisted killers. What do you think is going to happen?'

'Dammit, you're right.'

I'm already calling the chief as he speaks.

The chief listens, then puts Gaertner on the line again. He too listens to my theory.

When I put the cell in my pocket I have very little respect left for the FBI man. It's one thing him disagreeing with my theory – I could even stand a chuckle – but to be laughed at, and called a stupid fanciful idiot, takes the biscuit.

'You still got that tracker in my phone?'

'Yeah.'

'Well if it stops moving for more than twenty minutes, send the police and the FBI to wherever I am. I'll be in trouble.' I'm moving towards the door so he can't waste time trying to stop me. 'Check wherever you need to check and get me the coordinates for every abandoned bunker or building around here. You've got ten minutes before I'm out of signal.'

Chapter 77

The Mustang growls as I hurtle south along the forty-five. On the seat to my right, my cell is beeping as a series of emails come in. I guess they're from Alfonse. If I know him, he'll be sending each set of coordinates as he discovers them. I don't like the number of beeps it's making.

I pass over the Green River at twice the speed limit, with no idea of what I'm going to do when I arrive at my destination.

There are at least three killers, four if Young David is involved. Brian has a shotgun, I have fists and feet. The odds of me having a cell signal to call for help are slim to non-existent.

None of these negatives are enough to make me turn back. The more I think about Ms Rosenberg becoming their next victim, the angrier I become.

I round a corner and stamp on the gas once more. A Winnebago trundles along in front of me. As soon as we round the next corner, I drop two gears and rocket past the Winnebago. The driver flips me off as I pass.

Now I've crossed the Green River, I have to slow down. Where the exact location of every make-out spot was once committed to memory, time has blurred things for me. My recollection is vague and I have to look for familiar markers.

In-keeping with the base's secretive nature, it was never sign-posted.

I have to stand on the brakes when I do spot the right turning. A haul on the wheel steers me onto the new road where I feather the gas until the Mustang's rear straightens out.

A mile later, asphalt becomes gravel. Perhaps the military budget ran out when they got this far. More probable is that they hoped the lack of a decent roadway would prevent inquisitive visitors.

Another mile on is a sweeping bend the width of an interstate. It's here where all the parking takes place. If the number of used condoms littering the gravel are any indication— it's still a popular spot.

I push fond memories aside and fight to keep the balance between speed and control. A powerful rear-wheel drive Mustang is not designed for gravel roads. Every bend sees the rear step out in an effort to pass the front.

If the reason for my journey wasn't so important, I'd be enjoying the continuous sideways motion. Instead, the reduced traction is nothing more than an irritating delay.

The gates of the former military installation hang from their hinges. Beyond them, gravel returns to asphalt as the road continues to the actual base.

Two minutes after my tyres leave the gravel, they ease to a stop. I'm no special forces commando with years of training, but I know rescue attempts from armed captors are best conducted without announcing your arrival. The grumbling exhaust of the Mustang does a fine job of impressing pretty girls. It's not so good at stealth.

I get out and search the trunk for something I can use as a weapon. I'm looking under the spare for a tyre iron when I see the gun my mother gave me. If I was twenty years younger I'd facepalm. Instead I curse.

Half-forgotten instructions on how to use the pistol flicker through my mind as I pull it from its hiding place, check it's loaded, and stuff it into the back of my jeans.

Three paces towards the first building and it's in my hand.

As I search the deserted buildings, every action thriller I've read, or seen at the movies, has me peeking round corners and holding the gun at my chest with the barrel pointing upwards. When I round the corners the gun is extended in a two-handed grip. I'm not convinced I'd get a commendation from a drill sergeant, but it makes me feel safer to know I'm ready to shoot when I could encounter shotgun-wielding killers at any moment.

Every room, every corner or closet I examine is empty of life. There's plenty of human detritus left behind. Food packaging, soda cans and other litter abandoned by campers or partying youths decorates the floor in each room.

Not once do I encounter a door that hasn't been kicked in and left to hang on its hinges or lie where it landed.

Fifteen minutes after searching the first building I'm scrolling through emails. The number of beeps I heard was worrying, but I'm happy to find that most of them are junk or unconnected.

Alfonse has sent me two. I work out which of the abandoned bases is nearest and run back to my car.

Chapter 78

Ms Rosenberg lifts her head when she hears scraping. Light pours into her prison, forcing her to look away as her retinas contract.

Three men and a callow youth walk in.

Using what she can by way of speed and surprise, she throws herself forward and tries to claw at the nearest face.

She's a foot away from the bald man's face when he grabs her wrists. No matter how much she tries to wriggle, so her nails can collect that vital evidence, he thwarts her.

The handsome man stands back while the others help the bald man chain her to a hook in the ceiling. He's the obvious leader of the group.

It's him she addresses. 'Why have you got me here? You won't get away with this you know.' Her every instinct is telling her not to antagonise these men but she can't prevent herself. Deep inside, she knows they're going to kill her. If she can't stop them, the least she can do is harangue their worthless hides. 'You claim you're Christians. You'll spend an eternity in hell for what you've done.'

'I'd rather meet Beelzebub himself than live in a world where niggers, Jews and faggots infest every street. The United States of America was founded by brave men who followed the Lord's word. Not the lowlifes who're now usurping everything that once made this country great.'

Something about the man is familiar to Ms Rosenberg. A former story comes back to her – along with the man's name. 'You're Richard Anderson: your wife burned down your house.'

The man delivers a heavy slap to her right cheek. 'Leave her out of this. My name is Brian now.'

'Call yourself what you want. Your wife had mental health issues, didn't she?' Ms Rosenberg draws herself up as high as her bindings will allow. Whatever happens, she's determined not to show any fear. 'Was she your first victim?'

'I told you to leave her out of this.' Brian's hand wraps around Ms Rosenberg's throat.

She glares up at him. 'Why, who are you afraid I'm going to tell?'

He laughs and releases her. Takes a step back and brings himself back under control. She can see him working out whether he should continue talking to her.

It's an effort, but she manages to keep the fear from her voice. 'You said to leave her out of this. Is that because you feel guilty for killing her?'

'She's not dead. At least, not what society considers dead.' Ms Rosenberg detects sadness in his tone. 'I didn't kill Penelope. She's alive, but she might as well not be. She lives in an institution over at Salt Lake.'

'Is she ill, or was she hurt?' Somehow she manages to achieve a gentle tone. It's bad enough that she's going to die. To die without getting answers to her questions would be unbearable.

'Neither. Her mind went when that nigger bitch turned her down. Now she just sits there rocking.' His eyes flash as ancient hurt is exhumed. 'My beautiful, funny wife now spends her days either rocking in a corner or staring at her hands and crying. And it's all because she was turned down by that nigger bitch.'

Ms Rosenberg stays quiet for moment, then speaks in the softest tone she can manage. 'I don't understand. Why did the nigger bitch turn her down?' The derogatory terms offend her, but it's important that she connects with Brian on his wavelength.

'Penelope applied for a bank loan. The nigger bitch refused. Said Penelope would never manage the repayments. That her business plan didn't account for seasonal variations in prices.' The explosion of anger Ms Rosenberg expects doesn't come. Instead his voice falls to a whisper. 'She didn't have any faith in my Penelope.'

Again Ms Rosenberg lets silence fill the room. It doesn't take her long to recall that Sherrelle Fournier worked for a bank. After that, it's just a question of joining the dots.

'Why kill others and not just her? You're not a stupid man, you know it's not gays or Asians or Jews who turned down your wife. I guess you know the banks have criteria that potential loanees have to meet. The nigger bitch would have just been doing her job.' She knows there's little chance her words will affect his thinking, but she's willing to try anything that may just save her life.

Behind Brian she can see the two other men carrying in some kind of portable engine in a tubular metal frame. There are plug sockets on one side of it.

When she recognises it as a portable generator, she begins to tremble as fear makes her muscles judder. Her imagination is depicting a hundred and one power tools being used against her body.

Brian squints, then stoops to read what she's written on the wall. When he straightens, there's amusement on his face. 'Very good. I always did like your columns. You have an excellent way with words. The one you wrote last night was quite possibly your best.' He picks up a stone and scores out part of her writing. 'You'll understand how I'd rather your descriptions of my colleagues aren't left for the police to find.'

Ms Rosenberg finds his urbane nature unsettling. He's praising her writing while preparing to kill her. 'Then why have you brought me here?' She licks her lips and asks the question she most dreads the answer to. 'You are planning to kill me, aren't you?'

He smiles as he checks her bindings. 'You're here because you're the most high-profile Jew in the area. It's nothing personal. Only the nigger bitch's death was personal. Like you, the others were only chosen because they made the best victims.'

An abstract part of Ms Rosenberg's brain can follow his logic. The Asian girl with a pretty face, the well-known and respected ex-cop, the Mexican whose death could be made to contribute to their publicity campaign, and now her – a local journalist.

Every one of their deaths would speak to a different section of the community.

Another question pops into her head. 'How did you know where to find me?'

'I've been following you for the last two days. I knew you were staying at the hotel because I saw you put a case into the trunk of your car. I also knew you'd have to come outside for a smoke at some point during the night.'

Ms Rosenberg's head droops forward. She'd been chosen before writing the column; before it hit the newsstands.

The bald man approaches Brian. 'That's everything ready.'

Brian moves across to the generator. He bends over and gives the starter cord a strong pull. The engine fires first time, rumbles and then settles into a gentle putter.

From her position against the wall, Ms Rosenberg can see its controls. There are a pair of levers she guesses will control the throttle and possibly the fuel mixture. A red knob provides the on/off switch.

Ms Rosenberg's shakes worsen as she tries to keep the fear from her voice. 'What, no last cigarette?'

Brian laughs as he walks to the door. 'I don't think that's such a good idea.'

The door whispers as he pushes it to. As the light fades, it dawns on Ms Rosenberg how she'll be killed.

The fumes from the generator's exhaust are pulling at her eyes within a minute. She can taste them when she breathes. Her stomach heaves as the room starts to spin.

Not that it's in any way reassuring to her, but she knows carbon monoxide poisoning isn't the worst way to die. If it was, a lot fewer people would run a hose from their tailpipe.

As her chest tightens, silent tears run down her cheeks as she prepares for nothingness. Her last conscious thoughts are of Halvard. His smile. The way his arms would encircle her body. His laugh.

Chapter 79

The Red Wash Road isn't much of a road. The one thing it does have going for it is its destination.

It comes out at Jensen which means it's going pretty much where I want it to. The nearest former military base is along the forty. According to Alfonse's email, it's backed up against the Stuntz Ridge.

A heavily loaded semi chugs along in front of me, its driver creeping over the road just far enough to stop me passing. I flash my lights and give him a blast on the horn.

He moves over two feet. To his left. Any chance I have of passing him is cut off.

I bob right and try undertaking but he sees me coming. His blocking manoeuvre causes me to stand on the brakes.

He's treading a fine line. If I didn't have such an urgent mission, I'd follow him until he stopped and spend a moment or two shortening his nose.

I drop a gear, feint left, then duck right when he moves to block me. As soon as I've gone right, I weave left again and stamp on the gas. By the time he's realised his error I'm alongside his cab and travelling too fast for him to risk blocking me.

With him out of the way I can open the taps on the Mustang and get into three-figure territory.

Either side of the narrow road the scrub dissolves into a continuous green sludge as the bushes flash past my windows.

I get to Jensen and swing right onto the Forty.

While it's in much better condition, and wider than the Red Wash Road, it's also a lot busier.

Even while driving along, I'm thinking about why there are so many military bases in the middle of nowhere. I can understand them being near borders, or veritable targets such as Fort Knox, but why there would be three within an hour's drive of Casperton, is beyond me. For all I can imagine there would be a need for cold war monitoring stations and training centres, I still don't see the need for so many in such an empty area.

As I duck and weave between traffic, I keep a constant eye out for police speed traps. My cell is propped in a holder stuck to the dash. The GPS tells me that I have a half mile to go before I reach my turn.

When I leave the Forty, the road I join is a half-step above being a dirt track. It's twice the width of my car and is under encroachment from the scrub and rubble at either side.

None of these obstacles are enough for me to temper my speed. I'm working on the theory that anything coming towards me will be raising the same amount of dust I can see in my rear-view mirror.

When the GPS says I'm a mile from my destination, I ease off the gas and slow to the speed limit. Once again, I don't want to announce my arrival.

When I get within a half mile, I give the engine just enough gas to stop it from stalling.

Chapter 80

Even as I approach the base, I get a sense of foreboding. There are tracks in the road ahead of me where there shouldn't be any. Either I'm at the right place, or the military are still keeping an eye on it.

As soon as I see the rusted chain link fence, I pull over.

Behind the fence is a plethora of temporary wooden buildings jutting from the bottom of a cliff face. Each is around a hundred feet long and they are uniform in their appearance. There are rows of windows and metal chimneys at regular intervals.

Time, rather than vandals, has worn these once proud structures. Now they sag and droop where aged timber has been affected by the elements.

I'd guess at them being barracks if it wasn't for the lack of a parade ground, or any kind of sports field.

I get to twenty then stop counting. It doesn't matter how many huts there are. I will have to search them all until I either find Ms Rosenberg, or prove she's not here.

A set of tyre prints go through the gate and turn right. When I pass through the gates I notice the rusted padlock has a fresh cut through it.

I check my cell to find it lacking a signal. The only thing I can do with it is lay it against a gatepost and wait until its lack of movement prompts Alfonse to summon backup.

As I walk between the tyre marks, I notice one of the huts is constructed from bricks rather than timber. My immediate assumption is that it's the former officers' quarters.

A sign on the end of the building changes my mind. Underneath every line of English words are a row of symbols. I don't know their meaning, but guess they are an Asian translation of English instructions.

Their presence tells me that this isn't an army barracks. It's a former internment camp. Rather than spend money decommissioning it, the army have left it to rot because it's not in a place frequented by large swathes of the populace.

The tracks in the dust swerve towards what I thought were the officers' quarters, but are more likely to have been the guards' barracks.

I cross to the side of the nearest building and peek round the corner at the guards' barracks. I'm looking for movement inside the building; a change in light values when someone passes a window.

There isn't one so I creep across until I have my back against the barracks. Every sense in my body is heightened as I hear the murmur of voices. A whiff of rotting wood and decay fills my nose, but so does the pungent odour of a cigar.

I manoeuvre until I have an eye at the corner of the nearest window. The glass has half a century of grime covering it, but I can see enough to know there's no-one in the room I'm looking into.

My feet are placed with caution as I pad to the other end of the gable. Taking great care I inch my head across, bringing more and more of the space between this building and the next into view. Every muscle I possess is tensed, ready to snap me back to the cover of the building if I see someone.

The first thing I spot is a white panel van. It's too far away for me to read the licence plate, but the fact it's jacked up and parked next to a pickup truck identical to the one belonging to the Jones family is all I need.

It's decision time. I can go back and raise the alarm. Get every cop, FBI agent and state trooper in the area to descend on this place with their training and superior firearms. Or, I can play the hero, attempt a one-man rescue mission. I have a gun in my hand but I'm not sure I could point it at another man and pull the trigger.

If I knew Ms Rosenberg's life status, or had a cell signal, the decision would be a damn sight easier. The fact she can be killed at any moment, and her killers can escape along any one of the dozen tracks I'd passed on the way here, makes going for help appear selfish and cowardly.

The counterpoint to this is, there's nothing to be gained by me throwing my life away on a suicide mission.

I grip the gun in my hand a little tighter and think about putting a bullet into the front tyres on both vehicles. The idea is dismissed almost as soon as it registers. To be sure of hitting the target I'd have to get a lot closer. Plus, four gunshots are bound to summon, Brian and whichever members of the Jones family are with him.

Whatever my decision is to be, I know I need to make a choice and act upon it. I risk another peek around the corner.

The decision is made for me. Young David is now leaning against the pickup smoking. He sees me and lets out a yell.

I wheel round the corner aiming my gun at him. 'Freeze.'

He does. I'm not confident I could shoot him at this distance but at least I have one of them somewhat under my control.

'Down on the ground. Now.'

I find myself looking at Young David, through tunnel vision, over the sights of a shaking gun. Aware it could get me killed, I refocus my eyes so I'm looking at the whole alleyway.

Adrenaline floods my body. A coppery taste fills my mouth.

Shouts fill the silent air as the other killers react to my shouting at Young David. Kevin appears from behind the van; a shotgun held at his waist.

I see him find me and adjust his aim.

I'm back cowering behind the bricks of the barracks by the time he pulls the trigger. Lead pellets strike the wall but rebound away from me. If this was an action movie, the hero would dive out from cover and put three well aimed bullets into Kevin, before landing in a controlled roll, allowing him to drop any other combatants with a headshot.

It's not an action movie and I've never shot a gun beyond a rough practise with tin cans. Doing anything like that will result in several wasted bullets and one wasted life. Mine.

Kevin blasts away with the shotgun a second time. Perhaps he's under the mistaken impression I'm some kind of action hero.

As long as he's shooting at a place where I'm not, I'm happy. He's wasting ammunition with every shot he fires. At some point he'll have to reload which may be the only chance I get.

The issue there is that I don't know what type of shotgun he has, let alone how many cartridges it holds. To slow his progress towards me, I fire a shot round the corner.

Unless he's on top of the next building it has no chance of hitting him, but it'll give me chance to check none of his fellow killers are trying to flank me.

They're not.

This tells me one vital thing. The shotgun is the only real weapon they have.

Kevin fires another three shots while I'm checking my rear. That's five he's used.

I could now double back round the building and try to flank the others. The problem with that is I'll need to take either one of them hostage, and put a gun to their head, to persuade Kevin to lay down the shotgun. That means catching Brian or Young David without getting caught myself. There's also the chance Connor is around too.

One or two may be ambushable, but not three. I fire another shot, this time from a lower position. My aim is more threatening and, while I don't hear the thwack of a bullet hitting flesh, I hear Kevin curse before he pulls the trigger twice more.

I hear him rack the slide a third time. There's a faint click. The racking sound comes again as he searches for another cartridge. It clicks again.

I step round the corner and point my gun at him. 'You're out of ammo. Throw it away and lie on the ground.'

He's ten feet away. Even with my lack of gunmanship, I'm confident I can hit him at this distance.

Kevin complies with my demands with a deliberate slowness. When he's laid out on the ground I grab the shotgun and, using my left hand to hold the stock, swing it in a vicious arc so the barrel smashes into the sharp brick corner of the building. The barrel kinks as the reverberation shakes the shotgun from my hand. Even if they have extra ammo, the shotgun is now out of action.

I'm now at a crossroads; I have nothing to bind Kevin with, and I'm not convinced the others will give themselves up if I put my gun to his head. If captured by the police and FBI, they'll be looking at life imprisonment or Death Row.

A movement off to my left catches the corner of my eye. It's Young David, he must have circled the next building along to ambush me. His hands are empty but he lifts the shotgun and holds it like a bat.

'Drop it.' I wave my gun at him, indicating he should join Kevin. 'Do it. Now.'

He stands defiant until I point my gun at him.

I'm covering him and Kevin when I hear the insistent thudding of heavy footsteps. I whirl round just as Connor launches himself at me.

Somehow I keep a grip on the gun as we crash to the ground. I'm on top, but Connor wraps one hand around my right wrist and the other around my throat.

The gun is pointing at nothingness so I keep squeezing the trigger until the bullets are all spent. I'd rather the gun is empty in case I surrender the weapon to their control.

I drive my left fist into the inside of Connor's right armpit. The blow causes him to release my throat. I follow with a couple of lefts to his jaw. They're not as hard as I'd like due to him twisting beneath me. A third blow sees his fingers slacken on my right wrist.

Young David slams the butt of the shotgun into my back as I'm rolling off Connor. It lands on the same rib Crusher kicked last night.

I scramble to my feet in time to duck under Young David's next swing. As he has the weapon he's the most dangerous foe at the moment – if not the most intelligent.

His swing of the shotgun is so powerful, the lack of contact with me twists his body. With both hands on the shotgun he can't defend himself. An uppercut drops him in a heap at my feet.

I whip round and catch a right cross from Kevin on the side of my head. Connor is at his side. Both of them throwing punches in wild flurries.

I make sure not to trip over Young David's prostrate body as I retreat backwards. With my arms busy defending my head, I have only my feet left for attack.

As I back off from them, I'm sidestepping so Kevin has to move round Connor to get at me. My first kick misses, but the second connects with the bottom of Connor's left kneecap with enough force to tear cartilage and break bone.

He falls, clutching his knee with both hands. Pained screams replace the curses he's been uttering.

Kevin lands a body shot on my already damaged ribs. It's an effort to not double-up but, somehow, I manage.

His next shot lands on my cheek, before another body shot is thrown. This time I can't stop myself doubling over. He's too dumb to lift a knee into my face, and instead aims his blows at the back of my head.

I let out a scream of pain as I swing a vicious right at his crotch. Kevin drops to his knees, both hands cradling his damaged groin. I take a half step back, straighten up, and introduce the toe of my right boot to his chin.

He goes down. Hard. All three of the Jones family lay around my feet as I look round expecting Brian to join the fight.

Chapter 81

My gaze finds Brian sitting on the hood of the Jones' pickup. He's relaxed, casual, as he slides to the ground. I pick up the shotgun. His confidence as he approaches me is unnerving. He stops, pulls two knives from his belt, and tosses one towards me. It lands point first a foot in front of my toes and sticks in the loose dirt.

'You man enough, Boulder?'

I've never liked anyone who's challenged me. People who lay down challenges always have something to prove. Brian has seen me fight. Not just last night, but here today. He'll know my strengths and my weaknesses. I don't have a clue about his.

Another reason I don't care for people challenging me, is the fact that I'm self-aware enough to know I'm the kind of macho asshole who never backs down. Especially from bullies trying to get their own way through verbal challenges.

'One moment.' I don't wait for him to answer me. Instead, I bring the butt of the shotgun down on the left ankle of each of his three accomplices. 'I don't want anyone knocking my brains in from behind.'

I throw the shotgun off to one side and pull the knife from the ground. It's a hunting knife with a sharp blade and serrations on the back.

Even as we face off, I'm thinking about how Alfonse wanted me to kill the man responsible for killing his cousin. Now I'm locked into a knife fight with the person behind the heinous killings, I'm still not convinced I have the right to take another life.

That Brian deserves to die, is a given. His actions mean he's not fit to live in a decent society. By the time the world calms down from the anger his incitement has caused, there will be many more deaths than the ones he's orchestrated.

The nature of the kills is another reason he should be removed from the living. His victims would have died screaming. Not a quick and painless death for them. Instead they endured a slow, agonising demise at the hands of a monster.

I can't say I have the right to act as his judge, jury and executioner. All I know is, Brian deserves to meet the last of the three.

This knife fight is his idea, he wants to best me in single combat to prove his manhood to himself. He wants to kill me. I want him to die, but would rather the state appointed the person who ends his wretched life.

The counterbalance to this, is the way he's promoting his message on social media. To similar thinkers he'll be a champion for their cause. They'll rally to his side and protest outside courtrooms – raise money to fund his defence.

He's urbane enough to come across well in a courtroom. His poisonous rhetoric will be scribbled down by every journalist present and broadcast to the world. More innocents will die if he is given a platform to spread his vile opinions.

Brian gives a wicked grin and steps forward, his knife held in a backhand grip in his left hand.

I do the same but hold the knife in my right.

As he comes at me, he moves into a martial arts style crouch. Not good.

I fake a few wild slashes to see what he makes of them. The action also gives me a chance to rotate my upper body and find out just what damage has been done to my ribs.

They're sore as all hell but I don't think they're damaged beyond a crack.

Brian laughs at me. 'You ain't fooling me with them wild slashes, Boulder. I know you're better'n that. Saw you wince though. Your ribs hurtin'?'

His voice is more country than I'd expected.

He lunges at me and gives a flashing backhand swing from waist to shoulder.

I dance backwards, but in one move he's shown his speed. There was no time to counterattack as he moved away before I had chance to react.

Brian feints another sweeping diagonal attack, then throws a right foot into my bruised ribs while I'm off balance from my dodge. It sends me stumbling backwards, but the rush of adrenaline numbs the pain of his blow.

Instead of waiting for him to come at me, I advance – my knife hand weaving at the wrist.

I feint a slash to gauge the speed of his reactions. He's quick.

I try again, only this time I follow the feint with an attack. Brian counters by slamming another kick into my ribs.

It's a favoured move of his. The problem with favoured moves is once you know your opponents, you can use them to your advantage.

He comes forward, the knife in his hand slashing towards my face. I take a half step back and when he launches the kick to my ribs, I'm ready for him. I catch his leg and trap it against my body, making sure to lift it high enough to unbalance him without landing him on his back.

Brian thwarts my attempt to cut his Achilles tendon by kicking his standing foot at my head, forcing me to use my knife arm to defend myself.

Even as he's falling to the ground he's kicking out with his free leg. I slash at the leg and manage a superficial cut along his shin. Rather than have him stamp against my kneecaps, I drop his other leg and take a half step back.

The distance keeps me out of reach while also allowing me room to aim my own kick. The toe of my boot connects with his ankle. He grunts rather than yelps.

I repeat the kick but he rolls away and rises to his feet. Some bounce has gone from his step due to the injuries to his right leg, but they are too minor to have a telling effect.

He throws a punch and follows it with a slash of the knife. I feel the sting of his blade across my chest. My ribs stop the diagonal cut going deep, but blood soaks my shirt in seconds.

His next move opens a two-inch gash on my left forearm.

He lunges forward with cold steel flashing towards me. I parry the blow, knocking his knife arm high and wide. My left fist connects with the side of his head, but it's not the best punch I've ever thrown.

As he disengages, his knife stabs down into my shoulder. Pain shoots through me as the tip of his knife scrapes on bone. He's trying to draw it towards my neck where it can pierce soft flesh. I escape by dropping to the ground.

A thrust of my right arm towards his groin sees him draw back. An ugly cut on his thigh wells scarlet, but it's little more than an inch long.

So far our knives have drawn blood five times. His two wounds combined aren't as bad as any one of mine.

I need to shift the momentum of this fight but don't know how to. Accepting his challenge was an act of stupidity. I should have kept hold of the gun and used its longer reach to ward off his attacks. Instead, I let him choose the rules of the fight.

He catches the flick of my eyes as I search for the shotgun. Smiles. 'You should have kept hold of the gun, shouldn't you? You're losing. Don't worry, I'll take my time. Once your fight's gone, I'll peel you a little. Perhaps I'll keep peeling until you beg me to kill you.'

I'm expecting the lunge which comes at the end of his sentence. I've been in enough fights not to get taken by surprise anymore.

Instead of blocking him outside my body, I swipe his knife arm inwards as I wheel round him. The blood that has run from the cut on my left forearm makes my grip slippery, but I hold his wrist long enough to run my blade along the inside of his elbow.

I could have stuck him in the kidneys, but some primeval element of my psyche wants him to taste his own medicine. Choking on it would be better.

He yelps and drops his knife. The lower part of his left arm hangs useless as he spins away from me.

For the first time I see fear in his eyes. He backs away. As he goes, he's trying, and failing, to regain control of his arm.

I advance on him. Momentum has swung my way. A slash at him slices open his bicep. He counters with a hard right to my ribs. Breathing becomes difficult as he sidesteps around me and delivers a hard elbow to my head.

I whirl round to see him lifting the knife with his right hand. His grip is orthodox as he leads with his right foot like a fencer.

He's making wild slashes as he comes forward. I retreat; happy to wait for a safe opportunity; happy to let him tire himself out.

He puts in a quick step and stabs the knife forward.

I twist left and counter-stab as I back off. Steel collides with steel rather than flesh.

Brian pushes forward with a mixture of stabs and slashes. All thoughts of making me suffer must have been cast aside in a desire to kill me before I kill him.

Not sharing his urgent desire to kill, I keep myself out of harm's way.

It's a mistake. He's not been trying to get a quick kill. He's been steering me in a set direction.

A muscled arm snakes around my throat. Squeezes.

I'd stab the arm in a heartbeat if I didn't need the knife to keep Brian at bay.

With my eyes kept on Brian I throw my right heel backwards. It strikes bone.

I repeat the kick until I feel the grip on my neck loosen. I drop the knife, put two hands on the muscled arm, and fall to my knees twisting as I go. Connor Jones rolls over my shoulder and crashes into Brian's feet. There's a pained yelp as his broken ankle twists beneath him.

There's no way of knowing Connor's agony as he clambered from a prone position to stand on his one good leg to set the trap I've just fallen into. It doesn't matter. For his part in events, he deserves nothing but suffering and pain.

When I rise to my feet, I'm once again holding the knife in a backhand grip. Brian is upon me before I have time to set myself. Steel flashes and he opens a wound on my left bicep as I slash at his chest.

Connor's hand grasps my ankle and I fall backwards.

Brian follows me down. His left elbow slams into my face. The forearm still loose and uncontrolled.

My right arm is trapped between our bodies.

I manage to get my left hand onto his right wrist. He's pushing down. His knife three inches from my eye.

His weight is pinning my body. Pushing down on the knife.

Two inches.

Neither of us are using our dominant arm, though he's able to put his shoulder behind the knife.

One inch.

He smiles as he senses victory. Stale garlic pollutes his breath.

I twist my right hand and punch upwards. His eyes widen, and the pressure on his knife hand lessens, as my blade pierces his heart.

Pink bubbles decorate his lips only to be replaced with crimson ones.

I push him off my chest and leave him to gurgle. My knife protrudes from his chest so I lift his from where it dropped.

Young David is a moaning heap of undeserved self-pity.

His eyes snap open when he feels steel pressed against flesh. 'Where is Ms Rosenberg?'

If the ominous threat in my voice is a surprise to him, it's a shock to me.

Young David presses himself into the earth as if he can burrow away from the knife at his throat. 'The journalist?' I nod. 'She's in a fridge at the end of the building.'

I resist the temptation to punch him and stagger off towards the door of the guards' barracks.

Chapter 82

Drops of my blood leave a trail as I stumble towards the door of the guards' barracks. Some are larger than others and some are halfway to becoming clots.

I go up the three steps and burst into a hallway. To my left is a dormitory, a sign above the door to my right says 'Kitchen'.

The door is stiff. Aged hinges creak as I force it open. Everything smells dank. Dust motes that I've disturbed float across the beams of sunlight which manage to fight their way through the dirt on the windows.

A low rumble fills the air. It's the steady sound of an engine running a few beats above idle.

I cross the kitchen – past the old units, abandoned cookers and the serving hatch.

As soon as I haul the fridge door open, I cough and choke on the fumes that pour out to attack my senses. My eyes water as I peer into the fridge.

Ms Rosenberg is slumped against one wall. A chain through her bound wrists secures her to a hook screwed into the ceiling.

There's a portable generator in a corner. Its engine the source of the rumble; its exhaust the source of the fumes.

All this information is absorbed and processed in a fraction of a second. I screw my mouth tight and step forward.

I don't know whether she's alive or dead, but I do know she has to be removed from this fume-laden environment if she has any chance of survival. I stride to the generator, knock it off, then put my fingertips to Ms Rosenberg's throat.

I might be wrong. It might be wishful thinking, but I convince myself of a faint throb. Slight as she is, her unconsciousness makes her a dead weight as I lift her high enough to allow me to release the chain from the hook.

When she's free, I get her in a fireman's lift and rush outside.

I lay Ms Rosenberg down in the fresh air and look at her. Her eyes are closed, her lips are blue and there's not so much as the slightest hint of movement. She's covered in blood, but it's mine not hers. My wounds haven't stopped leaking just because I'm trying to save someone else's life.

There's no doubt she'll have carbon monoxide poisoning after being enclosed in such a small space with a running engine. I don't know how to treat it though.

Should I administer mouth-to-mouth to drive fresher, purer air into her lungs, or should I let the poison work its own way out of her system?

I check her pulse again. This time I'm less sure of its presence.

Again, I become stricken with indecision. Should I administer CPR or go for help? She'll be dead for sure by the time I return with help but, in my current bloody and weakened state, I won't be able to maintain the necessary treatment for more than a half hour without collapsing from exhaustion.

The wail of a police siren in the distance makes my decision for me.

I draw a huge breath into my lungs and blow it into her mouth.

When Chief Watson's truck roars into view I'm on my tenth repetition of chest compressions.

He jumps out and runs to the back of his truck. He reappears with a medical kit and what I hope is a portable defibrillator. A deputy appears from the passenger side.

'She's been gassed.' My words come between pants as I continue with the compressions.

The chief shoulders me out of the way, rips open her clothes and applies two pads to her chest. The pads are connected to the defibrillator by thin wires. He presses a button on the machine and her body jerks.

I check for a pulse then draw my hand back. 'Again.'

He does as I bid.

She doesn't respond.

Three more times we try.

Three more failures.

We look at each other and, in unison, stop our efforts at resuscitation.

The chief removes the pads from her chest, and I try to preserve her decency by fastening the buttons not ripped off by the chief's hurried efforts to get the pads onto her skin.

I look round as another vehicle approaches. It's Alfonse. After summoning the police he must have raced over here. I'm not sure how he planned to help, but I'm glad he's tried to come to my aid.

He runs across as soon as he sees me. Worry etched into his face. 'Are you okay?'

'I'm fine. It's just a lot of little cuts.'

The chief steps between us, gestures at the two dead bodies and the cursing Jones family. 'Want to tell me what went down here, Boulder?'

'These are the guys who've been killing people because of their skin colour, religion or sexuality.' I point to the barracks. 'Ms Rosenberg is their latest victim. They imprisoned her in an old fridge with a running generator.'

Chapter 83

I awaken to a nightmare of stiffness. Every part of my upper body aches. The bandages and dressings applied to my various wounds itch as well as restrict what little movement protesting muscles allow.

'Do you want some coffee?'

It's Taylor. Her voice as sweet and melodic as ever.

'Yeah please. Time is it?'

'Twenty after one.'

The light pouring through the window tells me I've slept for twelve hours solid – even if my body thinks otherwise.

The events of yesterday descend into a blur after the point where Alfonse arrived at the former detention centre.

I have vague memories of deputies having to restrain Alfonse from kicking Connor and Kevin while a paramedic fussed over me. Alfonse and the chief had bundled me into an ambulance once my various cuts were attended to.

Gaertner had been waiting for me at the hospital. He fired question after question at me as a doctor stitched me back together.

At some point Alfonse and Taylor appeared at the hospital. There was something of a disagreement when I left the hospital, but all I can remember about it was a determination to come home.

I remember failing to save Ms Rosenberg. Perhaps she'd still be alive if I'd driven there a bit faster, or shot Kevin instead of aiming wide, and claimed the shotgun. Letting myself get drawn into a macho situation by Brian had wasted minutes which could have made the difference. If I'd known first aid a little better, I may have been able to save her. Whichever way I look at it, I find I've made mistakes which could have been the difference between life and death.

Taylor puts a mug of coffee on the bedside table and drops a straw into it.

I lift the mug and am about to launch the straw across the room when I realise how much pain it'll save me.

'You're due two more of these.' Taylor rattles a pill bottle.

'Don't want them.'

'Cut the crap, Jake. You're lucky to be alive. Every movement you make hurts you. Why aren't you taking something for the pain?'

'I need to keep my wits clear.'

'What do you mean, keep your wits clear? You've solved the case. Disabled three sick killers and killed another. It's over, Jake. You've won.'

'Pass me my cell, will you?'

She frowns but hands it over. I show it to her. 'You see all these messages and missed calls? I'm willing to bet at least three quarters of them are my mother. She'll have heard about what happened and will want to tell me how stupid I am. I'm not engaging in a battle of wits with her at anything less than full strength.'

'You're scared of your mom?' Taylor dissolves into fits of giggles. 'That's priceless. Jake Boulder, the rough tough hero who keeps chasing killers is frightened of his mommy. Who is this matriarch and what makes her so scary?'

If her peals of laughter weren't so musical I might fall out with her. I'm not in the mood for levity.

'Don't laugh. We're having dinner with her and my stepfather on Friday.'

It's not the smooth way I had planned on telling her about the meeting, but it's fitting revenge for her mocking laughter.

'We are?' She leans over and kisses my forehead. 'Thank you.'

'You won't be thanking me after Friday night. You'll be ditching me for someone whose mother isn't an interfering narcissist.'

My words and tone are deliberately gruff. It's my way of stopping myself from saying the three words I want to say to her. So often when those words have been said to me, and I haven't reciprocated them, I've seen pain. Not the kind of pain prescribed drugs can fix. The kind only time and love can heal.

I'm not sure if I can face the pain of her responding to me with any other answer than 'I love you too'.

'Nonsense. Now just you lay back and let me take care of you.'

Chapter 84

It's dark when Alfonse draws up outside the Tree. The usual Sunday night crowd are hanging outside – smoking, laughing and filling the air with enough bullshit to give a horticulturist a wet dream.

Taylor skips ahead to get the door and Alfonse leads the way, making sure no-one bumps or barges into me. He's perhaps the smallest blocker I've known, but his heart's in the right place and I'm grateful for his help.

John is waiting for us in a quiet booth near the back of the room, his face pale and grave. The bottle on the table in front of him is sparkling water. Perhaps he too has issues with alcohol.

We go through the usual small talk greetings until Alfonse and Taylor make their excuses and leave us to it.

'You've come a long way to find me, John. Other than a desire to fill out another branch of the family tree, what brings you here?'

The question is a lot less polite than he deserves, or I intend, but I'm tired, sore and more than a little pissed at myself for not saving Ms Rosenberg.

He looks nervous. Like he's about to ask for something he's not going to get.

If it's money he's after, he's asking the wrong man. Other than the money I won betting on myself, I have little more than a month's salary to my name and I've already earmarked the sixty thousand I won for a children's hospice in Salt Lake.

'What is it, what do you want from me? If it's money you're out of luck.'

'It's no' money. I've got plenty o' that.' Nerves are thickening his Scottish accent.

'What is it then?'

'I've got leukaemia.' A lick of the lips. 'I need a bone marrow transplant.'

My bad temper evaporates as I digest this news. All of a sudden my long-lost, unknown-about half-brother is about to be snatched away from me before I get to know him.

The reason for his visit becomes obvious. Common sense tells me that bone marrow isn't something you can donate like blood so it can be stored until needed. He'll need to find a family member who's a match for whatever element needs to be matched.

I may well be wrong with my assumptions but they explain his presence here.

'You're asking me to donate. Your mother and sister aren't matches?'

'Mother died two years ago. Sarah is pregnant and both she and the baby would be at risk. I can't ask her. Won't ask her.'

I admire his stance. 'Cousins, aunts, uncles?' I would add grandparents to the question but guess they'll be too old.

He pulls a face. 'There are none. The old dear was an only child and well… you know about the old man.'

I struggle to keep a grin from my face at his use of the Scottish terminology for parents. It's not a smiling situation.

'You're wanting me to donate, aren't you?'

'Would you?' There's hope in his eyes. He sees a chance to watch his daughters grow up. Perhaps he's picturing himself walking them down the aisle in a typical Scottish kirk, or some grand cathedral. 'There's no great risk for the donor. The side effects are only bone and muscle pain, a bit of nausea, headaches and fatigue.'

It's clear he knows his stuff, but in his position who wouldn't? In these days of online doctors and medical websites it's only natural for the person with the illness to research everything about it.

This may be my chance at redemption. I've never been a great believer in karma or the yin and yang balance of life.

Yet twenty-four hours after taking one life and failing to save another, I'm being granted a second chance to be a saviour.

'If I'm a match, I'll do it.'

The End

A Note from Bloodhound Books

Thanks for reading The Kindred Killers. We hope you enjoyed it as much as we did. Please consider leaving a review on Amazon or Goodreads to help others find and enjoy this book too.

We make every effort to ensure that books are carefully edited and proofread, however occasionally mistakes do slip through. If you spot something, please do send details to info@bloodhoundbooks.com and we can amend it.

Bloodhound Books specialise in crime and thriller fiction. We regularly have special offers including free and discounted eBooks. To be the first to hear about these special offers, why not join our mailing list here? We won't send you more than two emails per month and we'll never pass your details on to anybody else.

Readers who enjoyed The Kindred Killers will also enjoy

Watching The Bodies , also by Graham Smith , the first book in the Jake Boulder series.

The Black Hornet by Rob Sinclair.

Acknowledgements

I would like to take this opportunity to say extend my grateful thanks to all at Bloodhound Books for their professionalism and hard work in bring this book out. Special thanks must go to Sarah Hardy for her excellent work in publicising my writing.

I'd also like to say a huge thank you to all the bloggers who've taken the time out of their busy lives to support me. They are the unsung heroes of the book world and their support really has made the difference. Noelle Holten especially deserves a mention as the self-appointed leader of my cheer. I may owe her an apology for what happened to her in the book.

Thanks also go to those who've supported me in my writing, my good friend and mentor, Matt Hilton, Col Bury who brainstorms ideas with me late at night over the odd glass of something hangover-making, the Crime and Publishment gang, all my writing and non-writing friends and of course my family.

Humble thanks also to Rebecca Higgs, who answered many stupid questions with intelligence and good grace.

Last but by no means least, my readers. Without your support, kind reviews and enthusiasm for my writing, I'd be nothing more than a stenographer for the voices in my head.